# FORBIDDEN LOVE WITH A THUG III

SHVONNE LATRICE

# About the Author

**<u>Other Works by Me:</u>**

Good Girls Love Thugs 1-5
Falling for a Hood King 1-4
Married to a Distinguished Thug 1-3
She's Gotta Have It 1-2
Me & My Dope Boy 1-3
Yazir & Nina 1-3
Forbidden Love with a Thug 1-3
You Needed Me 1-3
Shorty is in Love with a Real One 1-4
I Got Your Back 1-2
My Baby Is a West Coast King 1-4
Our Love Is the Realest 1-3
She Got It Bad for a Heartless Gangsta 1-4
She Got It Bad for a Heartless Gangsta: An AK Christmas
Hood Boyz Fall In Love Too 1-3
Nobody Can Love You Like Them Roughnecks Do 1-4
She Gave Her All to the Hood's Finest 1-5

**Visit TheShvonneLatrice.com for paperbacks!**

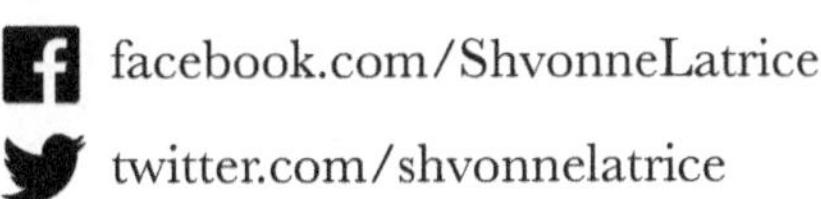

facebook.com/ShvonneLatrice

twitter.com/shvonnelatrice

$15.99

ISBN 978-1-966375-13-5

ONE

## Kilexis "Kill" Camren

---

The entrance dinged letting the store know someone was coming in, and when I looked towards it, I saw Sophie, Amelia's little home girl I fucked a while back.

"Hey Kill," she smiled and walked closer to me.

"What's good, ma?" I responded and took the bag from Ernie.

I put my hand up and he said, "See you later, son."

"I'm cool. How have you been?" she asked once I turned my attention back to her.

"Great. A nigga just had a baby," I cheesed as I thought about Alexsia. "I see you did too." I pointed to the little baby she was holding.

"Yeah, her name is Kilenna."

"Cute," I nodded. "Well it was good seeing you," I added and walked to leave out of the store.

"Kill, she's yours!" she called after me, and I snapped my neck to look back at her.

Shorty had to be fucking with me.

"Come here and let me talk to you for a second," I waved Sophie over to me.

She adjusted her daughter on her hip, and then followed me out

1

of the store. I opened the passenger door of my car for her, and once she got in, I jogged around to my side to get in as well. It was quiet for a few moments as I tried to figure out what exactly I wanted to say to her ass. Her daughter cooed, and she kissed her cheek before rubbing her back. The baby looked nothing like me, not even a small feature of mine was in her face, but that didn't mean shit these days.

"Are you okay?" Sophie quizzed.

"Nah ma, I'm not okay. How is that my baby? I fucked you one damn time and I strapped up. The shit didn't break either, I'm one hundred percent sure." I looked over at her, wearing a frown.

"I don't know. But a month after we had sex, I found out I was pregnant."

"Sophie, I refuse to believe that you didn't fuck anyone else after me. Didn't you say you had a boyfriend or some shit? Yeah, you did, so don't try to play me, shorty." I nodded as the scene of her mentioning she had a man came into my mind.

"We broke up, Kill! He found out that I'd slept with someone else and he broke it off with me. So no, I haven't been with anyone else after you. I was too miserable to go out and meet someone, and by the time I started to heal, I found out I was pregnant! And I can't believe you have a baby by someone else too!"

I wasn't sure who the fuck Sophie thought I was, but she had the game fucked up if she thought I was going for this bullshit. There was no way that damn baby was mine, and she wasn't about to try and pull a Margo on my ass. Nah, fuck that shit. Plus, Jersey would fucking murder my ass, even though Sophie was before her. How would that look? I was not the type of nigga that just shot my babies up in any bitch that I smashed. I was picky.

"I'm gonna need a DNA test, straight up," I responded, after a couple moments of silence.

"What? Are you serious?"" She looked to me with an angry expression as if I gave a fuck.

I didn't know her ass from a can of paint, and she really thought I was just gonna believe that her child was mine because she said it was? Hilarious.

"I'm dead fucking serious, shorty. I ain't doing shit until I get a test done. And don't even think about going on your own fucking time and showing up with the results. We're going to a for real doctor, and having it done with us both watching."

"Nigga, get over yourself! You think you're that much of a hot commodity to where I would need to lie about you being the father of my child? I mean you're fine, but not that fine."

"I must be, because you know you're lying like fuck. The baby looks nothing like me, and I'm not about to just take your word for it. Why would I? We weren't in some committed relationship. I fucked you the first night I met you!"

"Just like you fucked your baby mama the first night she met you!" she countered, and a smirk appeared on her face. "Yeah nigga, but somehow her baby is yours and mine ain't? Fuck out of here, Kill."

I had no idea she knew whom I was with, but then again, she was friends with Amelia who knew everything about me somehow. I wouldn't be surprised if Amelia knew what the fuck I ate for breakfast every morning. It was weird, but I was used to it by now.

"Let me tell you something, Sophie. For one, don't bring up my child's mother ever again. Secondly, I'd known her and come in contact with her a couple times before we engaged in sexual activity. Third, I fucked her more than one whack ass time, and I didn't use a cap every time. And lastly, I can spot a lying hoe any muthafuckin' where, so I see the difference between you two."

Tears slipped down her cheeks as she shook her head 'no' repeatedly.

"I fuckin' hate you, Kill. I wish I could take back that night we had together, but I can't. I will get a DNA test, and then you will see that Kilenna is yours."

"Sure. Is your number the same?"

"No, I had to—"

"Give me your damn number and get out my car."

"I ain't giving you shit, nigga, talking to me like that!"

"Give it to me willingly, or I will get it my damn self. And if I have to go out of my way to get it, it won't end well for you, shorty."

She swallowed hard, and then pulled her phone out since she didn't know her new number by heart. I typed her number into my iPhone, and then stored it right away. I then reached across her to pull on the lever of my door so that she could get her lying ass out of my whip. She looked into my eyes for a couple moments, and then finally got out of the car slowly. As soon as she closed my door, I peeled off down the street, headed to my crib on Saint Mortiz.

Although I knew deep down that I was not that child's father, a part of me wondered if I was. What if somehow I'd gotten her ass pregnant? In all my years of being on this Earth and fucking bitches, I had never gotten one pregnant because I wore a condom for that purpose. I didn't wear them to prevent STDs, because if I thought a bitch had one I wasn't fucking her period; with or without a condom. I strapped up because I didn't want a woman who didn't have my last name carrying my child. When Jersey got pregnant, I felt disappointed in myself because I had slipped up, but I was grateful that I had at least done it with a woman that I cared deeply for. Jersey was the first girl that had me feeling all warm inside and shit. I knew that I never loved Margo like I thought I had years back, when I met Jersey. Anyhow, this Sophie shit had me a little bothered because there was a slight chance that she could have had my baby because I did in fact fuck the hoe. That's what the fuck I get for slanging dick to these hoes out here, man. Something told me not to slide up in that trash ass puss but I went against my gut and did anyway.

I pulled up to my home, and just parked in the roundabout driveway instead of the garage. I didn't feel like putting my car inside, even though it was such a small task. That conversation with Sophie had completely drained me. When I walked into the home, I smelled something sweet, which made me smile at the thought of the small family I was creating.

"Is that cake?" I asked Jersey as I entered the kitchen. I spotted my baby girl, Alexsia, and picked her up from her little bed swing before kissing her plump cheeks. She was a mixture of Jersey and I, which I thought was cool as fuck. I knew she and I would make pretty babies.

"Yes, it's cake. Did you take care of that bitch?" she asked referring to Trixie, but wore that beautiful smile on her face. I chuckled because she looked so innocent but had just spoken some foul words.

"I did, baby, I did." I leaned down to peck her lips, and then placed Alexsia back into her bed swing. "Damn, I make some beautiful ass babies," I smiled while looking at Alexsia.

"You mean *we* make beautiful babies," Jersey giggled and walked over to me to kiss my lips again. "Go wash your hands so we can eat dinner, Kill."

"I wanna eat something else." I bit my lip before gripping her little ass in my hands, and sucking her lips.

"No, it's not time yet. And go, Kill!" She blushed and tried to pull away from me. I kissed her soft neck, and then let her go so I could wash my hands.

There was no way Sophie's baby could be mine; I would lose all of this, and that couldn't happen.

## TWO

## Cheyla Austin

---

Today was my first appointment since finding out that I was pregnant. This was so crazy to me because I never saw myself having kids and all that shit. I always thought I would be alone forever, just having a few male companions here and there. But just like Jersey's mother used to say, the people who say they aren't gonna have kids, always do. I thought I was an exception to that, but here I am.

"Kantwan, I don't need you to help me out of the car like that," I frowned as he held onto my hand, and closed the car door behind me.

Ever since I told his ass that the first three months were the easiest to miscarry in, he was always making sure I was careful. I couldn't wear heels of any kind unless I did it behind his back. He also would only smoke weed when he was out and driving his sports car, which I couldn't ride in, by the way. He wouldn't let me eat fish of any kind, because despite what I told him, all fish was bad for the baby in his mind.

"I do what I want," he responded as I slipped my hand into his.

"I would hate to see how you would act when I actually start showing. I'm probably gonna have to run off somewhere until I give birth," I half joked. Shit, I may *actually* have to do that.

"And you'll regret that shit once we come back together." He leaned down to kiss my temple, and then opened the door to the doctor's office for me.

I went to the counter to check in, and then sat back down next to Kantwan. There was a pregnant woman sitting across the room with her husband and two little toddlers running amuck. I shook my head as all kinds of thoughts ran through my mind. She looked so tired and miserable, while her husband or boyfriend scrolled on his phone. She yelled for them to sit down as she palmed her belly, but the two little devils paid her no mind. I'll be damned!

"That's gonna be us soon," Kantwan jokingly whispered into my ear.

"Nigga, no the fuck it isn't. This is gonna be our first and last baby, watch. Jersey said it hurt really badly when she pushed Alexsia out, and I refuse to go through the pain she went through multiple times."

"Yeah, yeah, yeah, you'll be pregnant again in a year or two, shorty, don't kid yourself. You love this dick too much," he grinned as I covered my mouth while laughing.

"I really don't know why I thought I could have a serious conversation with you, Kantwan."

"We are talking seriously. We fuck constantly and you think this is the last baby? I'm just trying to make sure you're being realistic. I think if we're careful it'll only be like three, but if we're heedless, I'd say like a cool six kids."

"Six? Hell no! Three is too damn much, but it's much more reasonable." I shook my head and then let out a sigh.

Kantwan was right. As much sex as we had, there was no way I wouldn't get pregnant again. I thought we were being safe before, yet I'm pregnant right now. I should've known that him pulling out, and me being neglectful to my birth control on some days would not keep me from having a baby. I think I was just so caught up in the moment with Kantwan, that the consequences of us fucking unsafely and like two dogs in heat didn't cross my mind.

"Austin!" The skinny nurse came out and called my last name. Kantwan helped me up, and I rolled my eyes so fucking hard as we walked to the back with the nurse. "Okay, just step on the scale for me, Cheyla."

The nurse weighed me and then took my blood pressure, before double-checking my reasoning for being there. Kantwan and I then followed her to another room, where she set my file down, and then gave us an estimated time on when the doctor would come into the room. I changed into the gown after removing my panties and pushing my dress up past my waist.

"You think we can get a quickie in?" Kantwan cheesed and I sucked my teeth.

"No, nasty." I climbed onto the examination table.

"What is she gonna do?"

"Just check and make sure the baby is okay, and tell us about how far along I am. That way we can see about how long it will be until the baby gets here."

"Cool."

My doctor finally walked in wearing a big smile on her face. Dr. Ronny had long, blond hair that she kept in a bun on top of her head, and her teeth were really big but white. I guess when your teeth were that large, you had to make sure they were white. There was no way I would be walking around with some huge ass yellow shits in my mouth.

"Good morning, Cheyla, how are you, honey?" she asked as she flipped through my file.

"I'm great. This is my boyfriend, Kantwan, and the one I'm pregnant by." I gestured towards him and he stood up to shake her hand.

"I better be," Kantwan joked, making us chortle.

"Oooh, nice and tall. Good job, now we don't have to worry about it being a short boy or something. I had a patient earlier whose husband was about 5'6, and she was so worried that their boy was gonna be small," Dr. Ronny joked as she washed her hands. "I think her husband's little ego was bruised, no pun intended." We all laughed. I loved Dr. Ronny because she was so sweet and always made little corny jokes. They weren't good jokes, but somehow they still made you laugh.

"Yes, I love tall guys and I'm happy I got one," I replied.

"Me too, sweetie, me too. Alright, let's see what's going on in there."

She turned the machine on, and then picked up some tool. She then placed one palm on my pelvis, while using the other hand to slowly insert the gray tool into me. I twisted my face up a bit, because it was slightly painful.

"I know it's uncomfortable, honey, but it will be over soon," she said as she looked over at the small screen. I could see Kantwan wearing a worried expression. My poor baby had no idea what was going on. "Okay, everything looks perfect, Cheyla. You're about seven weeks along, and the baby should come between forty and forty-two weeks, it all depends."

"So when would the baby get here?" Kantwan quizzed with furrowed brows.

"The baby should arrive at the beginning of May." She moved it around some more, and looked closer to the screen. "I'm gonna estimate delivery to be May 16 of next year."

"That's so far away it seems," I chuckled.

"I know, but it will fly by, and then soon enough, you'll be throwing the baby its twenty-first birthday," she chuckled.

We finished the exam, and then Dr. Ronny left the room so that I could clean myself and put my panties back on. Kantwan and I then talked with her in her office for a little bit, before leaving and getting into the car.

"So May 16, I will be a daddy," he grinned as he cranked up the car.

"Yep, I love you." I leaned over the center console.

"I love you too, ma." He kissed me a couple times, and then pulled out of the parking space so we could go get something to eat.

Boy had my life changed. At least it was for the better…

THREE

# Elijah Camren

---

*I* was sitting down chilling with my homeboy Blow, and my cousin Ka'Shea. Today was a relaxation day in a sense, so we were just kickin' back, smoking and shit. Blow lived in the hood, but since I grew up over here the shit didn't scare me. I did have to take more precautions because my status in the game had changed, but I wasn't tripping off that shit. If niggas were dumb enough to get buck, I had no problem pumping some lead into their dome. I stayed strapped.

"One of you niggas need to invite me over for dinner or some shit," Blow took a pull on his blunt.

"You know you're welcome in my crib anytime, man," Ka'Shea responded before stuffing some chips into his mouth.

Blow looked over at me suspiciously while blowing out smoke, causing me to break out into laughter.

"My nigga, do I have to say it? You know you can come through. You can have dinner with Ivy and my kid, bro. Ivy can throw down too, so don't be trying to come back for food every damn night," I taunted, making us all chuckle.

"Nigga, speaking of Ivy and her son, her baby daddy is coming up," Blow took another pull.

"Coming up on what?" I frowned.

"He don' scored a couple blocks and shit."

"He ain't do that shit himself, I know he's working with someone for sure. That nigga is a bitch," I spat.

Portland was a fucking idiot, and I refused to believe he'd come up with some plan and scored a supplier that damn quickly. Someone was helping his hoe ass and it wasn't just Sonny. Whoever decided to side with him was just as dumb as his ass.

"Nah, you right, he got his boy by his side too. They ain't moving weight like y'all and Kill, but they doing a little something. You know ever since he came into that money that his pops left him, he was able to buy a couple houses over in Eastside."

"Oh word, do you know if his shit is good or what? With the way that nigga was begging to get on, ain't no way he had contacts in his pocket like that, bro," Ka'Shea shook his head, saying exactly what I was thinking.

"I don't know. I do believe he has someone backing him, and Sonny like you said, but no one has said whom. All I know is that I saw some niggas selling, a couple different niggas actually, and they said they were working for Portland. I know y'all don't have much territory on Eastside, which is why I asked the corner boys about it."

Ka'Shea and I made eye contact, before we both looked back over at Blow. I knew Portland wasn't shit, and would never be shit, but something deep down inside of me was telling me not to ignore his ass. Something in my gut was saying that his efforts were finally gonna pay off, and that we would have to put in work to take him down. The worst part was that I was sure I would have to kill his ass.

"From what you observed, did it look like they were doing some shit? Have you heard about the quality of their product at all?" I questioned back to back.

"I bought some weed and that shit was fire. I got a couple homies who snort, and they said the shit was good as hell too. Makes me wonder where he got it from. It ain't no lowball supplier if he got some good on him," Blow blew out smoke. Despite his name, he wasn't a cokehead.

I just nodded in agreement.

Ka'Shea and I continued to talk with him, but I could tell we were both anxious to get up out of there and talk to Kill and Kantwan. They needed to know what the fuck was going on. Kill was smart and he would know how we should play this so that we wouldn't jump the gun, but also so that we wouldn't end up on the losing side.

Ka'Shea pulled up to Kill's crib, and parked right out front. We exited the car, and then jogged to his door before I rang the doorbell. Kantwan answered, and after we dapped him up, he led us to the den where Kill was finishing up a phone call. We sat down, and then Kantwan passed a tray of blunts around for us to partake in. As soon as I lit it and took the first pull, Kill was hanging up his call.

"Who was that little bro?" Ka'Shea fucked with Kill, as he cracked open a bottle of Hennessy.

"Stop with that little bro shit. And it was a contractor for the club we're opening. Everything is on schedule, and we can come by and see its progress by next Friday. I'm excited as fuck about it, because I know it's gonna be hella profitable." He took a seat on the couch next to me. "Also, we finally cleaned enough money using Axel's cleaners to buy the movie theatre." He sat down.

"Hi guys," Jersey smiled as she carried in a tray of sandwiches. Before she could even sit them down good, our high asses were snatching them muthafuckas off the plate like some niggas from a third world country.

"Thanks, shorty," Kill gave her a half smile, making her walk over to sit in his lap and kiss him.

"Aye, I came to talk, not watch y'all tongue fuck!" Kantwan barked. I was thankful because I was sure that in a minute, they were gonna start fucking in front of us.

"Fuck you, Kant." Jersey got off Kill's lap and then walked out of the den.

"What's good with you?" Kill looked over at me, prompting me to look over at Ka'Shea. I was eating this bomb ass sandwich, and since he was finished, he could talk.

"Blow was telling Elijah and I that Portland and Sonny are building a little empire over on Eastside," Ka'Shea explained, and after a couple moments of silence, Kill and Kantwan burst into laughter.

"Nigga, did you really call this impromptu ass meeting over Portland and Sonny? Them muthafuckas 'bout can't even pull a fuckin' trigger. I'll be damned if I'm losing sleep over them." Kill shook his head.

"That's how I feel too, but a part of me is wondering if we should be writing them off so soon. I mean, Blow said they had some pretty good shit Kill, and how would they get that when they have no reputation in the game? Good suppliers are not fucking with some niggas they have no resume on, no matter how much money their daddies left them," I said.

"So you're saying that you believe they have someone bigger helping them?" Kantwan inquired.

"That's exactly what I think. That nigga was able to take his dick out of these Wilmington hoes long enough to actually bond with someone who is well connected and has enough years in the game to get them good shit," Ka'Shea replied.

"You do have a point." Kill filled his glass with Hennessy. "You think it's Ahmad and Dante?"

"Nah, them niggas ain't got the connects to do some shit like that. Whoever they have knows something about the game, unlike them." Kantwan shook his head.

"Or maybe Ahmad and Dante got a good supplier off of their father's name. Axel is a household name in this drug shit, and mentioning that you're his son could get you a lot of shit." Kill sipped his drink, and squinted his eyes as he stared off at the wall.

"Dante and Ahmad don't even know Portland and Sonny, Kill," Ka'Shea chimed in.

I didn't know who Portland and Sonny had gotten to, but I was determined to find out. Ain't no way we were gonna lose our territory to some green muthafuckas like Portland and Sonny, or Dante and Ahmad. Ka'Shea had a point though, them niggas didn't know one another to be working together. Something wasn't right, and I knew sooner or later, shit would be popping off.

FOUR

# Sondre "Sonny" Austin

---

*S*hit had been going real well for the kid. I was making my
own damn money and plenty of it. With the help of Axel's
sons, and some cats they'd met through their father, we were pros-
pering very well. We'd set up a couple traps, and had hired on a few
corner boys over in Eastside to kind of test the waters. We were
being advised by this guy named Leroy that we should start in an
area that Kill and his crew hadn't quite used yet. I knew they were
planning to come to Eastside soon, but Leroy felt it was safer for us
to start small in a sense. We wanted to build and be strong before we
started any problems.

"Damn nigga, this is a lot of fuckin' cash," Portland chuckled as
we banded the money.

We threw our corner boys chump change but we made sure to
pay ourselves very well. Was it ethical? No, but we didn't give a fuck
about that, obviously, if we were slanging dope.

"I know, nigga. I'm thinking of getting me a house or some shit
with this bread," I nodded and smiled as I wrapped a rubber band
around a thick stack of money. I had never seen so much cash in
my life.

"Leroy said we need to have this shit cleaned first my nigga. We can't buy shit until we do that so relax. Plus, I just got you a crib with my inheritance."

"I know, but ain't nothing wrong with having two, especially now that Marley and my daughter live with me. I can't really get my dick wet like I want in this house," I chuckled.

My baby mama and daughter Sonaya moved in with me, and I loved having them around. Although that was the case, I was a nigga who couldn't be satisfied by one woman. And the fact that Raleigh no longer fucked with me, I had a little more time on my hands to entertain hoes outside of Marley. The chicks over on East-side knew that I was making a little bit of money, so they were throwing the pussy to me every where that I went. Wasn't nothing more exciting than new pussy, so you know I was indulging.

"Didn't you get some jawn pregnant?" Portland frowned.

Some bitch named Alicia claimed I got her pregnant, and I probably did. But I didn't have time to deal with that shit right now due to the circumstances surrounding it. All I cared about was getting this money, fucking a couple bitches, and taking care of the only child I would ever claim; Sonaya Austin.

"Yeah, but that bitch lying."

"Nigga, Alicia ain't no hoe, how the fuck is she lying? Didn't you take her damn virginity?"

"Yeah I did, but shorty is sixteen, they would throw me under the jail if the authorities found out she was carrying my baby nigga. We're about to be twenty-six soon," I sighed and shook my head as I began filling the duffle bag back up.

Since we had no businesses, we were currently using Dante's homeboy's burger spot to wash the money. The place made okay money, but not enough to clean our money at the pace we wanted. We tried to use Axel's cleaners, but he shut that down saying it was only for Kill's shit. I couldn't stand that nigga Kill with his greedy ass.

"You had no business fucking with a bitch that young anyways. Her damn body probably not even all the way developed. Ain't no way my dick would've gotten hard from looking at her ass." Portland turned his lip up.

"That's because you ain't seen her with her clothes off, boy!" I laughed.

"You're disgusting my nigga. If I have a daughter, remind me to never let you be around her."

"Aye, calm down. Worry about Breesha's hoe ass carrying your baby."

"Don't fucking remind me." He ran his hand over his face just as the doorbell rang. He went to answer it, and then came back into his den with Leroy, Ahmad, and Dante.

We dapped one another up, and then sat down to start talking business. Hopefully Ahmad and Dante had some good news for us. Our partnership was divided so that we could work better and smarter. Ahmad and Dante knew nothing about the streets really, so Portland and I took care of that part. They knew more about business, so we let them handle that. Leroy knew the most about being successful in this shit, so he was like out mentor in a sense, and he was trigger-happy so he would take down anyone we needed him to take out.

"Aight, so good news. Kill will no longer be using my dad's cleaners to clean his money. He's found another way to do it, but we couldn't care less. My dad is sick as fuck, and he doesn't mind us using it now," Ahmad grinned.

"You asked him if we could use it?" Leroy frowned. He used to work for Axel, that was until Kill took over and fired his ass. When that happened, Leroy began to hate Kill, despite them being cool in the past. The five of us were pretty much a group of niggas who hated Kill.

"Nah, but that nigga is sick as hell, he ain't gonna know." Ahmad frowned.

"I'm just not trying to step on your pop's toes. I mean, he still is *that* nigga, regardless of the fact that Kill is now the boss," Leroy exhaled.

"Chill, aight, we can use it," Dante sucked his teeth, backing his brother up.

"That's great news. But umm, Portland and I wanna know what y'all think about us setting up over in Browntown," I grinned.

"That would mean more money, but that's Kill's territory," Leroy furrowed his brows. "We would need to get rid of him prior to moving in on anything. It wouldn't be wise for us to try and compete, especially because they have some Grade A shit."

"Let's kill his ass then," I frowned.

"You know it ain't that easy. If it were, the nigga would've been dead. Kill ain't no damn fool, and we know that, everyone knows that. We need to be smart about the shit, and just tread very lightly," Leroy explained.

I was tired of treading lightly for this nigga! I wanted to make this bread, and get back at him and his brothers for fucking up my home life, and my boy's home life. Shit, I fucking loved Raleigh, and my heart still ached for her every now and then. The fact that she wasn't giving me any type of play, and when I say any I meant it, had me pissed as hell. I'd been with her for almost ten years, and she just left me like it was nothing. Then to make matters worse, that bitch nigga, Kantwan, was sticking his dick in my sister, got her pregnant and shit. The more that those thoughts raced through my mind, the angrier I got.

"Be patient, Sonny, we gon' do this shit." Portland tapped my arm and I nodded begrudgingly. "Aye, Leroy, let me talk to you for a second."

Portland and Leroy left the room, leaving me, Ahmad, and Dante to talk for a bit. After about ten minutes, Portland and Leroy returned, before Ahmad, Dante, and Leroy left out.

"What was that about?" I asked Portland as I reached for the bag of chips sitting on the coffee table.

"Gave him a knot to kill Elijah," he grinned and so did I. Hey. if we couldn't murk Kill, we could kill the niggas around him.

FIVE

# Jersey Warren

---

Two Days Later...

It was around 8pm at night, and I'd finally gotten my baby girl to go to sleep. She was wide-awake thirty minutes ago, and tried to stay that way for the longest. It was so cute watching her little eyelids lower, and then fly back up because she realized she was falling asleep. I swear, everything my little cutie did warmed my heart like crazy. I kissed her fat cheek, and then covered half of her body with her blanket, before taking the baby monitor with me to the bedroom.

After taking care of her all day, I needed to take a bath and relax my nerves. Since I was enrolled in online classes for my university, I had to make sure I stayed on top of my work. I thought it would be easier, and in a way it was because I could stay here with Alexsia, but damn I wished I would have known they gave so much damn homework in a small amount of time. By saying that, I wanted to take a nice bath and get a good night's sleep so that I could wake up in the morning and get some work done before my daughter woke up and took up all of my time.

I started the water in the huge Jacuzzi tub, and then put some of my bubble bath against the running water to make bubbles. I then lit one of my mood candles, and removed my clothing. Submerging myself into the water, I tightened my bun on top of my head because it felt like it was gonna fall. This damn water felt so good, and soothed every aching muscle in my body.

Like always, thoughts consumed my mind. Sometimes they were good ones, like about the life I'd built with Kill so far, but sometimes they were about my parents and brother. I'd lost them all in such a short amount of time, and it hurt badly. I thought about picking up the phone to call Portland every now and then, but I always changed my mind. Portland was an asshole and only cared about himself. And every time he fucked one of us over, we always forgave him, which is why he kept up his antics. I wasn't doing that shit anymore. Yeah, he'd reached out, but I knew it was only because he'd found out Kill was my baby daddy and wanted to get on. See what I mean? Portland cared about no one but his damn self!

I washed my body down, and then got out to brush my teeth. I then spread lotion all over me, before slipping into my nightgown. As soon as I walked into the bedroom, Kill was coming out of his bathroom with a towel around his waist. We both made eye contact and smiled. I noticed his was a bit weird, but it was probably because of the day's work, tiring him out.

"Hi baby," I chuckled shyly like a little girl, and rushed over to him after slipping into a short nightgown. As soon as I got to him, he scooped me up. "Are you okay?"

"Yeah, I'm good. I wanna talk to you for a second," he sighed dejectedly, and then walked me over to the chaise to sit me down.

His face bore a worried and distressed expression, which in turn worried me as well. What the hell could possibly be wrong now? My heart began beating extra fast, and he hadn't even said anything. I couldn't take anymore pain, I just couldn't. Not right now.

"Talk, Kilexis."

He got down onto the floor, wearing just his boxer shorts that he'd changed into. Looking up into my face, he said, "Jersey, I love you, shorty, so much, you know that, right?" I just nodded and began to slowly rub my palms together. "Just listen to me and let me finish before you say anything. So about a week ago, the day I handled Trixie, I ran into an old friend. Umm, that friend was a woman and she was someone that I fucked before, only once, and before you and I were anything. She umm," he looked off to the side and then back to me before saying, "she umm, told me that I was the father of her child."

"What? What the fuck!" I shot up off the chaise and tried to walk around him, but he stopped me. He was towering over me and holding me in place with his strong grip.

"I told you to let me finish."

"I don't want you to finish! You just go around making babies with every bitch you meet, Kill?" I hollered up at him as tears began to spill down my cheeks.

"What? I only slept with that hoe one fuckin' time, Jersey!"

"You're disgusting! And to think I—move!" I got away from him and started to walk across the large bedroom, but he hugged my body from behind. I couldn't hold it in anymore, so I just broke down and cried. "Kill, I can't do this! Too much is happening to me at once!" I sobbed.

"Baby, listen to me, aight? That baby is not mine. I only slept with her once and I used a condom, which did not break. I know what you were about to say baby and you *are* special. You are the only one I have ever gotten pregnant, aight?" he whispered as I cried, and then began kissing on my neck.

He turned me to face him, and then removed my gown swiftly. He pushed down my underwear, and then gently laid me back down on the bed. I was weeping lightly, so I covered my face. Removing my hands, he kissed the backs of them, and then resumed kissing my neck while lying in between my legs. I didn't see him remove his boxers, but I guess he had since I could feel his hard dick against my pussy.

"No Kill, move." I *gently* pushed his head as he trailed soft kisses down my flat stomach.

"Jersey, that's not my kid. I wouldn't have even told you, but I don't keep shit from you so I did. I ain't get that girl pregnant, only you. I want you to know this in case she tries to do some dumb shit like run into you and tell you."

Before I could respond, he'd taken my clit into his mouth. I arched my back, and then caressed his soft hair. He was licking and sucking like he was on payroll to do so, and I could feel it deep down in my bones. The way he ate my pussy showed me how much he cared about me. I could feel it with every slurp and suck, which made the feeling that much more intense.

"Aaahh, uuuh, shit," I whimpered.

He continued his tongue lashing, making me cum three hard times. I had to pull on his hair to get his mouth from between my legs because he was wearing me out already. Standing to his feet, he flipped me onto all fours, pressed my face into the pillow, and then slipped into me from behind. One thing Kilexis Camren could do better than anything else, was fuck. He gripped my waist tightly, and began winding his hips into me slowly, making me bite down on my lip and whine like a little baby.

"Kiiilll," I cried and balled the sheets up in my fist.

Suddenly, he gripped my hair into his hands, and began slamming into me with precision. He would beat it up, then move slowly as hell, and boy was it driving me crazy. He bent down while still stroking me from the back, and started sucking on my neck with his soft lips and tongue.

"You ain't going nowhere, Jersey," he whispered into my ear, and then pulled my bottom lip into his mouth to suck, all the while fucking the shit out of me doggy-style. "Say it," he growled and started going harder. I'd cum so many times I could feel it spilling down my inner thighs.

"I'm not going anywhere!" I called out. He smacked my ass, gripped it roughly, and then used his other hand to reach under me and grope my breasts.

"Tell me this is my pussy."

"It's your pussy, Kill, mmm, fuck!"

"I love you, Jersey," he said before leaning back up, gripping my waist, and pummeling into me. "Shit," he grumbled.

A few more thrusts, and he was nutting all inside of me. My

body quivered from releasing yet again, and he immediately flipped me over onto my back. Staring down at me, he panted heavily before licking his full lips.

"I love you too, Kill."

"That's not my baby."

"I know." I nodded as my chest rose and fell rapidly. He would never lie to me, so therefore I believed him.

# SIX

# Kantwan Camren

---

"*S*hit," I grunted as I let everything inside of me go into Cheyla.

As she breathed heavily, I kissed down her stomach while groping her smooth golden thighs. This had become a routine for me; getting some pussy before I went to meet up with Rachel and Tanya. Cheyla would always be dead tired at first, but after a couple minutes, she would be wide awake and into it. It seemed like I could never get enough of her, especially now that she had that infamous pregnant pussy.

I glanced at the cable box and saw it was time for me to get into the shower, so I rolled off of Cheyla and then out of the bed. I checked my burner phone, and saw that Rachel had sent a text over confirming the meet-up. Even though she didn't need to, Kill required it of her. That way, if one morning it didn't get sent, we would know something was up and know not to show up.

I loved that my brother thought ahead with shit, because you didn't feel unsafe and like you would be caught up. Elijah said when working for Axel, he stayed being paranoid because Axel only covered *his* ass. He couldn't care less about the next nigga, even if that nigga worked for him.

"Don't take a long time, Kantwan," Cheyla brushed her pointing finger across my lower back, right before I stood up to go into the bathroom.

"I'm gonna take as long as I usually do, ma, so expect the same, not a minute longer."

"Okay. Is there anyway you can speed it up?"

"Don't you have class today?" I laughed.

"Yes, I do, but I wanted to eat breakfast together before I go."

"What time is the class, Cheyla?"

"At 10am, and then I have nonstop classes until 4pm in the evening. I have a break in between, but it's no point in me coming home, so I just go to the computer lab and bullshit or do homework."

"Aight, I will try to work as fast as I can so that I can be back before 8:30am, and we can eat together. But if not, we can go to dinner when you get out of class so I can make it up to you." I spread toothpaste onto my toothbrush.

"That works. You always know how to please me, Kantwan. I love it." She laid back onto the bed and cut the lamp on in the room.

I gave her a small smirk, and continued to brush my teeth. I flossed then rinsed, before coming out into the bedroom to cut the lamp back off. Shorty had dozed off that quickly. I didn't need the light because the sun would be rising by the time I got out of my shower. After showering, I put on some deodorant and then got dressed in some dark jeans, a black shirt, a black hoodie, and some black low top Chuck Taylor's. I opted out of wearing jewelry whenever I went to meet up for some reason. After slipping my baseball cap down onto my head, I grabbed my personal and work phone before leaving.

On the drive there, Rachel entered my mind. After that ass picture she sent me, she kept sending little pictures every now and then. She would send ones of her in the shower, lying in bed wearing lingerie, just all kinds of shit and she knew she looked good. At first I would just ignore it, but once I started seeing that it made my dick hard, I knew I needed to have a talk with her. I never saw myself as the cheating type, and even if I was, I was gonna suppress that shit.

I dropped my whip off at the warehouse, and then hopped into the Nissan used for pickups. I pulled up to the location and noticed the truck was way bigger than the last time. Last time it was like a food truck, but this time it was just short of being an eighteen-wheeler. I was so confused as I threw the car into park.

"Hey boo," Rachel grinned with her fine ass.

"Sup, ma; Tanya. What is this shit? I can't fit whatever is in there in this little ass Nissan van."

"Kill wanted triple the product he received last time, so we had to get a bigger truck. We're instructed to trail you to the warehouse where we will help you unload there," Tanya replied.

"Why the fuck did y'all have me drive over here if y'all were gonna follow me back? We could've just met at the warehouse," I frowned.

"Because Kill told us to. He didn't want us possibly getting lost, so he wants us to trail you there instead of giving us directions. This is a lot of product Kantwan, and if we detoured somehow and fucked something up, Kill would do the same to us, fuck something up," Rachel explained.

She was right, too. My brother had become more vicious and I didn't mind it at all. At home chilling, he was still the same Kilexis Camren, but when it came to the business, he didn't play around at all. He gave no second chances, and he would chop your head off without batting an eye. Being ruthless had become a part of who he was. He was never scared to kill a nigga, but he would be remorseful afterwards. These days, he didn't give a fuck.

"Aight, I get you. Come on." I waved them on before jogging back to the van.

They followed me to the warehouse, and I got out to open the huge automatic door so they could pull the truck in. Once all the way inside, I let the door down, and the three of us began unloading. I saw that this time the keys were loaded up into barrels marked with beer brands. I swear my brother was smart as fuck. I was happy he was in charge because he was the cleverest, even cleverer than

Axel, oddly. The only time his "cleverness" annoyed me was when he would cancel out any ideas that I had, because he felt his were better.

Three fucking hours later, we were finally finished unloading and packing the shit away. I didn't mind the long work time too much, because the three of us made casual conversation, which was cool. Rachel and Tanya were pretty laid back and shit, so it was nice to have someone to talk to while I put this shit away. Listening to music wasn't cutting it anymore, because I'd gotten tired of my playlist as of late.

I went to sit down at one of the desks in the warehouse, before opening my laptop to log in the amount of bakery products. Kill hadn't changed the product listing to beer yet, so I just treated it the same. As I was typing, Rachel came over and sat at the edge of the desk. Although covered up completely, all I saw were those pictures she flooded my phone with.

"Working hard, huh?" she grinned down at me before biting her lip.

"I try to. Aye, what's up with you sending me pictures and shit?" I had to know what her intentions were. I was tired of pretending like the shit wasn't happening.

"You don't like them?" she cocked her head.

"Nah, that's not it, Rachel, I have a girlfriend."

"Oh shit! Why didn't you just say that? I would've stopped if you had. I'm not that type to go after another woman's man."

"My bad, I guess if I had just texted that, the pictures would have stopped." For some reason I didn't believe her pretty ass, but I was gonna give her the benefit of the doubt.

"It's cool, I'm sorry about that. I hope we can still be cool co-workers."

"Of course we can."

# SEVEN

# Ivy Horne

"$\mathcal{M}$mm, uuuh," I bit down on my lip to muffle my moans as Elijah pounded into me from behind.

I grabbed the pillow to bite down on it because I was seconds from screaming at the top of my lungs in pleasure. Donovan was still asleep, and I didn't want to wake him up just yet. I exploded again for the fourth time, and then finally so did Elijah. He showed no mercy in the bedroom, and I could not complain.

"Damn," he whispered as he slowly pulled out of me.

My body was tired as hell, so I collapsed onto the bed, lying on my stomach. Elijah just laughed at me as I laid there like a dead person. I was sore between the legs already, and knew walking around campus today would be a struggle. I rolled onto my back, and placed my hand onto my stomach, which was drenched in sweat. I loved cumming, but damn did I hate when he fucked me like this before class. How the hell was I supposed to trudge around campus with an aching pussy?

"Come on and let's shower. You can't be late for class, ma," Elijah patted my thigh. *Fuck you*, I thought.

"Why did you fuck me like that, knowing I have to get up and stuff?" I frowned but didn't move a muscle.

He scooped me up and then carried me into the bathroom. Sitting me on the closed toilet top, I watched him cut the shower on and test the temperature, before coming over to me and pulling me with him. We climbed into the shower, and washed off only, since I was too tired to get dicked down again. We stole kisses here and there, and it made me smile to think about how I'd finally gotten happiness with someone. Elijah was so perfect to me; well, perfect *for* me.

After showering, we brushed our teeth since there were two sinks in our bathroom, and then I got dressed. Since I would just be in class all day, I threw on some tights, a t-shirt, and some Adidas. I tied a sweatshirt around my waist in case I got cold during the day, and then put my long golden hair into two Pocahontas braids. Once I sprayed my body mist, and put on my deodorant, I was ready to go. I wasn't too fond of makeup, so I only wore it when Elijah took me out or when I used to work at Starzz.

"Have a good day, beautiful," Elijah smiled as he slipped his boxers on, looking like a sexy ass piece of caramel candy.

"I will try, baby." I leaned down to kiss his lips a couple times once he'd sat down on the couch in the bedroom.

I then went down the hall to get Donovan, before bringing him in the room with Elijah. After that, I was gone.

I pulled up to my school and was happy to park up close since I'd finally gotten enough to buy a parking pass. Before, I would have to hunt and search for a damn park around the corner because I refused to pay the fee for the lot. And don't think you could park for free, because they would ticket your ass in a hot minute. I parked my car and then grabbed my book bag from the back seat before exiting. I was here a little bit early, so I decided to stop by the food court so I could get a cup of tea, and some kind of pastry since I hadn't eaten yet.

I made it to the court, and after getting my snacks, I took a seat at one of the free tables and began tearing into the pepper jack croissant I'd ordered. It was so buttery and cheesy, which meant it was bad for me but I didn't care. Not like I ate this shit everyday.

"Hey, Ivy, right?" Some guy sat across from me. I recognized him from my class, so I just nodded since there was a whole bunch of croissant in my mouth.

"I'm Kevin, and I was wondering if you had all of the notes for biology class from earlier this week."

"Nice to meet you Kevin, and yes, I have them. I saw you in class on Monday though, why didn't you take them down yourself?" I questioned as I dusted the remnants of the croissant off my hands.

"I was dealing with some stuff, so my mind really wasn't in the class," he shrugged.

"Oh okay, I know how that can be. It's a lot of notes and we're taking more today, so when do you think you could have it back to me?"

"Umm, how about next Wednesday?"

"Could you get them to me this Friday? I don't have classes, but I will be up here typing a paper, if you don't mind driving up here."

"I have a class that day, unfortunately for me, so Friday is perfect. Do you not have a computer at home? I couldn't imagine having to type a paper up here, especially on a day I don't have class."

"No, I have a nice laptop at home, but I bring it up here to type because I need the peace and quiet. At home I get bothered by my son and boyfriend too much to get any work done," I chuckled.

"Oh, I get it. I like that you're dedicated to your work."

"Yeah, I have to be. I work for a call center right now which I hate, so every time I clock in, it reminds me to work harder to get the hell out of there."

"Makes sense. What days do you work?"

"I work on Tuesdays and Thursdays only, since I have classes Monday and Wednesday. I don't make as much as I used to because I'm off on weekends too, but my boyfriend helps me a lot," I nodded.

"Oh, dope. Yeah, I need to keep my head in the game like you, shorty, because my mind is all over the place right now."

"What is it? Your job?" I sipped my tea.

"Nah, my brother and his girl just got murdered about a month ago, and shit has been hard. He, my other brother, and I were real close, so it's hard being without him, ya know? I ain't used to this shit, so I can barely concentrate."

I shook my head slowly because I felt so bad for him. I could tell he was really hurting, and I couldn't imagine having to do all this class work while grieving. People and things didn't seem to matter much until they were nothing but a sweet memory. That shit taught me to cherish the little things in life.

"Well, I applaud you, Kevin, for being strong. Most people wouldn't even be able to make it to class, let alone go around asking for the notes to make sure they kept up. I'm sorry for your loss as well."

"Thanks, I just hope the person who did it gets caught."

"Well if they don't, karma is always waiting in the trenches to enact revenge for us. Just let it go and let life handle them."

"I like that. Shit, class starts in five minutes, wanna walk together?"

"Sure."

EIGHT

# Raleigh Warren

_______________________

"Wait, so you never told me how you got Trixie to get out of the house?" I smiled at my little sister Jersey, as we painted one of the bedrooms in my father's house.

"You have to promise to keep your mouth shut," she smiled and set the painting roller back into the tray filled with paint.

We had all the furniture placed in storage, except for the living room and kitchen things. We'd come up with a plan to make this place a boarding house in a sense. We were gonna rent the rooms out, and we'd already gotten someone to supervise, who we would allow to take up a room for free. It was a great way to make some extra money, especially because the inquiries for renting a room that we'd gotten so far, were from people who had a pretty good income. I guess because the house was located in a great neighborhood.

"I promise not to say a word. You should know that by now, babe," I replied and continued painting.

"Well, Kilexis took care of him, her, or whatever the fuck she went by. He just bumped her off and that's it."

"And no one has said anything? Her lawyer was pretty involved in her life."

"Was is the keyword, Ral. He jumped ship once she didn't get anything. He needed moolah to keep backing her, and once he saw she wasn't getting shit, he chucked them deuces up."

"Damn, that's what her ass gets! I'm just happy she chose *you* to blackmail and not me," I laughed and Jersey rolled her eyes.

"Me too, because if it had have been you, you would've let her tarnish Daddy's name for sure."

"You're damn right, fuck that nigga. Maybe if Trixie had have come out to the world and let them know what she really was, they would've gotten off mama's back."

"I doubt it. I think it would've made shit worse," she sighed.

Suddenly, the doorbell began ringing repeatedly. Whoever it was, was pressing it constantly, and obviously trying to get fucked up. Jersey and I looked at one another, clearly thinking the same thing, before putting down the paintbrushes and descending the stairs. When we made it to the door, I looked out the peephole to see Sonny's stupid ass out there pressing the doorbell.

"What the fuck is he doing over here?" Jersey frowned.

"Hell if I know." I snatched the door open, and Jersey and I stood there, waiting for his hoe ass to talk.

"Good morning, ladies," he grinned and lifted his hand lazily.

He was so basic compared to Ka'Shea, and I was starting to feel slightly embarrassed for fucking with him. Don't get me wrong, Sonny was handsome as hell, but Ka'Shea Camren was on some other shit. Jersey and I declined to respond, so there was silence as we waited for him to continue talking.

"Raleigh, baby girl, can I talk to you for a minute?"

"About?" Jersey raised her brow.

"I was talking to—"

"Nigga, I don't give a fuck who you were talk—"

"Jersey, it's cool. Go back and paint, and I will be up there in like five minutes. Go," I chuckled because she was staring at me with her eyes squinted. "What?" I stepped outside with Sonny and folded my arms.

"I ain't seen you in a while, shorty."

"So."

"Aight, I'm gon' come right out with this shit. I was embarrassed but now I'm not. I miss you and I want you back. I swear I'm done with all the games and bullshit."

"Oh you are?"

"Yeah, I am."

"Hmm, so you're not with Marley?" I smiled and he shook his head no. "Funny, because Cheyla said you had her in the club with you that night Kantwan fucked you up."

"Cheyla don't know what the fuck she's talking about! Plus, Marley and I have always been homies, she and I are not together though," he frowned as if I were out of my damn mind.

"And Alicia?"

I dropped that bomb on him, and by the look on his face, I knew he thought I didn't know. Wilmington was small, well the areas I hung in were. We all knew the same people, and everyone talked to somebody. Alicia's aunt worked at the call center with me, and she told me how Sonny's pedophile ass had allegedly gotten her niece pregnant. Sonny was for real a bottom feeder ass nigga.

"Who is Alicia?" he finally asked.

"Damn, how dumb are you, Sondre? It took you that damn long to come up with a response, and that's all the fuck you had to say?"

"Raleigh—"

"Stop, this is a waste of my time. I don't even know why I'm out here questioning you, when I don't even care. I just think it's funny that you try to pull little shit like we don't know the same people, Sonny! All of us grew up together! My brother is your best friend for Christ's sake!"

He pinched his nostrils as he looked off to the side, before turning his attention back to me.

"All the shit I've done for you, and just because this nigga got good hair and some bread, you saying fuck Sonny."

"Good hair, good dick, good money, good everything, and what do you have, Sondre? You ain't got shit but your dick going for you. Oh and excuse me, Shea has phenomenal dick. The least you can do is step your dick game up if you ain't got shit else going for you."

"Ah!" he rushed me, but I karate kicked his ass in the nuts before his hands could even make it to me. Dropping down to the ground, he gripped his nuts and rocked back and forth. "Fuck!"

"Make that the last time you attempt to put your hands on me, nigga. And instead of showing up here trying to convince me to let you fuck, you need to be worried about not going to jail over impregnating a little ass girl."

"Fuck you, Raleigh! When that nigga gets him a new bitch and starts cheating on you, you're gonna be back over this way," he panted as he finally stood to his feet.

"I would rather share his dick than have yours all to myself. Now get the fuck off the premises before I call your P.O." I slammed the door behind me, and then jogged back up the stairs to finish painting with Jersey.

"What did he say?" she asked when I entered.

"Same shit that he always says."

"You ain't thinking about it, are you?"

"Girl no, Shea has my fuckin' head gone, you know that. I talked to Sonny for pure entertainment and nothing else."

Sonny better make that the last time he pops up on me, because all I had to do was tell Ka'Shea's crazy ass, and homie would be six feet deep.

# NINE

## Kilexis

---

A Couple Weeks Later...

*I* hadn't spoken to Sophie since she dropped that bomb on me, so today I was gonna go to her crib in Elsmere. I'd found out exactly where she lived from Amelia, making me thankful for knowing her finally. I'd already knew the city, just not the address. I made Amelia agree to not letting Sophie know I was coming, and told her if Sophie wasn't home when I got there, she would pay for it with her life. I didn't like threatening people, but these days it seemed like I had to do it. I didn't mind following through with them threats either.

I fastened my chain link bracelet onto my wrist, and then brushed my fade a little bit, wearing a frown. I needed to get my shit cut, but I'd been too damn busy these days. I saw Jersey come from the bathroom wrapped in a towel, with her curly hair up in a bun on top of her head. I loved seeing her fresh from the shower, because the water droplets gave her golden complexion a bit of a glisten. My shorty was way too fucking pretty.

"Where are you going?" she asked and moved closer to me.

We hadn't had any problems after the night I confessed about Sophie. I wasn't sure if it was the way I fucked her, or if she just believed me, but I really didn't care. I refused to allow some one-night stand to interfere with a relationship I started *after* it occurred. And at the end of the day, that was *not* my got damn baby!

"I'm going to see Sophie." I turned to face her, and then leaned down to kiss her gently.

"What should I wear?" She walked to her dresser to grab some underwear and a little bra with no straps.

"Jersey—"

"I'm coming with you. I'm gonna be your wife, right? Then I need to be there and meet this hoe."

"Jersey, there is no need. I told you it ain't my baby, so why do you need to meet with her and shit? Y'all are never gonna have to communicate," I frowned as I watched her put on some jean shorts and a tube top. Her figure was back like it never left, and my dick always took notice.

"Because I need to come. Shit, why are you going if it's not your baby?"

"Because I want to talk to her about getting a DNA test, Jersey."

Sophie had been ignoring my texts and calls regarding the test. Now if I were any other nigga I would shrug it off and move on with my life, but if that was my child, I needed to know. I mean yeah, I felt deep down that it wasn't, but the fact of the matter is, I stuck my dick in her and that was how babies were made. My father always told me, if you fucked her it was possible.

"I thought you were so sure, Kill? If you're so sure, why do you need a test?" Jersey raised her eyebrow, pulling me from my thoughts.

"Just so I can be one hundred about it, Jersey. I'm 99% sure that I'm not the dad, but that 1% is fucking with me because I did sleep with her. Yeah, the condom was intact, but shit happens, and I refuse to leave a child of mine out in the cold.

She just shook her head and then tilted it back so tears wouldn't come out. I let out a deep sigh, and then made my way over to her. I pulled her close, and then kissed her full soft lips a couple times.

"Baby, this shit ain't worth your tears. All I'm doing is making sure of something that I already know. Wouldn't you rather us have it on paper than it just being a gut feeling?"

"Yeah."

"Aight then, and your little spoiled ass can come, just get Alexsia and quickly. I don't want this girl to get wind that I'm coming and bounce."

"Okay!" she said excitedly, and ran past me. I made sure to squeeze her nice round ass as she made her way by me and out of the room.

About twenty minutes later, my little shorty was bathed and dressed, looking so pretty. I swear I would kill anybody and anything for Alexsia. I loved her so much; her and her mother. The three of us got into my Denali, and after making sure Alexsia was buckled in, I opened the passenger door for Jersey. Jogging around to my side, I climbed in and then peeled out of the driveway. Here we go.

We made it to Sophie's house, and I felt relieved when I saw a car in the driveway. Someone was home and that was all I fuckin' needed. I didn't care who it was; they were letting me in the damn house. The three of us got out, then I hit the alarm on my car. I rang the doorbell, and waited while looking around at all the other nice houses.

"Who is it?" someone called out and I could tell it was Sophie. "I asked who is it?!" she hollered with an attitude before snatching the door open. Her eyes immediately went to Jersey and my daughter.

"Can we come in?" I quizzed and pointed behind her.

Sophie rolled her eyes and then looked behind her.

"Hey, look, now isn't a good time, Kill. You and her—"

"His fiancée, get it right," Jersey snapped. I pinched her smooth lower back, signaling for her to calm down.

"You and your fiancée need to come back another time," Sophie finished.

"No, we won't be coming back another time. Let me in because we need to talk about this damn DNA test." I barged in and then made sure Jersey got in behind me. Before I could say anything else, a man walked out into the foyer. *Well, well, well,* I thought.

"Baby, who are they?" he asked Sophie.

Sophie stood there, not knowing what to say as her mouth opened and closed repeatedly. Since she couldn't speak, I would do the shit for her because I was sure this was her dude. The same nigga she was badmouthing the night I fucked her.

"I'm Kilexis, and I'm here to set a date for Sophie and me to go and get a DNA test for her daughter, Kilenna. This here is my fiancée Jersey, and our baby girl. You are?"

"I'm Carter, Kilenna's *father*. Sophie, what the fuck is this nigga talking about?" he frowned and pointed towards me. *I thought they broke up after she and I had sex. Lying ass bitch.*

Usually I would've broken the finger he was pointing at me with, but I was gonna give him a pass since I'm sure this news was a bit infuriating. But just because I wasn't gonna snap that finger, didn't mean I wasn't gonna put him in his place.

"Well for starters, you need to address me with more respect than that, Carter. It's not my fault your bitch is running around here not knowing who she got pregnant by. Now I have shit to do and would like to get things started. Y'all can argue and shit about this on your own time. Show us to the living room or something, Sophie."

Sophie just nodded and started off, so we followed her. Carter was going off in her ear but in a low tone so we wouldn't hear them.

As soon as we sat down on the couches, Jersey whispered to me, "The way you just bossed up on them made me wanna give you some good ass head." A huge ass grin covered my face, as I squeezed her buttery smooth thigh. Some head sounded fire right now.

"Carter, I—"

"Ah! On your own time. Now my shorty has a doctor we can go to, and they have a slot for 11am next Friday," I cut Sophie off. I was not about to sit here and listen to her plead for his forgiveness or whatever the fuck she was about to do. She could do that shit once we left. "You're welcome to come for a test as well, Carter, but I'm not sure how that would make Sophie look."

"I don't want to use her doctor." Sophie looked to Jersey with an attitude.

"Well boo, unless you can find one right now who is willing to have this done in a week, you're gonna have to," Jersey replied.

"Why does she even have to be here? She wasn't there when I fucked you!" Sophie hollered.

I gripped Jersey's arm, because her leg was bouncing, which meant she was ready to fight. I saw her adjusting her grip on Alexsia's carrier, so I knew she wanted to use that same hand to punch Sophie's ass. Sophie was beneath her, and I refused to allow Jersey to stoop to her level and fight her.

"Sophie, she's my fiancée and she's here because I wanted her to be. Is 11am next Friday good or not? Matter fact, fuck that, and be there by 10:45am so we can check in. If you're late, you *and* him will regret it."

"Don't threaten me, boy!" Carter yelled.

"I just did. See you later," I stood up and so did Jersey. I made sure to guide her little ass in front of me so that we could leave, because I didn't want her to wail on Sophie's ass.

As she and I were walking out, I heard Carter and Sophie arguing. That nigga was mad, and I couldn't really blame him. However, if he came at me foul again, he would no longer be on this Earth, and I put that on my daughter.

The three of us got into the car, and then I drove off, headed to go get some food.

"That is not your baby, Kilexis," Jersey touched my hand.

"Told you, ma."

# TEN

# Cheyla

---



Few Days Later...

School wasn't as bad as I thought it would be. I just knew I would be stressed out and over it after just a few weeks, but here it was a month in, and I was good. I actually enjoyed having somewhere to be four times a week, because it filled the void of me wanting to work. I no longer felt useless and lazy. It was better than stripping though, because every morning that I woke up, I knew I was striving for something and not just getting out to make money.

It was Thursday afternoon and since today was my last day of classes for the week, I was in an extra good mood. I could not wait to get home, take a nice hot shower, eat, and watch TV. If tonight was real good to me, Kantwan would come home before I fell asleep, and we could cuddle and have sex. I swear I hated being away from him. I was in love with him, and I didn't mind being in his presence on a consistent basis.

I'd eaten lunch earlier, but now that I was pregnant it seemed like I was hungry all the damn time. I decided to go to the food court and get a deli sandwich since that would be quick, giving me time to eat it and chill before going into class. I ordered my sandwich, and then stepped to the side so I could wait for it to be prepared. Suddenly, someone came and stood extra close to me. When I looked, his smug expression was immediately recognizable. Before I could get a word out, he yanked me into a little hallway, and pressed me against the wall.

"What do you want?" I grimaced, even though I was scared out of my mind. I had to play tough, because if he knew I was afraid, I'm sure he would take advantage of that.

"You should know that I'm not gonna let you get away with setting up my brother and his girl," Monty's brother Isaiah replied. He looked so sneaky and conniving, that it was hard to tell if he was attractive or not.

"Nobody set him up. I don't even know what you're talking about. Monty will be alright, and if he has a problem with me, he knows where to find me all the fucking time it seems." I pretended as if I had no idea that Monty was killed.

"He's dead, bitch!" Isaiah slammed his hand onto the wall next to my head. I jumped so hard that I thought my head would tap the ceiling.

"Aye, what you yelling at her for, bro? You need to chill out before I call the campus police," some random guy who was passing by said.

"Nigga, mind yo' muthafuckin' business before I dead your ass!" Isaiah barked back at him.

"Yeah, okay." He gave a smirk as if he wasn't afraid, but you could tell that he was. I was afraid too, which is why it seemed like my feet were glued to the space he had me in.

The boy walked off, and Isaiah turned his attention back down to me, waiting for a response to his last statement. I was so busy being scared, that I hadn't thought of a good lie to tell.

"I didn't know he died Isaiah, he umm, what happened?" I continued playing the part.

"You know what the fuck happened! Someone told me your little bitch ass boyfriend is the one who popped him! You got some fucking nerve after all of the money my brother gave your hoe ass when you was shaking that skinny body in the clubs!"

"First of all, I'm not skinny, and secondly, I don't know what the fuck you're talking about. If Monty is dead, I'm sorry, but you need to spend more time figuring out who really killed him, and get the fuck out of my face, boy!" I nudged him and started to walk off, but he grabbed my wrist roughly. For some reason, him insulting my shape had angered me to the point where I'd gained some courage.

"Your days are numbered, hoe." He threw me into the wall and then stormed off.

A sharp pain shot through my stomach, and I just took a couple deep breaths to calm down. The pain soon subsided, and I just silently thanked God.

I rushed out and snatched my sandwich off the counter, which was waiting to be picked up. I didn't want to eat in the food court, so I just rushed to my class and ate in there before everyone started to come in. After class, I texted Kantwan to let him know I had some shit to tell him, and then I sped home. I made it home about fifteen minutes later, since it was no traffic yet, and pulled right into the garage.

Not seeing Kantwan's car there irritated me, because that meant he didn't take my fucking text seriously. I began to get paranoid because I realized I didn't pay any attention to my surroundings on the way home. I just sped here, and didn't even make sure I wasn't being followed. *What if he's here, outside waiting for me? What if I just gave up our home address to this nigga?* I asked myself as I damn near bit my nails down to the white meat. That evil looking ass nigga had me on edge. I quickly just hopped out of the car, ran inside, put the alarm on, and then darted up the steps as if I was Florence Joyner.

As I paced my bedroom, the door opened causing me to scream. When I saw it was just Kantwan, I placed my hand over my heart and exhaled heavily. I was not hip to this gangster life! By the confused look on his face, I could tell he thought I was losing my fucking mind. Shit, I didn't care what he thought, as long as he took care of Isaiah.

"You good, ma?" he asked.

"Kantwan, you have to kill Monty's brother!"

"What? Who the fuck is Monty?"

"The dude that you saved me from in the van that night! He... his brother... they—"

"Cheyla, sit down and calm the fuck down so you can talk properly. And calm down for the baby in your stomach, shorty. As hyped up as you are, it can't be good for my kid." Kantwan sat me down gently on the edge of the bed before he knelt down.

After a couple deep breaths, I said, "Okay, Monty is the guy that you saved me from that night. He has two brothers, and one of them, named Isaiah, threatened me today. He told me that he was gonna get me back for setting his brother up. I tried to explain that it didn't happen that way!"

"Cheyla, baby, please tell me you didn't say anything about what happened for real."

"No, I pretended to not even know his brother was dead. I acted as if I was hearing it for the first time. He said someone told him that my boyfriend did it though."

"Good job, ma. Where did this shit happen? You weren't home, were you?" he furrowed his brows.

"Nope! This was at school today, in the food court. He yanked me into some little hallway while I was waiting for my sandwich."

"I'm not too sure if he is anything to worry about, baby, but I will have someone keep an eye on him. Do you know his and Monty's last name or anything like that?"

"No. I only knew Monty as Monty. He was a faithful customer of mine at Starzz, and that was it. He hired me for that party at the Westin that night, the one you shot up."

"Hmm, maybe we can get his information that way, I will see. But relax your nerves, aight? He ain't gon' do shit to you, baby, I promise. Have I ever let anything happen to you?"

"No, you always save me or protect me."

"Aight then, so don't sweat it. This nigga ain't gonna do shit to you, and if I think he is, I will dead him like you asked. Cool?"

"Cool."

Thank God for Kantwan Camren.

## ELEVEN

## Elijah

———

Kilexis and I decided to stop and get some food. It was the middle of the day, and since all we'd been doing was working and having meetings regarding the new club we were opening, we wanted to just chill and get some grub. We decided to stop at El Diablo Burritos in Trolley Square, and sit down just to relax our nerves and talk.

"Feels good to talk about some shit other than work," Kill chuckled and glanced out the window.

"I know, man. Feels like the old days when we were just working the blocks and shit." I nodded just as a waitress came to our table to take our order. This was a stand in line spot, but because we knew the girl, she went out of her way for us. After we put in everything, we waited until she walked away to resume our conversation. "So what's up with that Sophie girl?"

"I pulled up on her ass and demanded that she show up for a DNA test. I wasn't fucking playing around with her ass at all. She really thought ignoring my texts was gonna do something. But get this, her nigga was there."

"Damn, and what the fuck did he have to say? That's grounds to get you killed. I wish I would find out my bitch got pregnant by another nigga, I'd kill all of their asses."

"I thought the same way until Margo got pregnant by that older cat. When that shit happened I was just over it. She wasn't worth any of that shit, and that's when I realized I ain't love her like I thought I did."

"That has to be it, because I can't see you keeping it pushing like that if it were Jersey," I chuckled.

"You damn right. I'd go insane if that shit happened with Jersey. But anyway, her nigga was perplexed because she'd been telling him he was the father so he was dumb confused."

"That's fucked up. Aye I know this is shady, but I'm glad as hell that you fucked her that night and not me, because she was almost mine. Remember?"

"Yeah, I remember, and fuck you," he laughed. "I should've just fucked Amelia's hoe ass and I wouldn't be in this shit."

"It ain't yours though, right Kill? I mean I know you strapped up."

Kilexis was never the reckless type, he was always careful. That's why it was a surprise when he got Jersey pregnant, but I knew he was feeling her way more than any of us knew, so he was probably in the moment. I just hoped that he was sure about Sophie and the fact that her baby wasn't his, because that would be all bad for more than one reason.

"Yeah, I fucking strapped up, man, ain't no way I was running up in her with no cap. I mean, I didn't plan to with Jersey, but a nigga was in the damn moment and it happened, I don't regret it though," he cheesed.

"Maybe you were caught in the moment with Sophie too," I said, and could barely get it out before cracking up laughing, because I knew that was straight bullshit. The waitress set down our plates and drinks before sashaying away.

"Fuck you, aight? Ain't no damn way that hoe had me caught up in shit. I remember rolling the shit down before telling her to hop on, because she was asking me to eat her out while I was doing it."

"You didn't?"

"Nigga, hell no! You the only nigga that let's these random hoes sit on your face," he taunted and I threw a tortilla chip at his lying ass.

"Fuck out of here, don't nobody sit on my face unless they got that Grade A, like Ivy."

"Too much information, but thanks."

We began tearing into our food and for some reason, this burrito was the best that I had ever had. I guess the fact that I skipped breakfast was the reason I was so got damn hungry, and now this poor burrito was getting devoured like a muthafucka.

"Aye, is this burrito the shit, or is it just me?" I asked Kill as I inspected my food, looking for a reason as to why it was so damn good.

"Nah, this shit is fire, low-key." He agreed.

*POP! POP! POP! POP! POP!*

Gunshots began flying through the window we sat by, as everyone screamed and hollered. Kilexis and I both dropped to the floor and put our bodies against the booth, hoping no bullets hit us. Once they seized, Kill hopped up with the quickness and ran outside, drawing his heat immediately while looking all around the shopping center for the culprits.

"Fuck!" he hollered and turned to me as he put his gun back in his waist.

When he did, I saw his right shoulder was soaked in blood. His once white thermal was a deep dark ass red up by his shoulder and collarbone. He was so angry he didn't even notice that he'd been hit.

"Nigga, they got you, let me take you to—"

"Take me home, Eli."

"Nigga, look at all this fuckin' blood! I'm not taking you home!" I started off after him, because he was booking it to my car.

"Fuck," he groaned in pain once he reached my whip. "Eli, man, just take me to my crib before the police make it here. Call this number so the medical professional I hired will come through, but do not take me to hospital, this shit was not random," he said once we were both in the car.

I stared at him for a bit before sighing heavily and taking the phone from him. I tapped the number he had cued up, then explained to the medical professional that we needed her because Kill had been hurt. I finished the call, and then sped out of there with one hand on my heat just in case. I stayed that way all the way until we reached Kill's home. When I looked over at him, the whole damn right side of his shirt was covered in blood.

"Fuck man, that nigga better already be here!" I shouted and jogged around to help him out of the car.

"Nah, I'm good, just go open the door." He handed me his key.

I shook my head at his ass, and jogged to the front door to open it. I looked behind me and saw he was struggling to make it over, but he was getting there. I knew he wouldn't allow me to help him, and that shit annoyed the fuck out of me. He never wanted help of any kind, from anybody. Finally, he made it, and just then, the medical person arrived as Jersey was coming down the stairs. Kill collapsed onto the floor, and groaned loudly as he held onto his shoulder with his eyes shut tightly and his teeth clenched.

"Okay! Get him on the stretcher!" the lady yelled out to her nurse assistants.

"Kilexis, what the fuck!" Jersey shouted as she tried to get closer to him. She was crying and so was little Alexsia.

"Jersey, get her out of here, shorty, please!" Kilexis hollered as I helped them lift him onto the bed.

"Baby girl, come on." I tried to turn Jersey away but her small ass was strong. She was trying to bypass me, and she was doing a pretty good job to be so little *and* holding a baby.

"Jersey, take yo' ass upstairs!" Kilexis barked once more as they rushed him to the back. He was in so much pain and I just hoped they could save his stubborn ass.

"Please go upstairs, Jersey," I begged as both she and Alexsia cried. I wonder if their daughter knew what was happening, or if she was just crying because of all the ruckus. "I will come and get you as soon as anything changes, okay?"

"Eli, just let me go back there, I have to—" she stopped talking when she saw me shaking my head no.

I picked her up while she was still holding her daughter, and carried her ass to the bedroom. I placed her down in it, and then shut the door, holding it closed. I could hear her crying and begging for me to let her out but I just couldn't.

How did this day go from sugar to shit so damn quickly? Someone was gonna pay for this bullshit for sure.

## TWELVE

## Ka'Shea "Shea" Camren

---

I pressed the back of my head into the pillow as I tried to hold my nut in. Raleigh was riding me all slow and shit, driving a nigga crazy. Her perky breasts were staring me in the face, making my mouth water. I wanted to devour them bitches, but I knew I would be bursting all inside of her if I moved too much. She was winding her hips, and her pussy was wet as hell like it always got for me. Gripping her hips, I attempted to control her movements. She hit the base of my dick, and when her body shivered from cumming, it was a wrap for a player.

"Shit!" I screeched as I filled her sexy body up with my seeds.

She slowly got up off of me, and then laid to the side to cuddle up to me. This was how we started every morning, and I loved the shit. Raleigh and I were close as fuck, so close that she never took her pretty ass home. She was always here, and if she did go to her house, she would be calling me to come spend the night. Usually I would cringe at the thought of spending all of my free time with the same woman, but I was feeling this shit. I was feeling it a little too much, and I was wondering what the fuck was wrong with me.

"You got me tripping, Raleigh," I whispered as my fingertips lightly brushed her small bicep.

"In a good way?" she quizzed.

"Good for you, bad for me," I chuckled and she hit my chest. "Nah, it's a good thing, only if you're serious as fuck with me," I sat up.

"I'm serious as fuck with you, you know that. You just better make sure all of your duckies are in a row, and that them bitches know whose nigga you are. Do they know your phone number is *our* phone number?" she joked... half joked.

"They know," I grinned and so did she.

I gathered the shit I would need to get cleaned up, before going into the bathroom to shower and brush my teeth. Once I was clean, I got dressed in some gray Jordan joggers, a black Jordan shirt, and some black and white retro Jordan 12's. Raleigh had just braided my shit up into two long ass French braids, and my facial hair had been freshly lined up.

"I don't know if I want you going out like that," Raleigh smiled as she picked some clothes out of her duffle bag. She then took what she needed to the bathroom so she could shower.

"I ain't even fitted, shorty."

"But you know even when you're dressed down, you still are fine as hell."

"True," I responded as she laughed.

"Let's go to the movies tonight, and then when we get back I can make you some dinner. You can have me for dessert."

"Sounds like a plan." I kissed her lips and then dipped.

I was on my way to go see my boy, Blow. I wanted to know if he had any more information on Portland and Sonny's little bitch ass operation. Hopefully he'd found out who was helping them. Maybe that would lead us to who the fuck shot my damn brother in the middle of the fucking day.

I got to Blow's home about fifteen minutes later, and as usual, he was sitting outside munching on some damn ranch sunflower seeds. This nigga's sodium levels had to be high as fuck with the way he ate them damn things.

"What's good with you?" he stood up and put his hand out to dap me up.

"Nah nigga, I ain't touching them hands. I saw you sucking the skin off them bitches when I pulled up." I sat down.

"Fuck you, bro. What brings you over here? Another dinner invite?"

"Nah, me and shorty doing a duo thing tonight. I was wondering if you heard anything about Portland and Sonny. Shit, do you know anything about my brother being shot at?"

"Yeah, I do. This cat named Leroy hit him."

"Leroy Leroy?" I frowned.

Leroy and I used to be cool when we both worked for Axel. He was always loyal as fuck, so this was a bit of a surprise. Then again, I did notice when I got out that he wasn't working for Kill like the rest of Axel's old team was. Maybe that's why he tried to come for my brother.

"Yeah, Leroy Yankee. They say he was trying to kill Elijah, but that doesn't make any damn sense. I know he has a little bit of animosity towards Kill, so why would he be looking to hit Eli?" Blow matched my frown.

"True. I don't think he was. I think his ass was trying to get at my brother for not keeping his ass on. But what did he expect, he was on that bullshit because he felt the crown should've been given to him or Axel's sons."

"Leroy is a fuck up and just like Ahmad and Dante, he has no business running a damn empire. Shit, he can barely carry out a damn hit," Blow scoffed making me laugh.

I chilled with Blow for a couple more hours, until the sun started to set a little bit. He was able to find out where Leroy was, and I wanted to pay that old hating ass nigga a visit. I knew Kill was capable of doing shit on his own when he got better, but he was my little brother, and this shit needed to be handled now.

I pulled up to the crib on Howland and Dupont where Leroy was. Just like Blow said, he was hanging in this little alley like area right next to the house. I kept driving and parked a little ways down, with my car facing Clayton Street, before exiting. I crossed the street, and then ran down towards the house while twisting on my silencer. As soon as I spotted that played out ass ducktail, I opened fire.

*PHEW! PHEW! PHEW!*

Each shot went straight into his ass, two in the back of the head, and one in his chest. Because the shots were low in sound, his people chilling with him didn't even notice he'd been capped until the third shot, where he slumped down in the chair he was chilling in. Screams broke out as I booked it to my car. I peeled out of there and hooked a left on Clayton Street so I could head home. That'll teach that nigga, and any other nigga to never fuck with a Camren. For now, I was gonna keep this shit from Kill, just until he recovered.

# THIRTEEN

# Jersey

---

*I* finished feeding Alexsia, and thank the Lord she was knocked out for the night. I then went to take a hot bath, before changing into a short nightgown, and making my way to the first floor. I finally made it to the back guest room where Kilexis was. He was propped up in the hospital like bed, watching TV and eating some chips. I hated him two days ago for making me go upstairs, but like always, I loved him again.

"Hey sexy," he bit his lip as I neared him with my cup of tea.

"What are you watching?" I asked as I looked at the TV. It was the only form of light in the room.

"Some show called *Homeland* or something. I ain't want to watch it but my arm started hurting when I was changing channels so, I just stopped," he responded and then set the chips on the nightstand next to him. "I'm sorry for yelling at you Jersey, I just didn't want you and the baby seeing me like that."

"I know. I was mad at first, but now I get it."

"Come lay in the bed with me, I miss sleeping next to you already." He patted the small space next to him.

"Should I be laying in the bed, Kill? I don't want to hurt your arm."

"Jersey, come on." I stood up slowly, and polished off my tea before getting into bed with him. I made sure to be careful, but he tugged me on top of him so that I was straddling him. "I should've had you take your panties off first."

I gave him a half smile, before standing up slowly on the bed to remove my underwear. I put them on the dresser, peeled the blanket off of his lap, and then pushed up his hospital gown. His dick was getting hard, but not all the way yet, so I bent down to take him into my mouth. I loved giving him head, because his moans were like a piece of music put together by Mozart.

"Shit, Jersey," he caressed my hair as I moved my mouth up and down his shaft. "Baby, fuck."

I continued working my magic as his dick became harder and harder in my mouth. Once it felt hard enough to chip my tooth damn near, I mounted him and then slowly slid down. Pain shot through my pussy with every inch of him that I took, causing me to dig my nails into his six pack. The pleasure and pain combination felt so perfect.

"Mmm," I whimpered as I sat still as a statue on him.

My center began to throb as he sat inside me. He then began pushing my gown up to expose the rest of my body, as I continued to stay paralyzed on his long thick member. Gripping my torso with his strong hands, he began moving me up and down slowly while biting his lip. Why was this man so damn fine? It really made no sense, and it was crazy that he was all mine.

"You get so wet for me, baby," he moaned and closed his eyes to enjoy the feeling of being inside of me. I loved hearing his voice when he had sex.

I finally gained enough strength to move up and down on him myself, while he held onto my ass cheeks lightly. His hands then roamed all over my physique as we both let out subtle moans here and there. He began thumbing my clit feverishly as I rocked my hips on him, and soon enough we were exploding together.

"I love you so much, Kill." I leaned down to cup his face and kiss his full lips.

"I love you too, ma." His hands wandered up and down my back slowly.

———

*J* finished changing my baby's diaper, and then picked her up so she could come to the room her father was in. We were all gonna watch some TV together since I was done with classes for the day.

"Is that my princess?" Kill smiled and reached for her. I could already tell that Alexsia was a daddy's girl, because she began moving wildly as if I was holding her hostage from him.

"I told you to stop doing that because she be fucking me up trying to get to you," I chuckled as I handed her over to her father. He blew on her fat belly, and she screamed and laughed loudly. "Too cute," I said before sitting down in the chair next to the bed.

Right when I did, my cellphone rang. I didn't recognize the number, but since it was from here in Wilmington, I decided to go ahead and answer it.

"Hello?"

"Baby girl, don't hang up Jersey, please!" Portland said. I rolled my eyes. After making sure Alexsia and Kill were good, I stepped out of the room to let this asshole humor me with whatever the fuck his stupid ass had to say. "Jersey?"

"What? What the fuck do you want? And you need to make it quick because I'm busy, nigga!" I barked.

"Baby girl, I miss you. I wanna see you and talk to you, I don't like us being estranged like this ya know? Especially because we used to be so close and shit."

"Well you fucked that up, Portland, so please miss me with the sob story. All you care about is yourself, and no one else, not even your dead father or incarcerated mother. You don't even give a fuck about your own son and his mother!"

"I do care! I care about all of y'all, Jersey, but that shit was too much. You know that you and Raleigh are much stronger than me, it's always been like that. I have a very fragile mind shorty. And as far as Donovan and Ivy, well they got that Elijah nigga."

"You sound stupid as fuck. Ivy did not get with Elijah to replace you, dummy." I rolled my eyes and turned my lip up in a disgusted manner as if he could see me. I wish he were here so that I could slap the shit out of his ass.

"She don't want me in Donovan's life. She prefers that nigga as her baby daddy, not me. I tried but that shit hurts my feelings knowing I ain't enough for her anymore."

"Here we go with another segment of Portland wanting someone to feel bad for his whack ass."

"Don't be like that, Jersey. But how are you? How is my niece?"

"She's perfect and I'm perfect as always as well."

"Oh, okay. Kill is her father, right?"

"Portland, you know who her father is, and that's probably the only damn reason you want to make up with me. Cheyla already told me that you and Sonny wanna be down with them."

"Well, Cheyla needs to update her information, because that's no longer the case. We got our own shit going on, and no longer need them Camren niggas. I'm calling you because like I said, I miss you."

"So."

"Maybe we can go to lunch or something, Jersey. I'm willing to do whatever it takes for your forgiveness. And even though Raleigh is fucking with me a little bit more than you, I still want to make it up to her as well. Please, one lunch date and we can go from there. You know Mom and Dad... Fuck Dad. You know Ma wouldn't want us apart and fighting like this. We've lost enough."

"Fine, Portland, I will let you know when I'm free."

## FOURTEEN

## Kantwan

___________

The fact that my brother got shot had me wondering if that nigga that threatened Cheyla was behind it. I wasn't too sure, but with all the shit going on I felt it was best to let my brother know about a potential enemy. Yeah I felt he was harmless, but shit, you never know. Niggas were acting bold these days and you could never be too sure.

I walked through Kill's home until I made it to the large room he'd been sleeping in while he recovered from being shot. When I entered, I was surprised to see him moving around and shit. He was using his arm like his shoulder wasn't just shot the fuck up a couple days ago. My brother irritated me sometimes with his always wanna be strong ass. He would never just sit down and rest, or be sad about shit that we knew bothered him. Nothing ever got this nigga down, or at least that's what he wanted us to think. I knew it wasn't healthy for him to be that way, but he'd been like that for as long as I've known him.

"Hey man, are you supposed to be moving shit around so soon?" I asked as I sat down on the couch in there. I smiled when I saw a baby swing bed, because I knew my niece had been in here.

"I'm feeling great, and this was in the way so I moved it." He pointed to the end table that he had pushed down some.

"How are you feeling?" I questioned.

"Bothered as fuck," he sighed and walked over to sit on the hospital like bed. "I don't know who the fuck it was that shot me, and would be foolish enough to shoot into a restaurant in broad daylight."

"Portland, Sonny maybe."

"I want to pin it on them, but I just don't see them being that bold. If they did have something to do with it, they definitely hired someone to do the work. They're not about that life like they try to pretend."

"I feel you. Cheyla told me some nigga threatened her at school and shit. I don't see how they would know you, but maybe that's a part of it."

"Why did he threaten her? I'm not following how some random nigga who threatened your girl would end up shooting at me and Elijah in the middle of a damn restaurant." He furrowed his brows.

I let out a deep sigh and said, "Nah, remember that night Cheyla got attacked and I had you come and get her car?" He nodded. "Well the nigga I killed, his brother is the one who threatened Cheyla. I'm thinking maybe he was just trying to get anyone of us."

"But me? Why would he choose me, or even Elijah? It would make more sense for him to come after you." He shook his head and then stood back up to pace the room. "What's his name?"

"Isaiah. Maybe he wanted you as revenge. I killed his brother, and he kills mine, you know."

"Do you have a last name on him or anything? We need something more to look his ass up."

"No, but I know his brother got a hotel room a couple of months ago at the Westin. His name is Monty and I'm sure they have the same last name; I hope they do."

"And how the fuck are we supposed to get ahold of some hotel records from the Westin, Kant?"

"I know somebody. He already told me he can get into any system from anywhere."

I met this dude name Ali, and he was a computer hacker. He told me he could get into anyone's system, including banks, colleges, hotels, and anything else. I wanted to use him but a few things had me a bit apprehensive. I needed to make sure he wasn't working for the government or anything, because that would get me in some serious ass trouble if he were to set my black ass up. My life would be over for sure.

"You met someone? Kantwan, we can't be fucking around with random niggas. Shit is too hot right now. Have Cheyla text me what the nigga looks like, and I will go up to the school and scope his ass out."

"I think it's better if we look into him privately, Kill."

"I didn't ask you what you thought, Kantwan, I gave you something to do. This is a monologue right now, not a dialogue. Get Cheyla to send me his physical description so I can look into him."

"I'm gonna do that, but I'm also going forward with the guy I met, Ali."

"Kantwan, you don't know this nigga! What if he's setting you up, huh? Then what? You want to risk going to jail over some nigga who we can catch without all that extra shit? Really?"

"I'm gonna look into him before I hire him."

He laughed and ran his hands over his face.

I understood that Kilexis was the boss, but I still had the right to think for myself. Every decision he made wasn't gonna be the end of the conversation like he wanted. I understood where he was coming from, but this guy, Ali, would be very useful to me; to us. I wasn't gonna let Kill's bullheaded ass fuck up something just because it wasn't his idea.

"Do what you want, Kantwan. Do what the fuck you want, but if you get caught up, you better not fuckin' mention me. And don't look to me to dig you out of some shit that you should've never been in, in the first place."

"I won't." I stood up just as Jersey was coming into the room.

"Kantwan, would you like some spaghetti?" she smiled up at me.

"Nah, I'm good. Peace."

I left out hot as fuck. I was a grown ass man and therefore I was gonna do what the fuck I felt needed to be done. I wanted to get this nigga's name so I could dig into his past and everything else I needed to know about him. As Kill requested, I was gonna have Cheyla text him the details of the way the nigga looked, but while he was fucking around trying to catch the nigga, I was gonna be doing what he should've been doing.

As soon as I got into my car, I pulled my phone out to dial Ali. I wasn't fucking around with these niggas.

FIFTEEN

Ivy

————

LATER THAT NIGHT...

*S*hamece and I were becoming pretty cool, and starting to talk a lot more lately, especially now that I was basically forced to quit the call center. Going to school, and having to keep up with them ten page papers and shit was really wearing me the fuck out. It came down to either keeping my job or staying in the school, and school won. I hated that Elijah was gonna be supporting me now, but it was just something I would have to deal with if I wanted to make something of myself. In the end, getting that college degree would all be worth it.

"Hey girl," Shamece smiled as soon as I got into her car. The smell of raspberries was in the air, mixed with a little bit of her perfume.

"Hey, how are you?"

"I'm okay, still trying to get like you and find me a good, fine man," she responded as we laughed.

"Well good luck, because it is pretty scarce out here, ya know?"

"I do. So do you wanna go to the movies first? Or get something to eat?"

"We can do the movies because if I eat, I'm gonna get sleepy as fuck in the theatre."

"Same!"

She sped off down my street, and we got to the movies in no time. We decided to see *X-Men: Apocalypse* and despite my reservations, it was a really cool film. I hated action and sci-fi, but this one actually had me interested. We then decided to just pick up some fast food, and go to her house to chill and watch some TV. I kind of enjoyed hanging with someone who didn't know certain aspects of my life like Jersey, Cheyla, and Raleigh did.

We made it to her house, and it was a pretty cool little place. She had it furnished nicely, which made me wonder if stripping was her only job. There was no way her ass was paying for all this nice shit from shaking her ass and swinging around a pole. I mean you made good money, but not that good unless you were selling pussy too.

"This is nice, Shamece," I said as I sat down in front of the coffee table with my Chinese food.

"Thanks, girl. Would you like something to drink?" she asked after she set her food down next to mine.

"Yes, some juice or water is fine."

"Okay."

She brought back the waters, and then sat down before we began digging in. This shit was so good, and for the first time in a long time I was gonna clear my fucking plate. *Damn bitch*, I thought to myself. Suddenly, Shamece placed a bottle of Vodka on the coffee table, and then grabbed some shot glasses off of the bookshelf she had them on for decoration.

"Let's take some shots!" she giggled.

"Shamece, no, how are you gonna drive me home?" I questioned.

"Can't your man come get you? Come on Ivy, it'll be fun!"

I stared into her eyes for a couple moments as she playfully pouted and begged for me to drink with her.

"Fine, Shamece!" I chuckled. She cracked the bottle open, and then began filling the double shot glasses with liquor. "Shouldn't we play some sort of game or something? Or are we just gonna take shots for no reason?"

"Okay, umm, let's play Truth."

"You mean Truth or Dare?"

"No, Truth. We will ask each other questions, and if we don't want to answer we have to take a shot. Cool?"

"Uh sure, I guess. But I don't think I will be taking many shots then," I laughed. I really had nothing to hide like that, so I was gonna be one sober bitch.

"We will see. Okay, is it true that you're over Portland?" she got right to it.

"It's very true! Extremely true!" I replied as we cracked up. "Is it true that you bought all of this by only stripping and nothing else?" I raised a brow at her.

"Oooh, starting off going for the jugular already I see. I will take the shot on that one," she grinned and threw back the shot. Once she gained her composure she asked, "How many dudes have you been with?"

"Just two," I shrugged. "How many have you been with?"

"Umm, like eleven," she said surprising the fuck out of me. "Have you ever been with a girl before?"

"Nope! And is that true? The fact that it's only been eleven guys?"

She poured and threw back another shot, making us both laugh loudly.

"Ivy, I'm losing terribly here, take two for me!" I just shook my head at her and then threw back two double shots, which burned the whole way down. I hadn't drunk in so long that the shit was scalding my stomach. "Have you ever thought about being with another girl?"

"Like a relationship?"

"No, just having fun."

I picked up the shot glass, which she filled, and then threw it back. I was gonna lie and say no, but I'd had a couple thoughts here and there so I decided to just keep quiet about it. I'd only thought about it because Elijah asked me if I would have a threesome with him.

"Oh shit! Anybody I know?" She cocked her head.

"Girl, I took the shot now it's my turn! Have you been with a girl? And if not, have you thought about it before?"

"Yes, I have. It was pretty cool actually; you should try it. Now is it anyone that I know that you've fantasized about?"

"I never said I fantasized about one. It has crossed my mind, and no it's not anyone you know. It's not even a person really. I should've just taken the fucking shot on this one!" I laughed and so did she.

We kept going and taking more shots, and the next thing I knew, I was low-key hella drunk. I got up to use the bathroom because in a minute, I would be peeing all over myself. Once I was finished, I washed my hands and returned to the living room so that I could call Elijah. I knew he was gonna be mad as hell, but I'd rather deal with him being mad than Shamece's drunk ass driving me home.

"He's coming?" Shamece asked once I finished placing the call.

"Yeah, he was a little upset but he will get over it once I give him some," I half joked.

I closed my eyes as I sat on the couch, waiting for Elijah to arrive, when suddenly I felt a hand moving up my thigh. I looked over drunkenly at Shamece, just as she got down onto the floor and placed my legs onto her shoulders.

"Shamece, move," I chuckled, thinking she was just being her usual crazy self. I knew I was wrong when she kissed my pussy through my panties, and then began to lick all over it.

My phone buzzed, and I saw Elijah's name pop up. I pushed her off a little more roughly than I had intended, and then grabbed my phone to answer it.

"I'm outside, hurry the fuck up," he hung up.

"Shamece, this was fun. I will see you later."

"I hope so," she licked her lips.

I rushed out to the car and got in on the passenger side. Elijah peeled off before I was even in good, and I just smiled at his sexy angry face. Reaching my hand into his lap, I leaned over and kissed his cheek softly.

"You smell like a fucking drunk," he spat but then a smile appeared on his face as I massaged his dick some more.

I dropped my head into his lap, and then removed his dick to start going in. Listening to his low moans really gave me some motivation, so I started giving him my drunken all. He was trying to keep himself in the right lane, but he barely could, so he pulled over.

"Ivy, fuck." He gripped my bun so tight I thought he was surely gonna rip it from my scalp. "Mmm," he moaned again right before he let off in my mouth. I took it back, and then sat up as he put himself away.

"She tried to eat me out, Eli," I admitted after rinsing my mouth with Listerine.

"Tried or did?" he asked as he pulled from the curb.

"Tried, she was kissing between my legs when you came."

"You liked it?"

"I don't know." I knew why his ass was asking.

He just squeezed my thigh and kissed my cheek. What a night...

SIXTEEN

## Portland Warren

One Week Later...

Fuckin' Leroy did a horrible ass job taking out Elijah. Not only did he hit the wrong nigga, but he didn't even kill the muthafucka he *did* hit. To make matters worse, everyone in the hood knew it was him, but thank God he didn't snitch on us, and the hood didn't snitch on him to the police. I had planned to hire someone to kill his ass, but someone had gotten to him before me. Sonny and I told Dante and Ahmad it was us who killed Leroy though, just so we wouldn't seem soft. I chuckled at my thoughts as I put my car in park.

I'd taken care of everything else in my life, somewhat, but now I needed to talk to Breesha. Ever since she told me she was pregnant, I hadn't said anything to her. I blocked her from contacting me on every outlet, and when she tried to send messages through the homies, I never responded. I know it was fucked up for me to do, but I didn't want a kid right now. To be honest, I barely wanted the little nigga I already had. I loved the thought of being a father, but I hated the responsibility it came with. Them little shits always needed something, and I was always expected to provide it. That was the only downside to being a man: you had to be the provider and the securer.

Knocking on Breesha's door, I waited for her to come answer it for me. She had better be here too, because a nigga did not leave Wilmington just for her not to be home. I couldn't call her beforehand because I deleted her number and didn't know it by heart. I was the grimiest nigga, I know, but look at my father.

I heard someone moving the locks, so I knew she was home. The door opened, and there she stood with her fine ass. Breesha was so damn beautiful, which is why I never understood her obsession with Ivy. Yeah, Ivy was beautiful and had my heart, but so did Breesha. The only thing that gave Ivy a little more leverage over her, was the fact that she had my kid and our history. But now that Ivy was out being a hoe, Breesha was on top. I just wished her ass wasn't pregnant, fuck.

"Yes?" she folded her arms and waited for me to speak.

"Hey baby, can I come in. I miss you and I wanna talk."

"Oh now you wanna talk? The same nigga who pushed me out of his lap when I told him I was pregnant? The same nigga who didn't even have the decency to come tell me to get out his house? I just woke up to niggas moving my shit onto a U-Haul!"

"I know, and all of that was fucked up, but shorty, I was tripping out. You know all the shit I been going through with my bitch ass daddy, psycho ass mama, and my jealous ass baby mama. You telling me about the baby was just too damn much, Bree. I need you now, though," I softened my tone. Her eyes became glazed over, and she looked to the right to wipe them.

"Come in," she scoffed and walked away from the door.

When I walked in, the smell of food hit my nose. I wasn't quite sure what it was, but it had my stomach grumbling like crazy. That was one thing I missed about having a main bitch, them damn home cooked meals. Both Ivy and Breesha could cook their sexy asses off, and they never left a nigga hungry either. The thought of Ivy now feeding Elijah my full course meals *and* my pussy, angered me for a few moments.

"What's that you cooking?" I sat down on the couch in Breesha's living room.

"Smothered chicken, green beans, loaded mashed potatoes, and strawberry cheesecake," she rolled her eyes as she responded to me before sitting down.

"Bree, how is the baby?" I rubbed her thigh.

"The baby is perfectly fine, despite it's no good daddy treating its mother like shit."

"I know I get it. I'm sorry for that bullshit, I was just tripping the fuck out. It was a lot of shit going on with my parents and baby mama."

"I know it's hard dealing with what your mother did, Portland, but that's what I'm here for. And as far as Ivy, what is she doing to you now?"

"She's doing what the fuck she's been doing. She wants to be a family but I ain't with that shit anymore. I can't see my son unless I agree to be with her either. She keeps blowing me up about leaving her nigga for me, and now he's mad and about to come for me," I lied right through my teeth. None of that shit was true, but I wanted Breesha to think it was Ivy coming after me and not the other way around.

"And you wonder why I don't like her! I'm glad you haven't succumbed to her advances Portland, she left you and you need to keep it that way. Only co-parent and nothing else."

"I know and I *am* only co-parenting. But what's up with us being a family, ma? You've always been a vacation for me and I wanna be on that vacation permanently."

"If we do this Portland, it can't be like the last time. I'm not the side chick anymore, I'm gonna have to be your girlfriend, like for real for real."

"That's what I want, shorty. I used to think I wanted you *and* Ivy, but now I know it was just my son that kept me feeling attached to her. But now that you're having my child, I think it's a sign for me," I grinned and so did she. It was so easy for me to lie, and that worried me a little.

"Well good, this can be our fresh start, Portland. No bullshit this time."

"No bullshit." I pulled her closer to me, and kissed her soft lips.

"And to think Ramia said you would bring me nothing but my demise," she said, referring to one of her hating ass friends. And to think I let that bitch give me some head.

"Ramia is just jealous," I smirked before pressing my lips against hers.

For now, I was feeling this thing with Breesha and me. But once the damn baby got here, I'm sure all of that would change. I wasn't meant to be the head of a household. I was meant to live like a king, fuck plenty of bitches, and spend plenty of money, nothing more nothing less.

# SEVENTEEN

# Kilexis

---

*K*antwan had me irritated as fuck. I knew he thought he knew what the fuck he was doing, but he didn't. He didn't understand that niggas were everywhere trying to catch somebody slipping. As much as I wanted to pay him no fucking mind, I couldn't let my brother go out like that. He would be mad that I stepped on his toes but oh well. This act would benefit us all in the end.

I'd just finished coming from getting the DNA test done, and Carter's ass came too. They said they would have them for me soon, and to come back with Sophie in a week. Speaking of Sophie, I had to reschedule the initial appointment because she claimed she couldn't get the day off. To make sure her ass wasn't lying, I showed up to her job, explained the situation, and lucky for her, the boss confirmed it for me. But, he also made sure to give her today off so we could get it done. I was a bit anxious to find out the results even though I knew deep down that baby was not mine. It just couldn't be.

Parking at Cheyla's school, I pulled out my phone and read the description of the nigga she said had threatened her. I then called my little homie that I had lurking up here all day, because I needed him to give me a location on the nigga so I could get at his ass. Once he gave me the spot, I hopped out of my whip and jogged over by the library. Leaning up against the outside, I checked my phone and saw my homie text me that Isaiah was on his way out.

"Isaiah?" I quizzed when some nigga with dreads came out of the library.

"Why you looking for Isaiah?" he countered.

"I'm looking for you because I wanna have a talk about some shit you've been spewing out."

He scoffed and then tried to pass by me like I was some bitch, so I grabbed him up by his collar and shoved him into the wall, after pulling him into some little alley like area.

"Aye man, back the fuck up off me!"

"Listen bitch, I don't appreciate you making threats to my little sister. I don't play that shit, and unfortunately you had no warning before making your big mistake." He tried to move but I was way stronger than him. And because the little alley was so small, people were just walking by not even paying attention. Due to him not wanting to relinquish his pride, he refused to call for help despite the fear that had filled his body.

"And what the fuck you gon' do, huh? That little hoe had my brother set up, and I'm gon' make her pay for it."

I just smiled and subtly removed my pocketknife.

"You thought I was playing?" I squinted my eyes and cocked my head as I repeatedly plunged my knife into his midsection.

He stared into my eyes as if I was his closest friend betraying him. Whenever he got ready to speak, I would stab him again, knocking the wind out of his stomach. I wiped my knife off with his shirt, and then let him slowly slide to the floor. To make sure he had checked out, I slowly slid my knife across his neck, slitting his throat. I then made sure no one was close by, and surprisingly it was rather clear. I guess this was a popular class time, which is why no one was outside. Making my way out, I walked to the car calmly as if nothing had happened.

Once I got to my car, I pulled out my dummy phone from the

glove compartment and dialed Kantwan. He didn't pick up the first time, so I called his ass right back.

"What's up?"

"Aye, no need to get at that Ali cat, I took care of the problem."

"Why? I told you I had the shit! Why the fuck did you go behind my back and do something you knew I specifically didn't want you to do, Kilexis?" he hollered.

"Nigga, calm yo' little ass down! Crying and shit like some little bitch! We on the same fucking team, this ain't no competition, Kantwan! Sometimes you have to do shit old school and not the way you're trying to do it! You don't know this nigga, and he could have you fucked out here!" I frowned as I removed my gloves.

"Fuck you, Kilexis." He hung up.

I clenched my jaw and just shook my head. I was surprised to see that no one had found Isaiah yet and called the police or some shit. I heard no commotion whatsoever, but that was fine with me because it just meant he hadn't been found yet. I sped out of there, and was gonna go see Kantwan but I decided against it. I went to Ka'Shea's house instead, because maybe he could get through to his ass. I wasn't gonna keep doing this bullshit with him. He needed to realize that we were on the same side and not competing against one another.

"What's good, bro?" Ka'Shea greeted me.

"Man, your little brother is on some bullshit for real. He out here mad because I took care of some shit that I warned him I was gonna take care of."

"Like what?"

"He told me some nigga threatened his shorty at school, and when I asked for his last name, he came at me talking about he's got some I.T. guy that can hack anything. He was gonna have him pull up the nigga's information so we could look into him more."

"Does he know the I.T. nigga well?"

"Hell nah he don't! And ain't shit we need to know about the guy we're looking for. Kantwan murked the nigga's brother, and he was trying to seek revenge. Why wait to look him up and allow him to possibly go through with something?"

"True. So what, he's mad because you handled the shit before him? Kantwan is stupid as fuck sometimes," Ka'Shea laughed.

"Hella stupid. Nigga hung up in my face and everything." I watched Ka'Shea roll a couple blunts.

"So what you do to old boy?"

"I stabbed his ass up in some little alley by the school."

"You wore gloves and shit right?"

"Fuck yeah I had on gloves. Matter fact, I need to torch the knife in your backyard or some shit."

"That's fine. Aye, I been meaning to talk to you about who shot your ass." Ka'Shea took a pull on the blunt.

"I know. We gon' find out, I just hope we do so before their asses strike again. I had someone watch Portland and Sonny, and they didn't see shit so now I'm really flabbergasted."

"Fuck." He rubbed his eyes and leaned back before passing me the blunt. "So it was Leroy."

"Leroy…Leroy?" I frowned and he nodded with his eyes closed. "How do you know?"

"Blow told me. He said every nigga in the hood knew it was him. I think homie was still heated that you fired his ass."

"No wonder he's been low-key as fuck as of late."

"Well, I popped his ass for you about a week and a half ago already, bro. I didn't want him trying to get your ass again."

"I just don't get why he would've waited so damn long to get me. Something ain't right here, Shea. If he was that pissed, he would've gotten me as soon as I let him go."

"I ain't even think about it that way. So you think someone put the idea in his head?"

"I am definitely feeling that way. He done hooked up with someone else who don't fuck with us, that's what I'm thinking. Leroy ain't no bitch, he wouldn't have waited this long if he was really feeling some type of way."

"I agree," he nodded and took a pull. "So who you thinking?"

"Nigga, I don't know. To be honest, Ahmad and Dante keep circling my mind. I'm feeling like they're working against us, but making silent moves in a way."

"This shit is just gonna get worse."

"I know."

The more I thought about the fact that Leroy was the one who shot me, the angrier I got. If that muthafucka was crazy enough to shoot me in broad daylight in front of hundreds of people, then he clearly had someone in his corner that he believed could protect him. I needed to find out exactly who that was, and the more that I did, the more in denial I became.

## EIGHTEEN

## Cheyla

_________________

Tonight, Ivy, Jersey, Raleigh, and I were gonna go out to this lounge. It was partially a club, but since I was carrying at the moment, we wanted to go some place where I wouldn't be shoulder to shoulder with a bunch of sweaty ass niggas who would be bumping into me. I chose to wear some pumps, along with skinny jeans, and a strapless top. My stomach wasn't bulging too much, so I was taking full advantage of that.

As I brushed my edges down, Kantwan walked into the room looking a little bummed. He'd been like that for the past couple of days, ever since he came back from seeing his brother. I'd been trying to just let him get over it, but now I decided to talk to him. I needed him to spruce up a bit.

Standing up from my vanity I asked, "What's wrong, Kantwan?"

He plopped down onto the bed, and then fell backwards to look up at the ceiling. He then massaged his closed eyes, before reopening them and sitting up straight again. I rubbed his bare back as he stared down as his hands.

"My brother is working my fuckin' nerves."

"Which one? Shea?"

"Nah man, Kill. I specifically told his ass I was gonna handle old boy who got at you, but he beat me to it. He went about it in a way that I didn't like, and that shit has me hot."

"Isaiah? Oh shit, that was Kill who got him?" I quizzed and he nodded.

There had been a stabbing at my school, and when they pulled the camera footage by that area, they realized someone had focused the camera's lens into the wall. By saying that, they had no idea who had stabbed Isaiah. I knew Kantwan or his brothers were behind it since I had texted Kill Isaiah's description, but I had no idea that Kill had done it his damn self. I just knew he'd hired a flunky to do the work.

"I just need to distance myself from him for a little bit so I can get my mind together."

"Kantwan, Kill was just trying to help. I mean you guys are brothers and you are working for the same goal. It shouldn't be that big of a deal, baby. You know he didn't mean anything by it."

"Don't fucking tell me what ain't a big deal, aight? I don't appreciate people stepping on my fucking toes! I don't give a fuck who it is! If I say I'm gonna take care of something, then let me fucking do it!" He shot up off the bed and barked down into my face.

I just stared up at him with a confused expression. Kantwan had never yelled at me like that, at least not while we'd been in a relationship. That's excluding the night he caught me stripping. This was still different though, because I really saw no reason for him to be this angry. He was acting like a bitch in my opinion, but I wouldn't dare say that shit right now. If I did, I would not be surprised if he backhanded me.

"Fine Kantwan, do what the fuck you want."

"I will do what I want! And since you're so team Kill, maybe you should start fucking him and spending his money." He snatched a shirt from his closet and stormed out.

"Whatever," I mumbled lowly as I grabbed my MAC lip lacquer to put on my lips.

Once I finished, I got up to check myself out in the mirror. I pushed my freshly pressed hair behind my ears, and then smiled at my appearance. I looked good and I was gonna have a good time tonight. I didn't feel like dealing with Kantwan's bratty ass attitude. Shit, and now that Isaiah was gone, I was gonna party even harder to celebrate. I don't know how I was gonna do it with no alcohol, but I would try.

My phone buzzed on the dresser, and I saw it was a text from Raleigh, letting me know Jersey was outside. I grabbed my phone and clutch, and then rushed outside. I hopped into the front seat, then turned my body a little to greet Ivy and Raleigh in the back seat. I then leaned over and kissed Jersey on her cheek before she pulled off.

"Where the fuck did Kantwan go?" Ivy asked as Jersey drove down my street.

"What? He's in the house," I replied confused.

"No bitch, he peeled out of here so fast that I'm pretty sure he was only driving on two damn wheels," Raleigh corrected me.

"Whatever, I don't care. He's mad at Kill about something. Tonight I want to have fun, so let's talk about something else, thanks."

I shook my head as I thought about Kantwan. Clearly he wasn't going to work or something, because if he were, Raleigh and Ivy wouldn't have been asking me where he was going. I would ask him where he went later—or shit, maybe not. Fuck him.

We pulled up to the venue, and Jersey drove right up to valet. Two guys approached the car, opening doors for the four of us. He handed Jersey a little retrieval ticket, and then once she stepped onto the curb in her tight red dress, we walked up to the bouncer.

"We're on the guest list of Shelby Waters," Raleigh told him. Her co-worker was fucking the owner of the club, so she promised Raleigh a table for her and her friends.

"Name," the bouncer asked.

"Raleigh Warren," she replied and then pulled the three of us closer to her so that he could see.

He looked down at the list, checked us off, and then let us in. Some girl with an earpiece told us to follow her and we did, all the way to this roped off area with plush white couches. There was a bucket of liquor, juice, and ice set down by a hostess as we entered, and a huge white card with Raleigh's name on it. The four of us took a seat and started making ourselves a drink; well, I just got some cranberry juice.

"It feels so good to be out," Jersey said into my ear and then smiled. She moved her wild curly hair to the other side, as she waited for my response.

"I know. It's crazy how we used to live the club scene and now we barely go."

"So true. But I can't say I'm upset about it. I prefer being a fiancée, student, and mother. But going out every now and then is nice." She sipped her juice and moved a little bit in her seat to the music.

"I *was* enjoying it but now I don't know."

"Girl, you guys had one damn fight. Relax, aight?"

"True. I just don't like fighting with him. I'm sure he will be over it in the morning. Come on." I stood up and then pulled her up with me.

The four of us began to dance and sing a long with "Panda" by Desiigner. Well, we sang along with as much as we could interpret. Ivy and Raleigh were throwing them back, and in no time they were tipsy as fuck. Some guys came into the VIP area, but Raleigh quickly shooed their asses away. We didn't want them problems, and with the way Kantwan's ass always had my location, I refused to be caught freaking one of these busted down ass niggas.

By the time it hit 1am, we were ready to go. The club was gonna close soon, and we didn't want to be caught in all the pandemonium that would occur when everyone was trying to clear the club. The four of us exited while laughing loudly and joking around. Seeing Ivy and Raleigh drunk was hilarious as fuck. I really had a good ass time tonight, forgetting all about my argument with Kantwan.

"We need to have a girl's trip, because tonight was not e-fucking-nough!" Ivy squealed as the valet guys helped us into the car.

"I know! Where should we go? I want something with the club scene!" I said.

"That, or something relaxing like Hawaii," Raleigh suggested and I nodded although she was in the back seat and couldn't see me.

"You have to drop that little one first, Cheyla," Jersey said.

"I know. And as soon as he or she is old enough to fly, or stay with his or her daddy, then we are going!" I replied as we all laughed.

"I'm hungry as fuck, let's go to Marsh Diner," Ivy sighed.

"I can always eat so I'm down," I said.

Jersey made a right, headed to Marsh. On the way there, I noticed a dark ass car was purposely trying to stay on the side of us in order to get our attention. I shook my head and stared straight, because I knew it was some thirsty niggas trying to get our attention. We came to a red light, and so did the dark car.

"Aye!" the guy in the car hollered. Still, I refused to look.

"What the fuck!" Raleigh yelled.

I looked to my right and saw it was that drug dealer Kantwan beat up. He was in the back seat with a long ass gun pointed at the car. Jersey sped off, running the red light, and they were right on our fucking ass.

*POP! POP! POP!*

He began shooting at the car as Jersey dipped and swooped at about one hundred miles per hour. The four of us were screaming at the top of our lungs as she made a quick right down some dark ass street.

"Oh my fucking gosh!" I shouted as I heard bullets start to rain on the back of the car.

"What the fuck! Who are they?" Ivy yelled so damn loudly that she almost drowned out the sound of our speeding cars and their bullets.

Suddenly the bullets stopped, and when I looked in the side mirror they were gone. Jersey pulled over to the side, because she was too shaken up to drive any further at the moment.

"What the fuck just happened?" She began to tear up like the rest of us.

"I have never seen them niggas in my life! Why were they trying to kill us?" Ivy questioned as she breathed heavily.

"Maybe some random niggas being dumb," I tried to cover my ass.

"No, they wanted us specifically." Jersey shook her head. "Thank the Lord my car is bulletproof." She hit the steering wheel with her fist.

"You need to mention this, every one of us needs to mention this to the boys so they can find out what's up! This better not be because of anything they did!" Raleigh spat.

"Look you guys, what do we need to mention this for? It's over," I shrugged.

"Even if I don't, Kill is gonna wanna know why there are bullet holes all over my fucking car, Cheyla!" Jersey barked.

"Okay, alright. Please tell him not to mention this to Kantwan. The guy who shot at us was someone Kantwan had beat up for me. I don't want him trying to go after him. He's saved me too many times, and I know he will get tired of it," I admitted.

"What did Kantwan beat him up for, Cheyla?" Raleigh questioned as Jersey cranked the car back up.

"He was my drug dealer, and I owed him money." I blinked away the tears as Jersey slammed on her breaks.

"Drug dealer?" the three of them shouted in unison.

"Yes! My drug dealer! I used to pop pills but now I don't! I don't wanna fucking talk about it anymore, just take me home!"

For the rest of the ride, no one said a word. Jersey pulled up to Kantwan's and my home on Augustine Road, and hit the unlock button for me to go ahead and climb out. I removed my seat belt, and then got out of the car.

Before I closed the door I said, "Not a word of this better get back to Kantwan. The three of you make sure of it."

I slammed the door, and then jogged into my house. I knew it was only a matter of time before Kantwan threw in the towel, right along with his captain save a hoe uniform.

## NINETEEN

# Elijah

———————

To keep some distance from the streets, Kill stopped me from picking cash up from the traps. Now my only job was to visit the warehouse and wait for the money to be dropped off once each house capped. I would then take it to this movie theatre that we'd recently acquired, so we could have the money cleaned. We tried using the cleaners that Axel used when he was the boss, but we were making way too much damn money for it to look legit, which in the end was drying our pockets up. Once we'd cleaned enough money, Kill bought out the theatre, so now that was how we did things.

Once I got the money to the theatre, I would supervise the count and make sure the money was banded and secured properly. I also made sure everything was split the way it was supposed to, so we would have Santana's, our supplier, money ready for him and in a different area than our money.

As soon as I slipped my SIM card into the day's dummy phone, a text came through from Navid. Navid was who we had making pickups from the corner boys and traps, and he would then bring it here to me. Navid would make the pick ups for the first half of the day, and then this guy named Leland would take the second half of the day, meeting Ka'Shea at the warehouse. I walked to the side door, and after peeking out the small rectangular window, I let him inside.

"What's good?" I put my hand out and we dapped one another up.

He brought the black bag into the warehouse, and I smiled when I saw it was about ready to burst open. I couldn't wait to get this shit clean and treat myself, Ivy, and Donovan to something nice. Navid and I began taking the money and placing it inside a box that read *Popcorn Bags* on the outside. Once we were done, there were about six big boxes full of cash and a few popcorn bags. We loaded them into the truck I was driving, and then we loaded some that were full of actual popcorn bags before closing it up.

"Aye, Eli, one of the dudes in the trap on Delamore Place, Sass, was telling me that someone came by and tried to rob him for a key," Navid said.

"The fuck? Why are you just now telling me this?"

"He just let me know today, and I wanted to pack up all the money and shit first. I didn't wanna ruffle your feathers beforehand or anything."

I yanked his collar and slammed him into the truck. He stared at me with fearful eyes, while panting heavily.

"The next time some information like that is given to you, you need to let me know right away aight. Someone coming to rob the fucking trap is big business," I gritted.

"I know man, I know and I got it. I swear I won't keep no shit like that a minute longer." He nodded as his face began to perspire.

"Good. Get the fuck out of here." I let him go and he booked it to the vehicle he drove. "Bitch ass nigga."

I hopped into the truck and drove the boxes straight over to the theatre, then loaded them in the back room with our workers Danny and Ranio. I went ahead and let them get started, because I had to go check out the trap on Delamore Place real brief before coming back.

"How is everything?" I asked as I stood by the door, waiting to leave.

"It's going good. Nothing looks fishy because the theatre is bringing in a lot of money. But I think soon we will need another business. Kill is pushing way more weight than Axel ever has," Ranio responded as he banded a thick wad of money.

"Aight, I will let him know. Get to these boxes and I will be back in like an hour, I need to check something out." They both nodded and I checked out the window to make sure it was clear before leaving.

Getting into the truck, I put on my seatbelt, and then sped down to the trap. As soon as I parked, I saw a couple niggas get up from the porch and run inside. I locked my gun into my waist, then jogged across and down the street to see what was up. I wasn't in the mood for any bullshit today, but I was ready to send a couple bullets through some skulls if I needed to.

"Yo, where is Sass?" I questioned the three niggas who were inside, trying to keep busy like I just didn't see their asses sitting on the porch.

"He umm, he went, he's in the bathroom," one of them pointed to the back of the house.

I knew some bullshit was going on, so I rushed to the back. Before I even got to the bathroom door, I heard a bitch moaning like she was being murdered.

*BOOF!*

I burst off into the bathroom, and almost shot his stupid ass when I saw him fucking some bitch on the sink. She screamed when I took my gun out, and hopped down off the sink.

"Eli man, what the fuck?" Sass hurriedly buckled his pants.

"Come out this fucking bathroom!" I barked and walked out with the chick right on my heels. "And you need to go!" She rushed out of the house before I could even finish.

"Eli man, what are—"

"Shut the fuck up and tell me what you told Navid!"

I knew now that the big dogs weren't dropping by, these fools would be acting a fucking monkey. They knew smashing bitches in here was not something that they could do. I wanted to slap his stupid ass across the face with my gun, but I decided against it since there were more important matters at hand.

"I told him someone came through trying to rob us for a couple keys. At first he was trying to be cool about it, but when we wouldn't budge, he got mad and pulled his heat out."

"Fuck did he look like?"

"White boy, skinny, and he seemed like he was some cokehead."

"Did you get the impression that he wanted it to smoke, or like he wanted it in order to sell?"

"Like he wanted to sell it, because he was trying to cut a deal and shit. Like on some repeated basis. He wanted to pay us some money weekly for product."

"And you didn't ask him any questions like why or who he was working with or for?" I frowned.

"Yeah, Mick did, and he just said he wasn't working with no one or for anyone," Sass shrugged.

"Fuck! Look, if you hear the names Portland or Sonny mentioned, let me know immediately. Hit my line as soon as you hear that shit aight?"

"Aight, I got you, boss."

I left out and then got into my car to head back to the theatre. I had no idea who was behind this shit, but I knew that white kid was sent to do what he did. Thank God Sass and Mick were seasoned and loyal, because any other nigga would've cut a deal. Someone was trying to sell our product and take our territory at the same time, and I wasn't sure who. Blow said Portland and Sonny had their own shit, so why would they send someone to get ours? Shit! I was so lost, and that was not a good fucking sign.

TWENTY

Jersey

———————

The Next Afternoon...

*U*nbeknownst to Kill, I was meeting with my brother to talk. Kill didn't want me speaking to my brother for some reason, and before we'd somewhat made up I was cool with that. I had a feeling it was because his cousin had stolen Ivy, and in my opinion that wasn't reason enough. But now, after thinking, I realized that being apart from Portland would make my mother very unhappy. Raleigh opened her big ass mouth when she went to visit her, so when I went she got on me about not speaking with my brother. I couldn't say I was only doing this for her though, because I did in fact miss him.

I walked into Firestone Roasting House on South West Street, and spotted Portland sitting down already. Adjusting my purse strap on my shoulder, I made my way over to him. We exchanged smiles, but when he got up to hug me, I put my hand up to stop him. We definitely were not there yet, and I didn't know if we would ever be.

"Okay," he chuckled lightly as he sat back down. "How are you?"

85

"I'm good Portland, you? Anything new going on in your life?" I raised a brow, wondering if he was gonna tell me he'd gotten some bitch pregnant. Ivy had already informed me, but I doubt his dumb ass knew that.

"Nah, just been living my life and shit, missing you though, Jersey."

"Whatever, Portland."

"Are you guys ready to order?" A waiter appeared and set down two glasses of fresh ice water. We put in our order, and then once he walked away, we turned our attention back to each other.

"So why am I here, Portland? I know you didn't miss me that much, you never wanted to hang out like that unless you needed something from me." I cocked my head.

"Not even, I just wanna know how life is going for you? Is that nigga treating you right or what? You've always been very easygoing Jersey, and from what I hear, Kill Cam isn't. I wanna make sure he's not taking advantage of you."

"He's not, and when have I ever been one that someone can walk all over, Portland?"

"Women change when they fall in love."

"They do, but you change for the better when it's the right man. I'm sure you would know nothing about that with the way that you've dragged Ivy through the mud." I sipped my water.

"Funny."

"Who is the girl having your baby, Portland?" He looked at me surprised, and then exhaled heavily. "Yeah, I knew, I was just waiting for you to tell me which you obviously hadn't planned to do."

"Don't worry, Jersey, it's not the same girl Kill got pregnant." He wore a smug expression before sipping his water. After looking into his eyes for a bit, I stood up to leave. He rose with me, and then grabbed my arm lightly. "Jersey, I'm sorry. Look, sit down so I can talk to you. I didn't come here to fight; I actually came here to talk about making peace, baby girl."

I snatched my arm and sat back down.

"What the hell are you talking about making peace? It's not that deep between you and me, Portland. You're making it sound like some fucking war or something."

"Look Jersey, you know who your man is, right?" He leaned in.

"No shit, Sherlock."

"No, do you really know?" He stared into my eyes, but I stayed silent, not sure what to say exactly. "Kill is a major distributor for Delaware shorty, and he can have someone killed with the snap of his fingers. Right now, he's kind of drumming up a war between his crew and me and mine. I'm begging you to talk to him, or I may end up dead."

"What? Kill wouldn't do anything like tha—"

"Jersey, you don't know the half of what your child's father is capable of. Do you know he just stabbed some guy up at Delaware Tech? Killed him in broad daylight, shorty, and came home to sleep next to you like nothing happened. Your man is unhinged, shorty, and I need you to help me out. I'm your brother."

I began to breathe harder than before as I processed everything Portland was saying. I knew Kill was doing something with drugs, but Portland was painting him to be some sort of murderous king-pin. He killed only when someone was threatening him or his family, like with Trixie. He didn't go around just shanking people. That wasn't Kill, he wasn't that type, and I would prove it. The stabbing at Delaware Tech was brutal and didn't connect to Kill at all. So if he did do it, he was cleverer and sneakier than I thought.

"I'm sure you're over exaggerating, Portland, but I will talk to him about you and see how he feels. If he's as big as you say he is, you shouldn't be a problem to him. You're not doing anything to provoke him, are you?"

"Hell no, ma, I was trying to work for the kid but he refused because of his brother and cousin. I tried to explain that I didn't care about his cousin dating Ivy, but they didn't believe me."

"That's not true though, Portland, you do care."

"I know, but I was saying anything to get down. The point here though, is that I'm scared for my life, and I need you to calm your boy down. He's not right in the head, Jersey. Just think, what kind of nigga would stab someone in the middle of the afternoon? What kind of man gets shot in the middle of a busy area? He's not what you think. He's way more vicious baby, and I need you to be careful. You piss a nigga like him off, and it won't matter that you're his baby mama and fiancée, he'll off your head in no time."

I swallowed hard, but then forced a smile on my face.

"Like I said, Kill is not what you think, but I will talk to him."

*'d finished having lunch with my brother, and had yet to stop thinking about what he'd told me about Kill. I knew Kill; he was my man, my baby daddy, and the guy that I loved. He would never do the shit that Portland said he would, and he would never start a war with my brother without my knowledge. I knew he didn't care for him, but that was where it stopped. Kill didn't seem to dislike my brother enough to murder him.

I entered the den to see Kill typing on his computer. When I got closer, he looked to me out the corner of his eye, and slammed it closed rather quickly. I ignored that and sat down next to him.

"Where is the baby?" I asked before he kissed me sensually.

"She's asleep. Where'd you go?"

"I went to school to work on some stuff and print a large document. I didn't want to use up all of our ink at home, I know you need it," I smiled and he kissed my neck. He then began unbuttoning my shorts, while sucking on my neck, making my pussy get wet immediately. "Kill, wait." I nudged him back.

"What's up?" he furrowed his brows.

"Did you stab someone at Delaware Tech?"

He chuckled and shook his head. "Why would I have done that? What could possibly make you think that?"

"It's just a rumor going around, that's all."

"Lies, but I won't press you. Why do you wanna know that? I don't even know anyone at Delaware Tech besides Cheyla and Ivy."

"I know, I just heard a rumor. Umm, everything at work good? No enemies?"

"That's not your job to worry about all that." He yanked my ankle so that I was now lying down, and then got between my legs to finish unbuttoning my shorts and kissing my neck. I guess I would have to find out once his dick wasn't hard.

TWENTY-ONE

# Raleigh

---

Jersey, Cheyla, and I were out to lunch at Walter's Steakhouse, because we just wanted to talk and relax. I was at a really good place in my life, just like them, so I wanted to get out in the sun and enjoy it. I also wanted to ask Cheyla about the guy who shot at us the night that we went out. I told Shea about it, and all he said was that he would have one of the little homies take care of it. I rolled my eyes at thought.

The waitress set down our food, and we all held hands and said grace before digging in. I loved Walter's, and I remember when my parents were still together, my dad would bring us here a lot. It was very nostalgic for me.

"So did anyone talk to their boyfriends about that night?" I asked before placing a piece of steak in my mouth.

"I told Kill, and all he said was that he would take care of it," Jersey shrugged.

"Same, Shea just said he would have the little homie do it. They clearly don't think it's a big deal," I shook my head.

"Because it's not a big deal. Loren is just a corner boy, and nothing more. I'm sure one of the little guys they send to get him will be just enough," Cheyla snapped a little, making Jersey and I chuckle lightly.

"Relax mama to be, that baby has you on one," I half joked with a smile, and Cheyla rolled her eyes as she ate some mashed potatoes.

"Portland was telling me that Kill and his brothers are starting a war kind of, with him and Sonny," Jersey sighed.

"Yeah right. Portland and Sonny are the least of their worries," Cheyla frowned and continued eating her food.

"I agree," I nodded.

We continued to grease down, when suddenly someone sat in the empty chair next to me. The three of us looked over at the pretty girl who was staring a hole through me. I looked to Cheyla and Jersey hoping they knew her, but when I saw they wore confused expressions as well, I knew they had no idea who this weird bitch was.

"Can I help you?" I covered my mouth since I was still chewing.

"Would you be able to talk for a few moments outside or something?" she smiled and pointed outside.

"What is this about?" I furrowed my brows.

"Shea." She stood up and then sauntered outside, giving all of us full view of her huge ass. I paused and closed my eyes, before getting up and following her outside. Once we were both out there, she cleared her throat. "How do you know Shea?"

"Excuse me? I know him because he's my boyfriend. How do *you* know Shea?"

"Your boyfriend?" she chuckled loudly, throwing her head back. "Girl, since when? Because I was his girlfriend before he went to jail, and I was still his bitch after, ask around about Mercedes."

"Oh, *you're* Mercedes. I know about you," I chuckled and shook my head. "Shea used to fuck with you, and now he doesn't so get over it."

"Oh he doesn't? Because I just fucked him a couple weeks ago, boo." She raised a brow. I couldn't tell if she was lying or not. I wished she had have said a date that wasn't so far away, because then I may have been able to remember what he was doing that day.

"I doubt it."

"Doubt all you want, but keep fucking with my man and we are gonna have problems! I'm the one who held him down, and I'm the first person he hit up when he got out! You should know firsthand how horrible it is to steal a man from his family."

"What?"

"Didn't your daddy get stolen from ya mama, Raleigh? Let Shea go so he can pay more attention to me and our unborn." She rubbed her flat stomach, and then turned on her heels.

I covered my face to get my emotions in order, and then went back inside as if nothing happened. I didn't know what to believe. Ka'Shea worked all hours of the night, and it was possible that one of those nights he'd slid up in Mercedes. I knew she wasn't pregnant though, just by the way she'd said it. It was obvious she just said that to get under my skin.

"What was that about?" Cheyla questioned while she looked outside as if Mercedes was still standing out there.

"Nothing."

We finished dinner, and then went to the nail shop and movies. I wanted to be out for as long as possible, because I didn't want to be sitting at home waiting for Ka'Shea that long. I wanted to only be there for a little bit before him, so that my mind wouldn't start drawing up scenarios.

When I got home, I took a hot bath, gave myself a little facial, and then brushed my teeth. After spraying on some body oil mist, I slipped into my pajama shorts and top, before crawling into bed. While I was lurking on Ka'Shea's Instagram, he finally walked in, making me jump slightly. Belly flopping onto the bed, he pulled my ankle and then kissed my thighs. I couldn't help but smile down at him.

"Wait Shea," I nudged his head once I saw he was about to get right to eating my pussy.

"What's up?" he frowned, and I could tell he was annoyed.

"You know we're exclusive, right?"

"We better be, because if not, you need to stop stashing clothes and taking baths at my fucking crib, shorty."

"Have you fucked with Mercedes since we've been together?" I asked and he exhaled before running his hands over his face. I already knew the answer. "Wow." I shook my head.

"Look, when you say together, do you mean like when we officially said the word and shit? After I was out of jail? Or do you mean while we were talking when I was locked up?"

"No, I mean after you got out and we started fucking."

"Okay cool. Nah, I haven't smashed her since we made it official. I fucked her as soon as I got out, and a couple times after that. But as soon as you came over that night and said you and Sonny were done, I haven't touched her."

"Promise?" I grinned and so did he. He was gorgeous.

"I promise, ma, I told you I'm all about you. Now come here." He yanked me down towards the edge of the bed, and then climbed between my legs to kiss me. "Oh, and we got that Loren nigga."

# TWENTY-TWO

# Kantwan

------------

*I* arrived at my destination, and made sure nobody was following me along the way. Before getting out, I looked around to also make sure I didn't see any of the vehicles that were in my brother's possession. I didn't want anyone in my fucking business. If I had to rock alone to get shit done, then that's what the fuck I was gonna do.

I exited the car and then jogged across the street to enter the car mechanic shop through the back. I spotted Ali sitting behind his desk, and we greeted one another once I neared him. I had him checked out through a couple of street sources, and niggas told me that they'd used him with no problem; he was just expensive. Money was no concern of mine if it got me results, so I wasn't tripping off of his high prices.

"You got that?" he questioned.

"Of course." I slid the envelope containing one thousand dollars across his desk to him.

"I told you my fee was two thousand."

"And I told you I wasn't paying the full price until I had the information I needed. You get half now and once I get what the fuck I need, you get the rest, aight? Now get to digging, I ain't got all fucking day."

"That's not—"

"Get to work," I gritted with my heat pressed to his head. He threw his hands up in mock surrender, and then inhaled sharply. "Now." I pulled my gun away and he powered on his computer.

I sat down next to him and watched as he typed in some codes and shit. Although Kill had caught Isaiah, I wanted to make sure Monty didn't have any more brothers that would spring up. After a few minutes, he finally started writing shit down, and then turned to face me. I bucked my eyes at his ass, signaling for him to get to talking.

"So Monty's last name is Smith. He should be easier to search on since his first name is not common, but if he has family members that you want me to look into, hopefully their first names are distinct like his, since his last name is common."

"You can't find his family by using his name?"

"I can only hack systems and trace names, I can't *find* the name. I have to be given the name first, before I can track their where-abouts or find them in a system."

"So if I get you some names, you can tell me where they are?"

"Yes."

I stood up, snatched what he'd written down and started towards the door.

"Aye! What about my money, Brick?" He called out the fake nickname I'd given his ass.

"I told you that you will get it once the job is complete. I need to get anybody that's associated with Monty. And if anything happens to my shorty before that, it's yo' ass. Keep hitting them systems until I get at you again." And with that I left.

I drove straight home, and called Cheyla on the way to make sure she was there. I needed her to tell me all the shit she knew about this Monty cat, and if he had any more muthafuckas that may be wanting to avenge his death. Was I gonna tell Kill this shit? Nope, because he shouldn't have stepped on my toes. If I gave him this info he would go behind my back and try to fuck some shit up just like before. As much as he liked to say we were a team, we weren't. We were his little flunkies while he ran around trying to do everything. I loved my brother with every inch of me, but sometimes I hated that he felt he was the end all be all.

I checked my texts and saw that Cheyla said she was almost there; she had just stopped to get food about five minutes from the crib. I went into the house and just sat at the bottom of the stairs, not wanting to go up. I wanted to talk as soon as she walked up in here. As I was waiting, my personal phone chimed, letting me know I had a text.

**Rachel:** *What you doing?*

I just scoffed and slipped my phone back into my pocket, just as Cheyla walked in.

"Hey baby," she smiled. She looked real pretty, and I noticed her skin had a natural glow to it. She was wearing a short ass dress though, and I ain't like that shit one bit.

"What's up, fuck you wearing that little shit for?"

"It's not even that little, Kantwan. It covers everything."

"Don't wear nothing like that to school, Cheyla, you got enough niggas on your bumper. If I have to beat one more nigga's ass because you walking around here enticing them, you and I are gonna be a wrap." She just chuckled angrily and headed to the kitchen with her food. I followed after her, and before she sat down, I hugged her from behind and began kissing her neck. "I didn't mean to be rude, shorty, I just don't want anything happening to you," I whispered.

"Get off of me please." She nudged me back, and then caught the lone tear cascading down her golden cheek. I forgot being pregnant made her a crybaby.

I sat adjacent to her and asked, "What do you know about Monty?"

"I don't know anything about Monty. Why? You think this is his baby or something?" she responded, her tone dripping with attitude.

"Nah, I know it ain't. I'm asking because I wanna make sure Isaiah was the only one trying to come for you. Does he have any more brothers, cousins, or even jump offs that would feel the need to avenge his death?"

"He has one other brother, I think his name is Kevin," she sighed dejectedly.

"Thanks." I stood up and then lifted her chin to look down into her eyes. "I'm sorry for being rude, aight? You know daddy loves you, shorty," I grinned before biting my lip.

She continued to chew her food, and once she swallowed she asked, "Where did you go that night I went out?"

"I don't even know what you talking about," I lied.

I went to chill with Rachel and Tanya for a bit, but nothing happened… nothing too bad happened. I didn't want to talk to Elijah, Ka'Shea, and definitely not Kill, so I went there. She'd been hitting me up despite her saying she'd stop, and since I was angry we chilled. All we did was smoke and shit, so I had nothing to worry about. Aight, she sucked my dick, but I didn't even nut, so in my eyes it didn't count. Cheyla wouldn't see it that way though.

"The night you blew up on me because you were mad about your brother getting Isaiah before you did."

"I must've went to the store or some shit, because I don't even remember like that. I smoked before we talked so maybe that's why," I lied again, but horribly.

She stared into my eyes and just nodded slowly, obviously aware that I was lying. I leaned down to kiss her, but she turned her face until I moved back. I walked like I was leaving but then came around and kissed her soft lips from the other side. She pulled away and pushed me lightly, before continuing to eat her food.

"Cheyla, so you're mad now?"

She just ignored me and kept eating, so I kissed her cheek and left. I didn't have the energy to beg. I put enough into this relation-ship, and it felt like I was doing all the work, as usual.

# TWENTY-THREE

## Sonny

A Couple Weeks Later...

*I* sat back and let the effects take over my body. I was stressing like a bitch, and the fact that I couldn't exactly pinpoint why, had me feeling even worse. It seemed like everything in my life was going wrong, and every time I attempted to fix one thing, I would be reminded that there were thousands of other things wrong.

For starters, this young shorty, Alicia, was swearing that she was having my baby. I denied it every chance that I got, but I knew her baby was mine. She was a virgin, and that was part of what attracted me to her. Like a fucking fool, I ran up in her ass raw, and she got pregnant. Then, our only connect to the streets and basically our damn mentor, Leroy, had been gunned down outside of his cousin's crib. Without him, we were out here like chickens with our heads cut off. Then on top of that, I didn't like the fact that Kantwan had my little sister with him.

"Yo, what the fuck is you doing?" Portland walked into my den wearing a scowl. "No need muthafucka, I already saw the shit." He shook his head at me when I tried to hurry up and put the coke away. I wished I never gave that nigga a key, but since he paid for the shit I felt like I had to.

"I'm stressing man," I sighed.

"Please tell me you bought that shit, Sonny." When I didn't respond, he ran his hands over his face. "Yo, you smoking our shit? You know that now that we lost Leroy, the supplier ain't fucking with us, and you got the nerve to be in here sniffing it up!"

"I know, man, shit! I don't need you coming up in here hollering in my fucking ear and shit! I'm stressed too, you need to hit this shit so you can calm down!"

"I got enough fucking problems, and becoming a coke head is not a new one that I need."

Him calling me a cokehead prompted me to lunge towards him. I landed on top of him, and we began tussling like some fucking fools. I was high as hell, and was no match for a sober Portland, so I threw my hands up after he landed his fifth right hook.

"Fuck is wrong with you, man? You on that bullshit! I did not get in this shit with you for you to be cracking under pressure! Yeah shit is off right now, but you need to suck it the fuck up! None of our lives is peachy, not even Ahmad and Dante!"

"I know." I nodded.

"Is this the first time?"

"Nah, man, but I ain't been doing it long so chill the fuck out!" I shouted the last part of my sentence when I saw him shaking his head and contracting his fists.

We used to clown the many dope dealers that went down because they couldn't keep their hands off their product. That was the number one no-no in this game, and I never saw myself being like the niggas who had fallen from grace, yet here I was. But regardless of me getting high here and there, I wasn't no damn cokehead.

"Whatever, the only good thing right now is that we don't need anything bigger than the cleaners to clean our money, since ain't shit gon' be coming in for a while," Portland sighed.

"So what's the plan as far as scoring product?"

"We tried sending someone to one of Kill's traps to cut a little side deal with one of the workers, but that nigga shut us down and snitched to his boss."

"You talk to Jersey about slowing Kill up?"

"Yeah, but she wasn't hearing me. So we may die before we even get some new product."

"Damn, we gon' get something, we always do. Plus Kill ain't really on to us yet, which buys us some time." I patted his back and he nodded in agreement.

Once Portland left, I invited Alicia over so we could come to some kind of agreement. I needed her to pin this damn baby on someone else, because too many people were finding this shit out and looking at me side ways. The last person that I wanted to find out was Raleigh, and when she threw that shit up in my face, I felt like all the blood in my body left. Marley's ass got the news and moved out of my crib for good, going right back to Wyatt's white collar ass. I don't know what was up with my bitches getting strong on me, but I wasn't feeling it.

"Hi." Alicia walked through the front door.

"How you get here?" I frowned, making sure her nosey ass auntie hadn't been the one to drop her off. I didn't need that loud mouth buzzard knowing where I laid my fuckin' head.

"Felisha brought me over, relax." She rolled her eyes and then started checking my house out with them. "This is nice, why have I never been here?"

"That's not what you came here for, come on." I walked to the back and she followed me. Once we got to my den, we sat down and she just stared at me waiting for me to speak. "So what will it take for you to stop running your mouth about us, Alicia?"

"What? You called me over here to figure out how to shut me up? I thought you were gonna finally have something to say about being in the baby's life!"

"If I admit to that being my baby shorty, I will go to jail. Don't you get that? Why are you not understanding that you and I having a child together is a violation of my parole?"

"You didn't care about your parole when you were telling me

you loved me and all that other shit you said! You lied to me just to sleep with me!"

"Alicia, please work with me. Look, I promise once you hit eighteen, we can work something out as far as me being in the baby's life physically. As of right now though, I need to be on some phantom shit. How much will it take for you to agree to that?"

She stared into my eyes, and then a small smirk appeared on her face. I knew that meant she was about to put a hurtin' on my pockets, but it was cool because I would pay whatever I needed to in order to stay out of jail.

"I want fifty thousand dollars in the next three days, or I'm going to the cops. And don't even think about trying to murder me, because I've already let my family know that if something happens to me it was you."

"Fine. But as soon as you get that money, pin the baby on someone else."

"I'll figure something out, just get me my money." She was texting on her phone, and then she stood up after slipping it into her purse.

As I walked her little ass to the door, I was shaking my head at myself. Why couldn't I have chosen to smash a dumber young bitch? Alicia was smart as fuck, and now I was about to have to pay up racks for her to keep her mouth shut.

# TWENTY-FOUR

## Ivy

———

"Hey, Ivy!" someone called to me, and when I turned around I saw it was my classmate Kevin.

"Hey, what's up?"

"I was wondering if you wanted to maybe partner up and study for the test. I can be at your place later; I'll bring snacks and stuff," he smiled. He was actually kind of cute, but too skinny for my liking. I liked a man with muscle, a nigga who could flip me in different positions in the bedroom like, Elijah.

"I don't think—"

"Ivy, please. I told you I'm dealing with some stuff, and I really need your help. Look, you're getting perfect scores on every damn quiz, and I can barely even finish filling in all the answers in enough time." He pointed to the test I had in my hand.

"But coming to my house? I don't know about that, Kevin. I live with my boyfriend and he wouldn't approve of that, no matter what it's about. And I know I wouldn't want him bringing a girl home."

"So what you like me or something?" he smirked. "I'm kidding, I'm kidding. That was a bad joke. But no I understand. I mean you can come to my place then if that's okay. I don't have a woman at home who will trip."

"How about we come back up to school and study here, that way we won't upset my boyfriend."

"Got a crazy one on your hands?"

"Just a little," I responded and we both began laughing.

"Aight, cool, so tomorrow?"

"No, Wednesday since I have classes already. I will just stay in the library, and you can meet me around six o'clock?"

"Works for me, and thank you again. I really appreciate the help, ma."

"No problem."

I headed towards my car, and boy did it pay to have early classes, because you could park right in the fucking front. I hated having to walk across this large ass parking lot. My feet were killing me, and I just wanted to go home, start dinner, and then soak my feet while reading a couple of my psychology chapters. Yeah, I'd chosen a major, and that was psychology. I wanted to work with families though, because hopefully I could save some from breaking a part. I knew there were plenty of families out there like Jersey's, and I think therapy would do them some good.

As I neared my car, I saw my stupid ass, trifling ass, pitiful ass, whack ass, lying ass, cheating ass, dusty ass, always so called getting his life together ass baby daddy, leaning on my damn hood like some fucking thug. I rolled my eyes once I got closer so that he'd notice, and then stopped right in front of him.

"I missed you," he grinned, and once I smacked my lips he began chortling loudly. "Nah, ma, I did. You're looking good. I'm happy to know old boy ain't knocked your pretty ass up yet."

"What the fuck do you want? Shouldn't you be worried about the bitches you knock up? Like the hoe in Lynford? Oops! That's right, she lives in Wilmington now, with you."

"Come on shorty, quit it. Ain't like I wanna be with her, and why you care? You miss me?" He moved closer to me, but I mushed his face.

"Again, what the fuck do you want, nigga?"

"I wanted to talk to you for a couple moments, come get in the car with me." He pointed to his Range Rover, which he clearly had detailed and fixed up. Anybody who drove it wanted everyone to know they had money; typical Portland. "Come on, I'm not gon' hurt you unless you want me to." He grabbed my arm.

"Fuck off of me, you couldn't even see my panties at this stage." I started towards his car as he followed me laughing.

"It's cool, I've seen all the ones you have."

"No, Elijah bought me all new ones, because he wanted to be the only one who has," I shot at him, and I saw his jaw clench a little bit as he hit the unlock button on his remote key.

"Get in the car, Ivy." Once we both got in he said, "Speaking of Elijah, that's what I came to talk to you about, and Donovan."

"I'm still changing Donovan's last name, so stop trying to change my mind."

"What last name are you changing it to? And Ivy I said I was sorry, I didn't mean it when I said I didn't want him."

"I have a couple options on last names. I didn't know my father too well, so I may change it to what I knew my mother's maiden name to be. That or Horne, or maybe even Camren."

"You better not change it to that last one, Ivy."

"I do what the fuck I want. Now you have two minutes to tell me why I'm in your fucking car, and not at home with my baby and man."

"I know you don't care about me anymore," he started, trying to make me say I did care, but I wasn't falling for that shit. "But does that mean you want a nigga to die?"

"What? What the fuck are you talking about? I don't have time for your stupid bullshit, Portland!"

"I'm talking about your man, shorty, he wants me and Sonny dead!"

"Boy please! Elijah doesn't give a fuck about your ass! Don't flatter yourself thinking he wants to take you out little boy."

"Then explain to me why he pressed a burner to my temple right in front of everybody out in Hilltop."

"You're lying."

"No, and he punched my ass too. Ask E-Way, ask anybody that lives on Franklin where his old spot is. He put a gun to my head, and he punched me on another occasion. Both times only because I asked him about getting put on."

"Why the hell would I believe anything your ass has to say? What would Elijah get from putting a gun to your head? He would've pulled the trigger if he had. Eli isn't the type of guy to draw his gun just for show. That's more of your style."

"Fine, Ivy, keep rocking with that nigga, but when he kills me and my sisters are crying, and my son is without a father, just know it was because you were thinking with your pussy and not your brain."

I didn't want to believe what Portland was saying. He was lying; he had to be. There was no way Elijah did that shit. The punch maybe, but pulling his gun out? And he would've mentioned these events to me I'm sure. Elijah wouldn't dare keep something like that from me, and ultimately I know he wouldn't kill Portland; he loved Donovan too much.

"Portland, you need to just get over the fact that I don't want to be with you, and quit making up lies. Ain't nobody put a gun to your head, and as far as the punch, you probably deserved it." I pulled the lever and hopped down out of his truck.

He reached across and grabbed my arm to stop me from closing his door just yet.

"Ivy, I love you and I want you to know, when you find out what that nigga is really out here doing, I will welcome you back with open arms. That's if I'm alive to."

"Suck my dick." I slammed the door and then rushed back to get into my Porsche.

Portland didn't mean shit to a nigga like Elijah, and I wasn't about to believe anything he was saying.

# TWENTY-FIVE

# Kilexis

---

Judgement Day...

Today was the day that I would be able to go on with a clear conscience. I would no longer find myself wondering if, and what would happen to my life. I was here to find out what I already knew, and I couldn't wait to hold that paper in my hand that told me I wasn't the fucking father. I knew I wasn't, so why was I so nervous?

I gripped Jersey's hand in mine, and then lifted it to kiss the back of it. She smiled at me, and I could see in her face that she felt nothing of what I was feeling. I was panicking just a little, and running over the details in my head of the night I fucked Sophie. I wore a condom, and a condom that was in tact when I pulled it off. There was nothing to trip about.

"I can't wait to read it, Kilexis," Jersey whispered as we stepped off the elevator. I declined to respond as I handed her the carrier containing Alexsia, and opened the doctor's office door for her.

"Jersey, you know only Sophie and I can go into the room right?" We sat down.

"Yes, I know. I will be right here with balloons when you walk out," she joked and I forced a laugh. She placed a kiss on my cheek, just as Sophie and her boyfriend, Carter, walked in. "Does he get to go in?"

"I think so, because he took a test, too."

"Good morning," Sophie half smiled and sat down across from us in the waiting room.

"Morning," I replied, but of course Jersey ignored her, and played it off by kissing Alexsia's fat face. I looked over at my baby, and when she saw me she laughed and covered her little eyes with her small hands.

"That is so cute how she acts towards you," Jersey said as we chuckled.

"Sophie Borden!" A woman walked out holding a clipboard. Carter, Sophie, and I stood up and made our way towards her. "Are these the potential fathers?" the lady asked, and Sophie nodded. "Okay ,come on back to Dr. Menales' office."

I looked over my shoulder at Jersey, and she was wearing a closed mouth smile. Even in just jeans, sandals, and an oversized sweater with her dark curly hair all over the place, she still looked gorgeous to me. Again, the day when I got used to her beauty still hadn't come.

The three of us walked to the back, and then the lady opened a door to an office. There were three chairs set up, so we all took a seat, leaving Sophie to sit in the middle. We waited in silence, since neither of us had any words for one another. My heart was beating so damn fast that I felt like it was gonna come out of my chest at any minute. *Please God, I was safe.* I said a silent prayer as I clutched my iPhone in my hand. My palms were a bit sweaty, so I decided to put my device up before it slipped out of my hands.

"Good morning, Mr. Camren, Ms. Borden, and Mr. Rays." The doctor shook each of our hands before walking around to sit behind her desk. "Okay, so we are here to determine the paternity of Kilenna Marie Rays," she said as she pulled a Manila envelope out. "Now *I* can read the results, or I can give you your copies, and you guys can open them and read them yourselves, either right now or once you leave here."

"Let her decide," I said referring to Sophie.

"We can each take an envelope and just open them here," she sighed and I could tell she was nervous. "No, just read it Dr. Menales, so we all can hear it together I guess." She quickly changed her mind, as she rubbed her hands up and down her thighs. As skittish as she was, I was starting to believe that maybe I was the father.

"Very well. So we tested both Mr. Camren and Mr. Rays for paternity..." My mind began to drift as she spoke, using all of these medical terms about what they did and how they did it. I just didn't want this to be my child. But what if it was, and I was speaking ill of it. *Calm the fuck down, Kilexis, come on man. How could it be yours?* "So Mr. Rays came back as not being the father, unfortunately," she continued. I began breathing harder, knowing that if he wasn't, I was. A real nigga wanted to cry right now. I looked over and saw Sophie wearing a small smile, and Carter sitting still like he was paralyzed from the neck down. I was in his place once, so I knew exactly how he felt. Hopefully his feelings weren't too strong for Sophie's hoe ass. "And Mr. Camren came back as having a zero percent chance of being the father as well," the doctor finished, catching me off guard.

"What!" Sophie shouted.

"So wait, I'm not the father?" I grinned and palmed my chest.

"No, I'm afraid not, Mr. Camren. Neither you nor Mr. Rays is the father of little Kilenna. Now Sophie, was there anyone else you'd been with around that time?" So much for her being too depressed to go out and get fucked with her lying ass.

"Yo, can I have my paper, I have to go and show my shorty- my girl outside," I said before Sophie could answer. I didn't give a fuck about what she was about to say, a nigga was just happy he wasn't the damn father.

"Sure, Mr. Camren." She handed me my envelope.

I ripped that shit open as I left her office and rushed down the wall. As soon as I walked out into the waiting room, Jersey stood up, and I scooped her little ass into my arms before kissing her full lips.

"What does it say?" she giggled as I placed her back onto her feet.

"That Alexsia is my only child, and that you are the only woman who will be the mother of my kids." I leaned down and kissed her harder. "Fuck, I love you."

"I love you, too," she chuckled and took the paper from me as I grabbed Alexsia's carrier. "I knew it! So I'm sure her man is happy," she said as we walked out of the doctor's office, ready to get on the elevator.

"Get this, he ain't the damn daddy either."

"Really?" She bucked her eyes as we got onto the elevator. Before she could speak, Carter and Sophie came out of the doctor's office arguing, and then got onto the elevator with us.

The four of us stayed quiet, and then once we stepped off, we started to go our separate ways in the parking lot. I felt like someone was walking behind me, so I turned around to see Carter. Sophie had continued on to her car.

"Take the baby to the car, Jersey." I handed her the carrier, but she didn't move. "Go now." I pecked her and then she walked away. I made sure she was gone, and then turned to look down at Carter. "Is there a problem?"

"I know who you are."

"I know who *you* are. Now that we got that out of the way, the fuck do you want? Shouldn't you be leaving, your girl is peeling out of the parking lot without you."

"We drove separately, and when I say I know who you are, that means I know you're Kill."

"Okay, bye." I turned to walk away.

"And I got something for yo' ass since you wanna bust down other niggas' bitches, homie!"

"You got something like what, huh? Fuck you got for me that won't get your ass killed?" I neared him and got right up on him.

"Just know, you need to watch your back. I know more about you than you think, homie." He backed away and then rushed off. I pulled my phone out to shoot a text, and then walked to my car.

"What was that about?" Jersey asked as soon as I got in my whip.

"Nothing major, just wanted to know if I knew anybody else that Sophie could've slept with."

"Let's go out to eat to celebrate!" Jersey beamed.

"Okay."

A couple moments passed before she said, "Drive, Kill."

"I am, just let me finish sending this text to Shea. He wants the info to my Hulu account," I lied and chuckled. I looked out the corner of my eye, and as soon as Carter started backing out of his parking space, two black trucks came up on each side of him and began filling his car with bullets.

"Oh my gosh!" Jersey screamed.

"Get down, shorty!" I hollered as I sped the opposite way out of the parking lot. After a few moments of driving, Jersey sat back up and looked around. "It's cool, we're away." My phone buzzed and once I got to the red light, I opened it to see a picture of a dead Carter.

"Was that Sophie's man?" Jersey panted.

"Not sure, where do you wanna eat, baby? We need to take our mind off of that crazy shit."

"It doesn't matter. I swear I hate it over here," she shook her head.

"I know, and don't worry, I'm never gonna let shit happen to you."

That'll teach that nigga, Carter, for stepping to me. Too bad he's not alive to have learned his lesson.

## TWENTY-SIX

# Cheyla

Tonight Kantwan was going out, and the nigga tried to lie like he had work to handle, but I quickly disproved that shit by calling Jersey, Ivy, *and* Raleigh, who said that their men were at home. So now he and I were going out together. I didn't know what the fuck was wrong with him, but this shift in his character was not cool. However, I loved him and I wanted to be with him, so I would stick this little rough patch out with him. As long as he wasn't fucking around on me or hitting me, we were good.

"Ready," I walked down to the den. "Where are we going?" I asked him.

"Strip club," he sighed and got up from the couch. I knew he thought I was gonna back out, but he must've forgotten I used to live in the damn strip club, so I didn't care.

"Cool, let's go."

A smirk covered his sexy ass face as he walked by me, hitting me in the face with his intoxicating cologne. I followed him out as I took in his clean, yet simple attire. He wore dark gray colored jeans, a red polo shirt, and red and white Nikes. He wore a silver watch with diamonds in it, the matching chain, and small diamond studs in his ear. He was too fine; too fine for me to walk away just because he was acting a little different.

He opened the door for me while stroking his neatly trimmed facial hair, and I stopped once I got in the doorway to look up into his smooth, deep, caramel face.

"What," he frowned.

"Aren't you forgetting something?"

He smiled and chomped on his gum, before pulling me close by the waist and kissing me. He kissed me so softly that my clit tingled. Being pregnant made me so much hornier than usual, even when Kantwan did the smallest things. After a few more pecks, he let me go, and we left out to head to the strip club.

"Did you have to choose Starzz?" I quizzed once we pulled up.

"This is the best strip club out here, ma. Just because you don't work here anymore, doesn't mean that niggas stopped coming aight? Now come on." He got out of the car, and then came around to open my door before taking my hand into his. He hit his alarm, and then we strolled to the entrance.

The bouncer just greeted him by name, and didn't even make him pay. Now, either that meant he was a regular, or he was just well known. Either could be the case because now that he worked with Kill, it seemed like everybody knew him. People always called me Kantwan's girl instead of my name. All I know is he had better not been a regular now that I was no longer an employee.

"When was the last time you came here?" I quizzed as we walked in.

"When I came through and fucked you," he smiled, licked his lips, and then kissed my cheek. We kept walking and I smiled when I saw the homegirl, Gretchen, on stage. We stopped when we got to a table with two girls sitting down, which confused me a little. I know his ass wasn't about to meet up with these two hoes without me. *I'm glad I fuckin' came.*

"Cheyla, these are my co-workers, Rachel and Tanya," Kantwan introduced me. I remember those names from when they popped up on his phone every morning.

"Nice to meet you," they said almost at the same time, except

Tanya was smiling and Rachel wasn't. Rachel looked from me to Kantwan, and he cleared his throat before helping me up into the booth to sit down. Something was not right here.

The four of us sat there and watched some of my old associates on stage, and when Pound Cake, aka Shamece, walked by, Tanya waved her in. She greeted me, and then began to dance for Tanya. I started feeling nauseated, so I decided to go to the bathroom and splash some water on my face.

"Baby, I'll be right back, okay?" I said to Kantwan. He just nodded and continued sipping his drink while watching Pound Cake do her thing. I had to admit, I hated seeing him so enthralled by her moves.

I went to the bathroom to pee and put water on my face to calm myself down. I was hot as fuck, hungry, and about to throw up in a second. As soon as the thought crossed my mind, I felt my stomach bubbling, and my mouth become salty. I rushed into the stall and hurled all of my insides it seemed into the toilet. Once I was finally finished, I dug into my purse to quickly brush and rinse my teeth. I had thrown up in public a couple times before, so I was used to this and therefore prepared.

After washing my hands, I came back and started over to the area we were sitting in. When I got closer, I recognized a familiar faced stripper in Kantwan's lap; Miami, the bitch I fought over his ass. Except tonight, I couldn't whoop her ass because I was carrying his fucking baby. Tonight seemed to be getting worse by the damn minute.

"Really ,Kantwan?" I folded my arms as Miami put her all into the lap dance. I also noticed that Rachel and Tanya had switched seats, so now Rachel was sitting next to Kantwan, enjoying Miami as if she was Kantwan's bottom bitch or something.

"It's a strip club shorty, what the fuck?" Kantwan frowned as if my existence irritated his soul. That shit hurt, but I chucked it up to me being sensitive.

"Yeah, chill, Cheyla," Miami smirked as she reached behind herself to caress Kantwan's beard.

"Fuck you, bitch! You better be lucky I'm pregnant!"

"I hope you know who the father is," she whispered and continued to dance on *my* muthafuckin' man, who didn't stop her.

I felt tears welling up, so I just turned to walk towards the exit. When I got outside, I pulled my phone from my pocket so that I could dial Jersey. Hopefully, she could come give me a ride. I felt like an outcast right now, despite me being here with a man who supposedly loved me. I just kept taking deep breaths so that I wouldn't cry. As the phone rang, I felt someone snatch it from me. I looked to see it was Kantwan.

"Can you please give me my phone back so I can call my best friend for a ride home?!" I was so angry I could spit! Whatever the fuck that meant.

"Fuck do you need a ride home for, Cheyla? You said we could come out, so why the fuck are you mad?"

"Because you got a bitch that I fought over you in your got damn lap taunting me! Then when we get here, it's two bitches waiting for you! This is where you were gonna go nigga? To chill with them two? And what, have a fucking orgy afterwards with Miami and them?" I hollered so loudly, I felt a rumble in my chest.

"Aye lower yo' muthafucking voice when you talking to me shorty! I was coming out to have some fucking fun! Yes, I have females as friends, and I met them because I work with them! How in the entire fuck was I supposed to know that you fought that bitch? Huh? And why would you be fighting her over me, when I don't even know the hoe?" he barked down in my face, causing me to cower a bit. I saw something scary in his pretty, brown eyes, and I didn't know what was next.

"Take me home, or if you wanna stay here and carry on with your new Kantwan Camren persona, go ahead. I should've known your ass was gonna change once all this shit happened! So fuck you! Do what the fuck you want, my baby and I do not need you, okay?" I shoved him, but he didn't really go anywhere.

"You don't need me? How the fuck you gonna pay for them classes huh? What you gon' shake your ass? You can maybe do it now, and that's a big maybe, but what about when you start showing more huh, Cheyla? You think niggas gon' tip you crazy when you shaking yo' ass with a big belly?"

"Don't worry about it, nigga," I began to sob more. "Ju-just give me my phone and go back in there with your bitches." I stuttered as I began to cry harder. I loved him. The old Kantwan would never speak to me this way. The old Kantwan Camren loved me and would never be hanging out with some females while trying to lie about it. The old Kantwan would never put me down, especially while I was pregnant.

"Nah, I'm not giving you your phone, come on." He lightly tugged on my arm until we got to the car. We got in, and then he sped out like a madman. "See, this is why I wanted to go out alone. You fucked up my night with this bullshit. I ain't never fucked around on you! I'm the fucking good cop in this relationship! From the very start I've been all about you and what you need and when you need it! You ain't once gave a fuck about what the fuck Kantwan wants! I'm always saving you and having your back, yet all you care about is yourself. When I wanted to be your man, it wasn't cool because you didn't want it. But oh, when Cheyla wanted to be in a relationship, it was expected of me to just oblige. I'm tired of this shit! Sometimes a nigga needs something back. You just take, take, take and fucking take!" He roared as I wept the whole way home. I'd never seen him so angry. He was angrier than the time he caught me stripping.

I said nothing in response to him, and it was quiet until we made it home. I knew he would get tired of me, and that's why I never wanted this shit in the first place. I knew he would make me fall in love, and then leave me with a broken heart, just like Jersey's father did her mother. We entered our home, and I went upstairs while he went to the den. After taking a bath, I climbed into the bed, and cried myself to sleep.

⎯⎯

"I'm sorry, baby." I was woken up when Kantwan hugged me tightly from behind, kissing my shoulders and the nape of my neck. The tears came immediately after. He caressed my small bulge, and continued kissing my neck.

"What is wrong with you?" I questioned.

"Nothing, baby, I've just been in an irritated mood that's all. I'm gonna collect myself though. I don't want to upset you while you have my baby in there. I love you, shorty, and I know you don't need me. I need you though." He turned me onto my back and pulled my panties down slowly, before tossing them to the side. "I need you bad. I don't know what I would do without you." He dipped under the covers and then placed my legs on his shoulders.

Taking my clit into his mouth, he began sucking gently. He spread my legs wider, bringing my center more into his face as he flicked his tongue and sucked on my clit.

"Mmm, shit," I panted. I was still angry, but this was too good to stop him. He continued devouring me as if his life depended on it, making me cum four times back to back. "Okay, okay, I accept your apology," I whimpered for him to stop. I'd cum so many times my box was aching.

"I ain't mean nothing I said in the car." He threw the covers off of his head.

"Yes, you did, and from now on I'm gonna make sure that I put more effort into us." I caressed the side of his face as he kissed up my stomach. Once he reached my face, he dipped his tongue into my mouth and entered me slowly. My legs trembled as he invaded my body with his long, thick rod. I felt shocks of pain mixed with pleasure every time he pushed himself inside of me. "Baby, I love you," I whispered as he sucked my lips, and pounded me slowly.

"I love you more, and I'm sorry."

TWENTY-SEVEN

# Elijah

"*D*oes he know why we're here?" I asked Kill as we sat in my car, parked a little ways down from Axel's house.

"Not necessarily, I just told him that we wanted to get at him about some things."

We weren't too sure about who had Leroy shoot Kill, nor about who had sent someone to try and cut a deal with Sass and Mick, but we wanted to find out. Sass said Portland and Sonny weren't mentioned, so we were racking our brains trying to figure out who else would possibly come for us. It wasn't some new muthafucka, because they knew where our traps were and shit. This was someone who knew us, and we had a feeling that maybe Dante and Ahmad had somehow linked up with Portland and Sonny. I'm not sure how, but shit, anything was fucking possible.

I ashed the blunt, and then Kill popped some gum into his mouth before passing me the box to get a piece for myself. Once I handed it back to him, he shoved it into his pocket and we got out of my car. Nearing Axel's house, we both gave each other a knowing look before approaching the gate to be buzzed in. After we got through, we jogged up his walkway, rang the doorbell, and then strolled inside once his housekeeper greeted us.

"Follow me," she smiled and began switching towards the back of the house.

When we walked into the den, Axel was sitting there hooked up to some machine. It looked like an IV, but I wasn't too sure. He was in his usual business casual attire, it's just his sleeved was rolled up, and some tubes were going into his arm, which was much skinnier than before. Upon entering, he looked to us and gave a huge grin.

"Welcome, boys. I would get up, but I'm not the strongest right now," he cleared his throat. "Have a seat, anywhere. Catharine, please bring the three of us some scotch."

"But Mr. Johnson, the doctor said it's not good for you to have any scotch. I can bring you some tea, how is that?"

"That's good." He nodded and then half smiled at us. I could tell he was embarrassed, but there was really no need to be; he was sick. It reminded me of my uncle. Because he was sick, he felt like his illness negated all of his accomplishments as a man.

"Okay, I will be back with some scotch, and then some tea for you, Mr. Johnson."

"Can I have some water, too,please?" I chimed in and she nodded with a smile.

"To what do I owe this pleasure Kill? Eli?" Axel looked at us as we took seats on his huge leather couch.

"Well, Axel, I wanted to ask you something, but I want you to remember that this is just a question and nothing more," Kill explained and Axel nodded, giving him permission to continue. "I'm not sure if you know, but I was shot a little while ago, while sitting in a restaurant eating. It was around one in the afternoon, and in a pretty busy area."

"What the fuck? What psycho muthafucka would do that?" he furrowed his brows.

"It was Leroy."

"Leroy? Why? Because you fired him? Why the fuck did he take so long to do something about it?" Axel frowned.

"That's the thing, I'm not sure. See I know my fiancée's brother and her best friend's brother don't really fuck with me, but something tells me they weren't behind this. Well, something tells me that someone they're working with was behind it."

"Really? Who did you have in mind, Kill?"

"Your sons," I answered for him since Kill was a bit hesitant.

"My sons?" Axel chuckled as if he were waiting for us to say we were kidding. "Dante and Ahmad? That's actually hilarious. My sons couldn't pull a trigger if you paid them. So one, they would never be bold enough to shoot in broad daylight, because they're not well trained with firearms. And two, everyone knows my sons because of me, so they'd be too easy to identify."

"I already said Leroy shot me, so I know it wasn't them, Axel. I'm thinking they got in his head and had him do it."

"No." Axel shook his head repeatedly.

"So there was no way you think they could've asked Leroy to get at me? You don't think that because I declined to give Dante and Ahmad a job, they may have linked up with him?" Kill inquired.

"I mean, where is this coming from? Why out of all the people in Delaware, do you choose my kids?"

"They inquired about working for me, Axel, and I turned them down. I didn't have anything for them except block work, and you and I both know they are pretty green when it comes to the business. I fired Leroy because he was insubordinate. I feel it in my gut that he linked up with someone who convinced him to come after me, us," Kill replied.

"So you think they're *that* angry about not being down with you?" Kill and I nodded. "Well, can you blame them? You let your little brother get down and he's just about as green as them, maybe even more."

"Kantwan is naturally street smart, Axel," Kill said.

"Exactly, most of this shit is common sense, and despite its name, most people don't have it. Kantwan does and he knows a hell of a lot more than your sons honestly. That was even before we showed him anything," I backed Kill up.

"Well—" Catharine walked in with our beverages, and Axel waited until she left before continuing. "I understand your concerns, gentlemen, but my sons are not the vengeful nor jealous type. They may have been a little bothered by your declining of their application to work, but they're smart enough to know not to go against someone of your caliber."

"I hope so." Kill stared into Axel's eyes as he sipped his drink.

We changed the subject and talked for a little longer about random shit. Axel updated us on his condition, explaining that he had really good doctors who were keeping him alive, but he was very weak. It was crazy to see the man that the streets once feared become so meek and feeble. It just made me want to live life to the fullest.

After leaving Axel's, we met up at Ka'Shea's to talk about what had just happened. I wasn't too sure if I was convinced that Dante and Ahmad weren't coming for us, and I wanted to still keep an eye on them niggas.

"Fuck he say?" Kantwan asked as he sparked a blunt.

My little cousin had been on edge lately, and Kill said it was because he felt he emasculated him in a way. Ever since we were kids, Kantwan hated for Kill to help him with something. I remember when Kill and I were like seven years old, and Kantwan wasn't quite six yet, we were swimming at one of my aunt Laurie's friend's houses, and when Kill tried to help Kantwan he didn't want it. That nigga almost drowned like a muthafucka, and my uncle had to jump in fully clothed to save his stubborn ass. I guess that incident did nothing to change him. I laughed at my thoughts.

"He claims he doesn't think his sons would go that far, because they're not the jealous type," I replied.

"Shit, money and status change people. I bet you them niggas mouths were watering thinking they'd inherit that empire, and now that they haven't, they're mad." Ka'Shea took the blunt from Kantwan.

"But damn, I'm wondering if we have two sets of enemies, or if Portland, Sonny, Dante, and Ahmad are all a fucking team." Kill stared down at his feet thinking.

"How the hell would they know one another though?" Ka'Shea frowned.

"I'm gonna get someone on them, and see if we catch them doing anything. Shea, get Sass up out of the trap and have him trail one of them niggas and find out if they're doing anything."

"Got it."

TWENTY-EIGHT

# Ka'Shea

One Week Later...

 was leaving the jewelry store because I'd bought this bracelet for Raleigh. I wanted to get her something other than the watch she'd gotten, and I felt this was perfect, just like her. I laughed as I thought about how Mercedes tried to fuck all my shit up, but it didn't work. That hoe knew she wasn't pregnant, and if she was, it was about one hundred niggas who could be the dad.

Speaking of Mercedes, that scrape had been blowing me up as of late, and I had to let her ass know she was getting blocked. She knew full well that she and I were never gonna be anything, even before I went to jail. I stayed smashing other hoes, but I guess that's what I get for allowing her to tell people she was my girlfriend. I really didn't care at the time because it was just a title, and it didn't stop me from doing what the fuck I wanted to do.

*WEE-ER! WEE-ER!*

"Fuck!" I shouted as I looked in my rearview mirror at the police trailing me. I pulled over to the side, and then reached into my glove compartment for my proof of insurance and registration. "This is some bullshit."

"License, proof of insurance, and registration please." The officer approached my window.

"Sure." I handed it over. "May I ask why you pulled me over, officer?"

He ignored me and walked away with my documents. Exhaling heavily, I laid my head back on the headrest, and waited until he was done. Finally after an eternity, he walked back over and handed me my shit back.

"I need to search the car, Mr. Camren, please step out of the vehicle."

"Search the car for what, man? You ain't even told me why you pulled me over!"

"We heard you might be carrying illegal substances and firearms in the car, and we need to check it. Exit the vehicle please, before I am forced to take further action," he stated sternly and stepped back to allow me to open the door.

I clenched my teeth and then got out of my car like he'd asked. His partner lightly pushed me into the car, and began patting me down as the initial officer searched my whip, including the trunk.

"Aye, what the fuck you doing?" I yelled as the partner placed handcuffs on my wrist. He said nothing, and then pushed me down to sit on the curb, so he could help the other officer search my vehicle.

Fifteen minutes later they came up empty, and then removed the cuffs from my wrists. I rubbed my shits since they were in pain, and then got into my car to get ready to leave the area.

"Sorry about that, Mr. Camren, you have a good day." The initial officer tapped the top of my Porsche after handing me my documents back.

I just rolled my window up on his ass and pulled off. At first I planned to head home to see Raleigh and give her this expensive ass gift, but I needed to make a quick pit stop in between. Once I got to where I was going, I opened the passenger seat of my car and removed my handgun. Locking it into my waist, I exited the vehicle.

"What's good!" Blow hollered from his porch, before stuffing a sunflower seed in his mouth.

"What's up? She in there?" I pointed at Mercedes home, whom he lived across the street from. He nodded in response, and then shook his head at me. "Ain't even like that. Aye lookout for me, aight?" I said and he nodded again.

Rushing up the porch steps, I beat on that bitch's door like I planned to break it down. She finally answered wearing a scowl on her pretty face. When she saw it was me, her expression softened, and she stepped back to let me in.

"Finally, you come see me, asshole!" she shouted and hugged me from behind. "I missed you, Shea, I love you," she whined.

"Get off me, ma," I replied dryly while prying her small hands from my six-pack. "Come take a ride with me, shorty."

"I hope you're taking me shopping, Shea, you haven't bought me shit in a cool ass minute," she giggled and grabbed her big ass purse from the couch.

I ignored her and then opened the front door. I made eye contact with Blow, and he nodded to me to say it was cool. Mercedes and I walked to my car, and once she got in, I went around to my side. Peeling off from the curb, I turned up my music loudly. Mercedes swayed to the Kevin Gates song as she rapped along with her sexy ass. I hated her, but I loved looking at her.

"Where the fuck are we?" she frowned when I pulled into the warehouse, underground.

"I have a surprise for you, come on." I exited the car, and so did she. Once we got to the room I was looking for, I closed the door behind her.

"I swear if you propose right now, I'm gonna slap the shit out of you, Shea. I need something way more romantic than this. And my family needs to be here."

"Mercedes, I know what you did."

"Huh? You better not be talking about me approaching that hoe of yours. You damn right I came at that bitch! I thought about leaving your ass, but I didn't! Leaving me for months to shack up with that girl, there aren't too many more times that—"

"Nah, bitch you set me up. You set me up when I went to jail some years back, and you gave a tip to the police today." She opened and closed her mouth, confirming everything I'd just said. "Yeah, I didn't wanna believe you set me up the first time, but I realized it was you after the fucking cops searched my shit today. It was like an epiphany."

My brothers and cousin swore up and down that Mercedes had set me up, but I refused to believe it. Even when I got out, I just couldn't see her doing me like that. But today, as I sat on that curb cuffed, it all hit me. A couple days before I got sent to jail, Mercedes found out that I'd slept with a couple other girls and was heated. She got mad at me about it, but was even madder because I didn't give a fuck. Just like last time, she was mad about Raleigh and me, so she tried to do the same thing. Lucky for me, and unfortunately for her, I was smarter this time and didn't drive shit around in my whip. Only thing I kept was a gun, but that was stored in a place they'd never find. Also, I was in a much higher position that rarely called for me to touch or transport product.

"Okay, Shea, look. I promise I will never do no shit like that again, babe. But what do you expect from me when I hear from everyone that you're out here cheating on me!"

"Cheating on you? Cheating on you, Mercedes? When have I ever been just about you? From day one I've been fucking other bitches! I never told you it was just me and you. You took it upon your fucking self to assume the position as my girlfriend. And regardless of whether you and I were exclusive or not, I now know that you're a grimy ass bitch."

"Shea—"

*POP!*

I cringed as I saw the bullet pierce her smooth forehead. She fell backwards, with her eyes wide open. I hated to do that to her, because she was cool or so I thought. I enjoyed fucking the bitch and she could actually hold a conversation. I never understood why I couldn't make her my girl like that, but now I realize it was because I knew she was a shade monster.

I called clean up, and after clearing her hoe ass out, I finally took Raleigh her gift. Now that Mercedes was gone, shit could really get popping!

TWENTY-NINE

# Jersey

_______________

My body was back to normal, but since I wasn't stripping anymore, I decided to take up working out. I almost chose to do a pole dancing class, but I felt that was too much like what I'd already done half of my life it seemed. Stripping was my past, and so the fuck were poles. To assist me and keep me on track, I hired a trainer. Because I had Alexsia, I knew it would be easy for me to blow off the gym because I was too tired. I had a lot on my plate from school, being a mom, and basically a wife, so the gym could easily get pushed to the side. I needed someone to stay on me.

My trainer's name was Harold, a black guy in his early thirties. I met him in my English class, and since he was a professional I agreed to let him train me. He offered me a discount, too. He was nice looking, but not really my type I guess. He was way too buff for my liking, and he was about 5'11, which was too short for me. I know I'm only 5'5, but I liked my men to be six feet or higher, like Kill, who stood at a nice 6'3. And Kill had muscles, but it was proportioned and lean. In addition to Harold's height problem, chocolate was my preference, and Harold was caramel.

We'd just finished running around the track eight damn times, and boy was I tired. That was what I liked about Harold though, he always came up with new ways for us to work out, because I told him I became bored easily. He knew keeping me on the same routine would not be good in any way, shape, or form.

"Nice job," he smiled as we leaned against the fence on the track.

"Thanks," I panted as I downed some of my Gatorade. I had two big cases at home; I was dedicated.

"We've only been working together for a few weeks, Jersey, and I can already see a difference. Your body was perfect before, but now it's even more perfect," he grinned as we walked around the fence to sit down.

"Shut up!" I chuckled and hit his arm.

"Let me stop complimenting you before you terminate my services, Lord knows I don't like to lose money."

"No way, I like working out actually. I didn't think I would, but I guess since I miss being active, I'm enjoying it."

"What made you want to get into the gym? Because like I said, you looked perfectly fine when we started."

"I told you I had a baby," I laughed.

"Shit, you sure did. It's hard to believe from looking at you. How old is he or she?"

"She's only five months, but I want to keep my body together, you know? I want to entice my man to keep making these babies," I half joked and we both chuckled.

"So, you're with the father of your child?"

"Yes, thank God. I was blessed, because I know plenty of girls who have babies by niggas they wish they hadn't had them by." I shook my head as I thought about Portland and Ivy.

"Ain't that right. Like my damn mama, it's eight of us, and my dad never shaped the fuck up. He was the worst nigga all the way up until he died. My mom did a great job, but I'm sure she wishes sometimes that she'd gotten pregnant by someone else."

"I would hate to feel that way. I'm happy I don't though. I wouldn't want to have a baby with anyone else." I smiled at the thought of Kill.

"Please tell me that's an engagement ring on your finger, and not some promise ring."

"It is an engagement ring, asshole," I chuckled.

"Good, that shit is huge though. That nigga must really love you or some shit. What's his name if you don't mind me asking, Jersey?"

"Kil-Kilexis," I stammered a bit. Kill advised me to stop telling people I was with someone named Kill, and to use his full name. I wasn't sure why, but I just decided to comply.

"Kill?" He bucked his eyes.

"No, I said Kilexis."

"Oh, aight, I was about to say, we can cancel this contract we got right now, shorty," he snickered.

"Why?"

"You've never heard of Kill?"

"No," I lied, anxious to know if he felt the same way Portland did. Kill was the type who only killed for good reasoning, I just couldn't see him stabbing someone at a school, or threatening to kill his own fiancée's brother.

"He's a big time distributor for Delaware, ma, and he's crazy as fuck. He can have you tracked down and killed just by snapping his fingers, and at any time of the day. The worst part is that he's smart though. Usually niggas in his position are idiots, but not him. Every move is calculated and that's why when niggas come up dead on his watch, ain't shit people can do about it. For one, no one ever sees shit, and if they do, they're too scared to run their mouths."

"The police can protect them."

"Yeah, certain ones, but what about the niggas he has on payroll." He sipped his Gatorade.

"Kill has police on payroll?"

"You damn right. So like I said, if that was your nigga, I'd have to let you go, ma."

I just chuckled lightly and fake smiled. The Kill he was talking about was not the Kill I knew. This Kill was a murderous, vicious, ruthless, kingpin, but my Kill was kind, thoughtful, and a hero.

I stood up and squinted my eyes at the sun before beginning to stretch. Between Harold and Portland, they were gonna have me scared to sleep next to my own damn man. As I was stretching, I looked back to see Harold checking my body out with a lustful stare. The bulge rising in his basketball shorts let me know he was enjoying everything he saw.

"Should we go run some more?"

"Who? Oh yeah, umm, let's go." He shot up and tried to low key adjust himself, before running off. I followed behind him with all kinds of thoughts floating through my mind. Was this why they called him Kill?

THIRTY

# Kantwan

___________

*I* was sitting in my den, pondering over the shit my brother and cousin brought to me. They were still skeptical about Ahmad and Dante, but I wasn't. Them niggas were up to something, and while Kill, Elijah, and Ka'Shea sat on their asses wondering, I was gonna take care of the shit. I knew I was supposed to follow my brother's lead, but sometimes he needed to follow mine.

I ashed my blunt, and then leaned back on the couch. Picking up my game controller, I began to play my video games. I wanted to clear my mind a little bit, because I'd been losing a little bit of sleep over this shit. As I was getting into it, Cheyla walked in wearing shorts and a little ass top with no straps. Her stomach was protruding way more now, but she didn't look bad at all in what she had on. In fact, my dick got hard immediately upon seeing her. My shorty was so sexy to me.

"Thirsty?" She reached out a beer to me, and a sandwich on a plate was in the other hand. Ever since I voiced my opinion about her not being as invested as I was in the relationship, she'd been doing way better. I liked her just fine before, but she didn't believe me.

"Thank you, shorty, why all this?"

"I can't feed you?" she grinned and sat down.

I pushed her hair behind her ears, and then brought her closer to peck her lips. I then paused the game so I could tear into my sandwich. As I was eating, I felt her staring at me, so I turned to look at her. I smacked my lips and then reached my sandwich out to her mouth, in which she took a bite before smiling with her adorable ass.

'I'm sorry, you just make it look so good. I actually ate the first one I made you."

"It's cool," I chuckled and sighed.

"What's wrong?" She scooted closer to me.

Cheyla was like my best friend, and she had my back more than anybody I felt. I didn't hide shit from her, as far as work goes. The only thing I kept from her were things that would involve her some kind of way if she knew about it. Other than that, my girl knew everything.

"You know that nigga who threw us that party when we first got started a while back?"

"Yeah."

"Well, I think his sons are trying to take us out, but discreetly. We don't quite have any proof, just a gut feeling, but I know them niggas are behind who shot Kill." I was gonna mention her brother, but decided to omit that.

"I wouldn't be surprised."

"What do you mean?" I finished my sandwich.

"When we were at the party that night, they gave you guys these little looks before whispering amongst themselves. It was a look of jealousy, and like they were being fraud with you."

I pulled my phone out and text Ali, because I needed him to track down Dante or Ahmad Johnson. I could've easily hit Sass, since Kill already had him tailing them, but I wanted to do this shit on my own. I felt like I needed to prove something. I wasn't gonna do anything, I was just gonna talk to the nigga and see if I saw what Cheyla saw. I would then go back to my family, and let them know my thoughts. Nothing too detrimental.

"Thanks, baby, aye, I'm gonna head out in a little bit."

"Why? Kantwan where are you going?"

"I'm going to meet someone." I stood to my feet.

"Kantwan, do not go meet with Axel's sons alone. Call Kill—"

"I ain't calling no fucking Kill! Why you always bringing that nigga up and taking his side? Whose girl are you huh?" Maybe she didn't have my back like I thought.

"I'm yours' Kantwan, but—"

"Aight then, act like it! Quit always cheering for this nigga when you're supposed to be my bitch, aight?"

She opened her mouth to speak, but decided against it. I was annoyed now, so I just rushed out and up the stairs to go hop in the shower. When I got out, I saw her bathroom door was closed, so she must've been doing the same. I slipped into some black joggers, black New Balances, a black t-shirt, and a black hoodie. I opted out of wearing jewelry. I snatched my phone, keys, and some cash before leaving out.

Ali texted me while I was in the shower, and let me know that Ahmad was doing something at his father's cleaners, the one that we used to clean our money in. I pulled up to it, and parked across the street. I chose to drive this 2001 Toyota Camry that I'd purchased for five thousand, because I didn't want to use my precious Mustang or any of the luxury cars I'd purchased recently. After discreetly making sure my Rhode Island plates were on correctly, I headed over to the cleaners.

When I walked in no one was in front, so I just slipped past the counter and headed to the back, securing my gun on the way. I was just here to talk, but in case someone tried to run up on me, I wanted to be prepared. I went into the back office, and when I opened the door, Ahmad shot up out of his seat frightened.

"Oh shit, it's just you," he chuckled and then sat back down.

"Yeah, just me. So how you been, man? I ain't seen you around."

"I been good, just working on making this Johnson's Cleaners better than it was the day before, ya know?"

"Cool, you know, I came to talk to you and see if you knew anything. My brother got shot, and someone came by our traps trying to make a deal with one of our workers for a couple keys.

Have you heard anything? Like have you witnessed someone talking slick about one of us?"

"Nope, but you know I don't do too much hanging out in the streets. I'm more of a business man than a street thug."

"Fuck is that supposed to mean?"

"It means just what I said. I don't dibble and dabble in the streets like you and your brothers, so it would be hard for me to hear something about you, ya know?"

"Yet, you were begging my brother for a fucking job though, right?"

"I didn't beg. I simply offered my assistance to someone that I felt needed it. I was trying to assist him and clearly he needed me if he's out here getting shot at in broad daylight."

"How did you know he got shot in broad daylight?"

"Huh? I mean you sai—"

"No, I said my brother was shot, I didn't say when he was shot, you bitch ass nigga." I rose to my feet as I felt a sudden rush of anger flow through me.

*POP! POP! POP! POP!*

As soon as he reached for something, I pulled out my silenced gun and popped his ass four times. I gave him two to the head, and two to the chest. He fell backwards, and his blood splattered all on the blinds behind him.

"Fuck!" I shouted.

Rushing to the camera room, I retrieved my pocketknife and slit every got damn wire in that bitch. I busted out the screens of the televisions with the butt of my gun, and then completely ransacked the room, damaging any recording devices they had. I then rushed to the very back where we used to band the money, and grabbed a lighter with gasoline. I poured and poured until there was no more left, and then went back into Ahmad's office to get some matches. I lit one when I got a little closer to the back room, and dropped it before running out. I hit the block and came back around to my car as if I wasn't just inside Johnson Cleaners, then slipped into my whip. The flames were already in the front of the place, and once I saw the windows break, I sped out of there.

I didn't feel like going home because this night had turned out to be a fucking disaster. I went there to talk, and ended up killing this nigga and burning the damn cleaners down. I knew Cheyla would try to reprimand me for not waiting for Kill, and I didn't want to deal with that shit. I drove to a nearby hotel, and quickly checked in before going up to shower. When I got out, my phone was ringing off the hook, and I saw it was Rachel.

Kill had moved me from meeting up with her and Tanya to get the product, to a new position. Now, I was to wait at the warehouse for one of our workers named Doley to drop the product off. I would then supervise a team of four in dividing and delivering. Ever since that change, it was like Rachel had been having withdrawals. We'd become cool… homies, and I guess she missed it. Or maybe she missed sucking me off.

"What's good?" I answered.

"Hey, I miss you."

"Oh, word?"

"Yes, can you come over? Since I can never come to your house."

"Yeah, because my girl lives there. But uh, I'm in a hotel tonight, so you can come through here. I will text you the address and shit."

"Okay," she responded excitedly.

Twenty minutes later, Rachel was knocking at my door. Since I didn't have a change of clothes, I just put on the same thing I was wearing, minus the shirt. I let her in, and that's when my phone began ringing again. I saw it was Cheyla, so I hit ignore and then silenced my phone.

"Had a nasty fight with your baby mama?" Rachel walked into the room looking sexy as fuck and carrying a bottle of patron in her hand. She was wearing a short ass dress with no straps that accentuated her perfect D cups and nice fat ass. Shit.

"Don't worry about that. Sometimes a nigga needs to just get away." I plopped down on the bed and closed my eyes for a couple moments.

"Why did you have to bring ya girl to Starzz that night?" she quizzed in her thick Caribbean accent.

"Because I wanted to hang with her. Why else?" I lied. Cheyla's ass forced herself onto my night out, but I wasn't gonna say that. I already felt a little bad about letting Rachel give me some top.

"You know how I feel about you, and you knew that would hurt my feelings, Kantwan."

"Shorty, she's my girl, fuck do you want me to do, huh? Be with the both of y'all or some shit? I ain't that type of nigga."

"Or." she walked over and straddled me on the bed. My hands immediately began rubbing her smooth golden thighs as if they had a mind of their own. Fucking her had crossed my mind, but I'd always only settled for head. "You can give me more attention." I had never cheated on Cheyla, but damn was I craving shorty right now.

"What kind of attention do you want?" I bit my lip and let my hands go up her dress. She had on no panties, and it caused my breathing to become heavier as I squeezed on her ass. Moving her dress to her waist, I looked down to see her pussy, which was neatly trimmed, not bald.

"I want the attention you're giving me right now." She gulped some of the Patron.

I sat up with her still in my lap, and then took the bottle from her. I took a couple sips, and then passed it back to her before pulling her dress over her head. *No bra, fuck.*

"Let me get a cap." I moved her off of me after sucking the life out of her nipples.

"I'm clean, Kantwan, and I haven't fucked anyone since my last boyfriend three years ago."

"I know, but I have enough kids."

"You only have an unborn."

"And that's all I want right now."

I stepped out of my joggers, and my dick was standing at attention already. I waved her over, and she took my dick into her mouth to begin working. I threw my head back as she pleasured me with her warm wet mouth. Gripping her hair, I began humping her face, hitting her tonsils every now and then. She was moaning as she gave me the sloppiest fucking head in the world. I felt my nut rising, so I pulled her off, and then got on my back to roll the condom down.

She straddled me, and then slowly moved down my pole, whimpering the whole way. Once she made it to the base, she cried out and her body shivered. I could tell by how tight her walls were that she hadn't been fucked in a cool minute. I began guiding her up and down my rod slowly, and that shit felt so damn good. I knew she had that bomb between her thighs.

"Baby, uuuh shit," she moaned and knotted her face up.

She finally got used to my length and girth, so she started to rock her hips back and forth, and up and down. She was so damn wet, and I was about to lose my mind. Her pussy was fire, and definitely second runner up to Cheyla's. Cheyla's pussy was molded just for my dick it seemed, so she was slightly better feeling.

I flipped her onto all fours, and when I got inside I began beating it up. She clenched her teeth together as I pounded her feverishly, and I could feel her nectar dripping down her thighs. I delivered her some more long hard thrusts, and then finally I filled the condom up. She just collapsed onto her stomach as I climbed off the bed and went to flush the condom.

I wiped my dick down with a warm, soapy towel, and then went back to the bed where she was. She was breathing hard still, but able to turn onto her back. Her legs were trembling, so I scooped them up and put them under the covers for her. She snuggled up to me, and kissed my jawline before exhaling.

"You got me sprung that quickly," she whispered and chuckled. "It could always be like this, Kantwan, she would never know."

# THIRTY-ONE

## Ivy

———

That Same Night...

Tonight my baby and I were gonna go hang out with each other, since Donovan was spending the night with Jersey. Most of the time, we usually went to dinner, the movies, or little places for Donovan, but tonight we were gonna party together. Elijah had become my best friend, and who better to party with than a sexy ass best friend that can dick you down?

I finished fastening my necklace, and then ran my hands down my camel colored dress as I observed my appearance. I wore matching camel stilettos, and since my golden blond hair was freshly pressed, I let it hang down. I spritzed some of my Chloe perfume on, and then turned around to see my love smiling as he watched me near him.

"What you looking at?" I asked as I approached him. He was sporting a navy blue button up, dark jeans, navy blue Adidas, and just the right amount of jewelry.

"The prettiest girl in Delaware?" he grinned and rose to his feet. I pushed his dreads from his face, and then stood on my tiptoes to kiss him. Yes, even with heels on, I had to get on my tiptoes to kiss his ass.

"You ready?"

He nodded and then we left.

On the way there we listened to Pandora, letting it get us in the party mood. It did us right, because the whole way there we were grooving to all kinds of club jams. By the time Elijah pulled up, we were both ready to go inside and have a good ass time. After giving his keys to valet, we held hands and then walked straight to the front. The bouncer let us by, and then Elijah led me right to the dance floor. Tonight, we had a table, but we really wanted to just dance.

"Bad Ass" by Kid Ink blasted over the club, as I moved my ass against Elijah. I was using all the moves that got me good ass tips while working for Starzz. I smiled when I felt his dick get hard, because that meant I still had it. It was nothing to get a random dick hard, but the ability to get a nigga hard that has fucked you one hundred different ways to Sunday was really an accomplishment. After dancing to a couple more songs, we went to our reserved VIP area, and ordered drinks and wings from the hostess.

"Who knew my shorty could be so much fun?" Elijah cheesed as he got comfortable on the plush couch.

"Yeah right, you knew you would have a good time. You probably are having more fun with me than you do with your friends."

"You're pushing it, but I will say I haven't had this much fun in a very long time." He pulled me into his lap and kissed my shoulder gently. I moved a little in his lap to the music as we waited for our food and drinks. "This is what had me on you in the first place," he said, referring to my dance moves.

"I know, and I'm sure it was better then, since I had on way less clothes."

"I think it's better now, because I actually know what the pussy is like," he whispered on the nape of my neck before kissing it, making chills trickle down my spine.

"Ivy?" I heard a voice say. I looked up to see Shamece standing by the bouncer guarding our VIP.

"Hey, girl. She's cool," I told the guy. He let her by, and she came and sat across from Elijah and me. We'd text here and there since our last awkward encounter, and we kind of just acted as if it never happened. "Baby, this is Shamece, we used to work at Starzz together remember? Shamece, this is my man, Elijah."

"Damn, you look even better in person. She showed me pictures, but they do not do you justice," Shamece giggled.

"Thanks, ma, and nice to meet you." Elijah nodded.

"So, who are you here with?" I inquired.

"Nobody, I just wanted to get out, and shit, sometimes you can't wait for others to have fun."

"I understand. Elijah and I kind of wanted to party, yet spend time with one another so we came here together."

"Uh oh, I know people have been trying to get at both of y'all all night!"

"Nah, I think everyone knows better. My shorty is off limits and I don't mind telling that to anyone who wants to know," Elijah corrected her, and I just smiled before pecking him.

"Get Busy" by Glasses Malone suddenly came on, and that was my song so I stood up to dance. The hostess brought the drinks and food in around the same time, so I picked my martini up and began sipping and swaying. Elijah bobbed his head, and then Shamece came behind me, wanting me to dance on her. I was in the zone, so I just kept moving as she gripped my small hips. We danced together until the song went off, and then both plopped down on the couch.

"Thanks for the show," Elijah chuckled and I playfully rolled my eyes.

"You liked what you saw?" Shamece quizzed Elijah.

"Of course. Two beautiful women dancing together." He frowned and nodded as if Shamece was a fool for even asking him something like that. I didn't like him calling other girls beautiful, but I was starting to feel my liquor, so I was chill.

"Can I get you guys some more cocktails? Or would you like me to open the complimentary Grey Goose for you?" The hostess showed back up, smiling. She was skinny as hell, kind of tall for a girl, and had long, red hair.

"Pop the bottle, please," I answered her. She did so, and then poured some into three glasses. She put juice in my drink, and in Shamece's, but not Elijah's since he wanted it plain.

I downed mine, and then leaned over to kiss Elijah. Because I was a bit tipsy, I kissed him nastily, not even remembering Shamece was on the other side of me. He moaned from the kiss, and that turned me on like crazy.

"Damn, can I get one?" Shamece joked and I chuckled. "I'm serious." She bit her lip.

I looked to Elijah to silently ask if it was okay, and he shrugged wearing a half smile, meaning he was more than okay with it. I turned my attention back to Shamece, and then pressed my lips against hers. It started slow, but then we really got into it. She was a good ass kisser, and I surprisingly enjoyed the shit. I finally pulled away, and as I was about to say something to Elijah, he stood up off the couch.

"Let's go," he said and polished off his glass of our vodka.

"What? Okay," I replied and stood up. I hoped he wasn't upset, he *just* said I could kiss her. I was gonna have to suck a lot of dick tonight to make it up.

As we were walking out, he turned to look back at Shamece and said, "You too."

That shit caught me off guard. She hopped up and followed us out where we both retrieved our cars from valet. Shamece trailed us home, and the whole way there, Elijah had his hand on my thigh just rubbing up and down, getting me hot. I loved his strong touch against my soft skin. He was a pro and always knew where to touch me and when.

We made it to the house, and both Shamece and I followed Elijah to the guest room. He dimmed the lights, and the three of us immediately began undressing. I had never had a threesome before, but I guess there was a first time for everything. I was horny, and I loved pleasing Elijah, so if this was what he wanted, then so be it.

"Leave your shoes on," Elijah directed the both of us. I did as he asked and then climbed onto the bed.

Elijah walked to the edge of the bed with his dick standing at attention, and when I saw Shamece about to suck it, I nudged her lightly. This was *my* dick and I was gonna be the only one putting it in my mouth. I heard Elijah chuckle lightly right before I took him into my mouth and began pleasing him. Shamece got behind me, and laid on her back, pulling my pussy down to her mouth, so that I was sitting on her face.

"Mmm shit," I moaned as Shamece sucked on my clit. I could barely give Elijah head, because she was doing such a good job.

Elijah noticed I was having a hard time, so he gripped my hair and pushed himself inside of my mouth. He humped my face slowly, and the sound of him moaning had me even wetter than before. His dick got harder, and so did my clit, right before we both exploded. Sliding a condom down, Elijah got on his back, allowing Shamece to mount him. She bit down on her lip with every inch of him that she took in, and I was slightly jealous. I could see all in her face that she was enjoying my dick. Suddenly, Elijah yanked me over to him, and made me sit on his face as Shamece rode him, moaning like this was the best dick she had ever experienced. She and I both appeared to have cum at the same time, because we both trembled violently while screaming out loudly. My nigga was a beast if he could make two bitches cum that hard at once.

I wanted my turn, but Shamece kept riding, clearly wanting another hit of my man. I continued to rock my hips on his face as she continued bouncing on him and hollering. I knew that feeling and I wanted to make sure Elijah didn't cum again before I got mine.

"Uuuh oooh fuck!" she yelled as she released and collapsed on his chest. *No bitch*, I thought as I got off his face.

He knew, so he moved her off of him gently, and then put me on my knees. After removing the condom, he slid into me from behind, making me quiver lightly. As he rammed into me, Shamece and I kissed feverishly; or at least tried to. I was crying out so much that I could barely fix my lips to kiss her. It was all so much going on as she played with my clit and kissed me, while Elijah beat it up doggy-style. After feeling like Elijah was fucking me for forever, he finally released and so did I for the sixth got damn time. I instantly turned to face him, and threw my arms over his shoulders to kiss him. His strong arms snaked around my small body, holding me in place since I was trembling so. While he and I kissed, Shamece planted pecks all over my back.

Tonight was fucking crazy. Once we caught our breaths, we went at it again, and then Elijah and I went to our bedroom upstairs, allowing Shamece to sleep in the guest bedroom.

"Did you have fun?" I asked Elijah once we got out of the shower and climbed into the bed.

"Man, too much fun."

"This will not happen again for a long time, Eli, so don't get excited."

"I know, and I don't need it to. You've had a threesome before?"

"No."

"I can tell by how petty your little ass was being," he chuckled and so did I.

"She looked like she gave good head, and I didn't want you getting sprung off her head game. Have you had a threesome before?"

"Only like four times."

"Four? Nigga that's including tonight or no?"

"Not including tonight. Tonight makes five."

"Ugh, you're nasty," I giggled.

"But tonight was the best one, because it was with you." He kissed me as I caressed his face.

What a night...

THIRTY-TWO

# Portland

___________

"This shit is not going as planned, and I need to know what the fuck you niggas plan to do about it," Dante barked.

I understood and shared his frustration. We had no connect, which meant we had no new product, barely any niggas working for us, no Leroy, no place to clean our money, and to top it all off, Ahmad was killed. Then my plan to get Ivy and Jersey to slow Kill's team down, failed like a muthafucka. At a time like this, we would need Leroy to guide us, but his ass was dead.

"Y'all need to find out who the fuck killed my brother and get him!" Dante added and pouted like a little ass girl.

"Nigga, we know who the fuck did it, and that's the problem. We can't do shit about it with the way we're working right now," Sonny frowned.

"Do whatever you did to Leroy, to the nigga who did this. Who was it exactly? Y'all saying it was a Camren, but I just don't believe that shit." Dante quizzed.

"I'm telling you it was one of them. We just ain't know Ahmad had any known beef with any of them. He didn't, right?" I looked to Dante.

"Nah, I mean he got into a little tiff with Kill, but other than that, to their knowledge we're still cool with them. And I doubt Kill would do it since he see's my father as his father."

I didn't know what to think, and I was tired of sitting here with these niggas discussing it. I wanted to go home, get some head, and eat. My mind was tired and I was over this shit, I really was. A part of me wanted to just give up and find some way to get back into the Camren's good graces. I didn't want to die, and it was looking pretty possible at this point. As the old saying goes, if you can't beat them join them.

"Alright, y'all, let's call this shit a night. I'm tired and I need to think with a clear head." I rose to my feet and stretched a little. By the look on Dante's face, I knew he wasn't okay with what I'd just said.

"Nigga, my fucking brother is dead and you trying to go home to lay up with that hoe of yours?" Dante grimaced.

"Dante, we've been at this fucking shit all damn day, my nigga. All he's saying is we need to go home to rest so that we can come back with some fresher ideas," Sonny tried to assist me.

"Like I'm gonna listen to some base head," Dante scoffed and waved Sonny off. Before I could even say anything in his defense, Sonny's ass was across the table and choking Dante.

"Aye, y'all what the fuck! We got enough damn enemies out here!" I barked as I yanked Sonny from Dante. Thank God I was pretty muscular and Sonny was skinny, or I would have had to call for back up.

"Hey, Portland," one of my guys, Ezekiel, walked into the warehouse, and by the worried expression on his face, I knew some more shit had hit the fan.

"What's good?" I asked, still lightly holding onto Sonny's collar. He and Dante were staring one another down angrily, so I knew if I let his ass go they'd be back to boxing.

"We think them Camrens are on to us and y'all being a team," Ezekiel replied.

"What? How? They would have no proof, no one knows we

know each other, unless someone has been running their damn mouth. Sonny yanked from me and neared Ezekiel.

"Nah, no one has. But E-Way just let us know that the Camrens have gotten wind of this foursome y'all got. He was basically telling us to dip on y'all."

"Oh word?" I raised a brow. E-Way was my nigga from way back, so to hear he was trying to go behind my back and jump ship not only infuriated me, but it hurt.

"Word, P, he said if they come to him, he's acting like he don't fuck with you and is gone tell everything. He's gonna try to link up with them somehow since he knows Shea's homeboy, Blow."

"Thanks for that, Ezekiel," was all I said as I booked it out of the warehouse. Sonny was right on my heels, because he knew what we had to do.

"This nigga E-Way, man," Sonny sighed as I peeled out of the warehouse area. I was going 90mph trying to get to E-Way's house before he did some dumb shit and got me killed.

About fifteen minutes later, I was pulling up to his home. I parked a little ways down since I knew he was on his porch. As soon as Sonny and I got to his steps, he attempted to run into his home, but we were too fast for his rotund ass.

"For real, Eldrick?" I gripped his collar, calling him by his government name. "You trying to switch sides?"

Sonny closed his front door after making sure no one was outside. It was around eleven at night, so the streets were pretty clear.

"Look, Portland, it would be smart for us all just to bow the fuck down, my nigga! This shit is stupid! We don't have the team or the resources to be going against Kill and you know it!" E-Way hollered and pulled himself from my grasp.

"Nigga, shut up! Quit acting like a fucking bitch right now! Get off Kill's dick, my nigga!" Sonny roared, expressing some of what I felt. I agreed with them both to be honest. I shuddered at the thought of waving my white flag and surrendering to Kill, but I knew E-Way was right, our resources were far and few in between.

"It's time to shed some pride, y'all, and you know it. I'm not down with this no more. You both were in here on some shit, talking about y'all would have the streets under control, and how the fact that you had Axel's sons meant the world. I should've known that wasn't true! There is a reason why Axel gave his shit to someone other than his offspring!" E-Way shouted.

"Man, calm your ass down! We just need some time!" I shouted back, not liking the way he was coming at me. He was making it sound like I came up in his broke down ass crib selling wolf tickets. I would've never tried to do all this shit had I not felt that my plan would work.

"Whatever, you just better hope they don't come to me asking about you because if they do, I'm gonna sing like Mary J. Blige on you niggas!"

*POP! POP! POP!*

"Nigga," Sonny whispered after witnessing me send three bullets into E-Way.

His plump ass hit the ground so hard, I thought he was gonna fall through the wooden floors. Panting heavily, I stared down at his lifeless body feeling all sorts of emotions. I was enraged at the disrespect, but I was saddened because he was my nigga. Did he really deserve that? Or should I have just taken his advice? I had never pulled a trigger in my life, and I felt some kind of way about the fact that my first bullet went into a childhood homie.

"We really have to come out on top now, Portland. We just killed the homie," Sonny said after a few moments of silence.

"I know. I know."

# THIRTY-THREE

## Kilexis

_____________

e'd just found out that Axel's cleaners had been burned down, and I was perplexed wondering who it could be. That was until Kantwan's ass ran up on me and confessed about how not only had he burned the cleaners down, but he killed Ahmad prior to that. Axel was furious about his cleaners and the fact that they'd found the burned skull of his son. I knew now, that any ties we had with Axel would have to be severed. I couldn't smile in his face knowing my brother murked his son.

"What the fuck happened, my nigga? How did it even get that far?" Ka'Shea frowned as he looked at Kantwan.

"I walked in just to see if I got a guilty vibe from him, and I promise that was it. I wasn't gonna kill him if I did feel he was guilty, I just planned to come back and tell you guys. But when he and I got to talking, he started taking little jabs, and then he slipped up and said Kill got shot in broad daylight. I never mentioned when you got shot, I just said you did."

"Kantwan, it wouldn't be odd for him to know about it," Elijah responded.

"Nah, because when I asked him how he knew, he was stuttering and shit like he knew he was caught up. Otherwise if he wasn't guilty, he would've came right out and said he'd heard it or whatever." Kantwan shook his head 'no' repeatedly, signaling his mind was made up about Ahmad.

I can't lie, from what my brother was saying, it definitely sounded like Ahmad was behind getting Leroy to shoot me, and probably the white boy showing up as well. The room fell silent as the four of us sat there processing what Kantwan said, and thinking about the next move.

"So, y'all do know that we need to get Dante now too, right?" I asked the room and they nodded. "I think it should just be Shea and I who get him since Kantwan you've done enough, and Elijah your face is more familiar to him than Shea."

"Sounds good, but what about Axel?" Elijah questioned.

"I'm trying to spare him, because the nigga is dying and ain't much he can do, especially now that I have his whole team. But if it comes down to it, we'll murk his ass, too." I shrugged like it was nothing, but the thought did bother me somewhat.

After going over some more details, I hit up Rogue and told him to try and get a location on Dante. I knew since he was probably moping around about his brother, he wasn't thinking about hiding out or some shit, or at least that's what I hoped. Plus, he had no idea who to hide out from anyway.

I waited until Kantwan and Elijah left, before turning my attention to my brother Ka'Shea to explain some shit to him. I wanted this shit with Dante to be quick and clean.

"So what's the plan, bro?" he asked once I closed my office door.

"I'm waiting for Rogue to text me back, and once he gives us a location, let's just trail him all day until he gets home. If he is already home, then we're gonna break in his shit once night falls upon us."

"Cool, well it's already 7 PM, so it should be dark pretty damn soon." He looked at his watch.

"You right. Go ahead and go so you can change and load up, then meet me back at the warehouse."

As soon as Ka'Shea left, I ran upstairs so that I could change. Jersey was napping in the bed with Alexsia, and they both looked so peaceful. I walked over to the side of the bed that Jersey was on, and then leaned down to kiss her cheek gently. She opened her eyes and jumped back hard as fuck, making me frown.

"What's wrong?"

"No-nothing, you just scared me," she stuttered.

"Oh, my bad, shorty, go back to sleep."

"Where are you going at this time, Kilexis?"

"I need to handle something." I pulled up my black sweats and then threw on a black shirt as well.

"I heard about Axel's cleaners being burned down. Is someone mad at you or something like that?" she questioned and climbed off of the bed.

"No, Jersey," I turned to look at her as I pulled my hoodie down and grabbed my keys. I stuffed them into my pocket, and then unlocked my top drawer using a code, to get a dummy phone. As I placed a battery and SIM into it, Jersey's eyes were locked onto me.

"Why do you want me to stop calling you Kill?"

"I didn't tell you to stop calling me that. I said when people wanna know who you're with, tell them Kilexis and not Kill. That's two totally different things."

"But—"

"I have to go, baby." I leaned down to kiss her cheek lightly and then left. I don't know why she had the sudden urge to question me so much, but I wasn't gonna give her all the answers. I was protecting her, and that was how it was gonna be whether she liked it or not.

Once I made it to the warehouse, I saw Ka'Shea's car was already out there, so I climbed out and went inside. He was in there face timing like some little hoe, so I shook my head as I sat down adjacent to him.

"Aight, baby, I have to go, see you later," he grinned and hung up.

"Who the fuck was that?"

"Raleigh, who else?"

"Yo, I'm sure you just came from seeing her, so why did you feel the need to FaceTime her my nigga? You're pussy whipped like a muthafucka," I chuckled and he smacked his lips.

"Whatever, what did Rogue say as far as Dante's location?"

"He said Dante is staying at some hotel. That's risky if we try and get him while he's there, so I'm wondering what other way we can get his ass. The last thing I'm trying to do is go down for murking his ass. I mean, I can pull it off, but it would take more planning. We wouldn't be able to do it tonight, and I need to get it done *tonight*."

"How about we get him to come through over here? We can tell him that we have a plan in place to help find out who did his brother in. Once we get him over here, we can get in his head and find out for real if he was behind you getting popped, and if Sonny and Portland were in on it too."

"I knew you were good for something," I chuckled.

I switched the SIM back in my phone and then called Dante. To my surprise, the nigga agreed to meet and said he was ready to find out who would do such a thing to his brother. I made sure to make him agree to keep this meeting a secret, just because we didn't want Ahmad's *assailant* to get wind of us coming, and end up fleeing or retaliating before we could even touch them.

"What's good?" I greeted Dante as soon as he entered the warehouse. "I'm sorry to hear about your brother, man," I added as we walked to the back room where Ka'Shea was. "Dante, you remember my brother, Shea. Shea, Dante." They shook hands and then we all sat down.

"So, what were y'all thinking? I'm trying to take these muthafuckas out ASAP!" Dante ran his hands over his face.

Ka'Shea stood up and said, "We were wondering what you was thinking when you had Kill and Elijah shot at." He pressed the barrel of his gun to Dante's temple, prompting him to freeze up.

"I... aye man, I don't know nothing about that!"

"Oh, yes you do. See, Ahmad admitted to Kantwan that he was behind it, right before he was taken care of." I half lied as I twisted the silencer onto my gun with a smile. Tears began to fall down his cheeks as he watched my every move.

"Aight, wait, wait, shit okay. Look Ahmad wasn't the one who set it up, but he did know about it. The both of us knew about it. Portland was the one who brought up the idea, but his intention was to kill Elijah. Instead the shooter hit you, and when he said he didn't kill you, Portland and Sonny had him taken care of. But look, fuck what my brother and those two were on, I'm trying to be down with y'all."

"Wow, so y'all are working with Sonny and Portland. How do you even know them?" I frowned as Ka'Shea adjusted the grip on his burner, which was still prodding Dante's temple. I couldn't believe Sonny and Portland had him thinking they killed Leroy.

"Ahmad and Portland have a mutual friend named E-Way, and we met him at a party. Bu-but he's dead now. Anyway, the four of us got to talking, and Sonny and Portland started telling us they were building, because they didn't fuck with y'all."

"Thanks," was all I said before nodding my head up to Ka'Shea. He pulled the trigger, making a big ass hole appear in the side of Dante's head. I dialed Rogue to come in with his clean up crew, and then headed to Kantwan's so Ka'Shea, Elijah and I could discuss what we'd just heard.

I left Kantwan's after making sure everyone was abreast, and then went right home. As I was preparing for a shower, Jersey walked into the bathroom smiling. I smiled back at her, and then began undressing. She picked my clothes up, so that she could wash them, and then left out. I cleaned up, brushed my teeth, and then climbed into bed with my shorty.

"Why was there blood on your sweater, Kilexis?" she inquired as soon as I hugged her small frame. I just sat up and grabbed my phone before heading to the door. "Kilexis, where are you going?"

"To sleep in the guest room, goodnight."

# THIRTY-FOUR

# Cheyla

---

$\mathcal{I}$'d just finished spreading lotion all over my body, so I slipped my dress over my head. My belly was sticking out more now, so it made my dress rise up a little in the front. Blowing out hot air, I removed the dress and put on a longer one. Today I had a doctor's appointment, and Kantwan was supposed to come with me, but he said he had to work. Since it wasn't anything special, only a check up, I let it go. Plus, afterwards I wanted to go talk to my brother, because I'd overheard the boys last night, saying that they were gonna have to get him if he kept fucking with them. I wanted to hopefully convince him to cut out whatever the fuck he was doing to them.

My gray t-shirt dress was long in the front and back, but short on the sides so it was perfect. I put on some low top Air Force, and then let my hair hang down. I made it to the doctor's office about fifteen minutes later, and as I was getting out, I saw Miami walking out with a smile on her face. This building was a cluster-fuck of doctors, so it's no telling what she was here for. I'm sure it was the infectious disease doctor she was seeing though.

"Hey, Cheyla," she waved and then began laughing.

I was gonna keep walking, but I just turned around and asked,

"What the fuck is your problem? Why can't we just not talk to one another? Why can't you just keep it pushing, oh it's because you're jealous."

"Jealous? Jealous of what Cheyla?" She folded her arms and cocked her head.

"You're jealous of me. You're envious of the fact that I no longer work at Starzz, that I didn't have to sell pussy while I was there, and of the fact that you can't have my man."

"Oh, honey, you're so oblivious that it's a shame," she pouted playfully. "Your man is not as exclusive as you think. I know you thought because you have that baby growing in there that he was gonna be well behaved, but you're wrong."

"What are you talking about?" I frowned.

"He's fucking my homegirl, Rachel, and we even had a three-some two nights ago. Just think, I'm sure he told you he had to work or something, but that was a lie. Rachel and I were sucking and fucking your man all night, baby, and didn't let him leave until the morning," she giggled. "I told you I was gonna fuck him."

"Oh, okay." I turned to walk away, because I refused to let her see me cry. She was telling the truth, because two nights ago, Kantwan claimed he had to work, and he didn't come back until eight the next morning.

I just entered the building, and got onto the elevator. I breathed heavily and constantly, trying to keep the tears from coming out. I needed to be strong until I could get somewhere and cry like I wanted to. The elevator dinged, so I stepped off and went into my doctor's office. I walked straight to the counter, because I needed to talk to the nurse.

"Hi, I was wondering if, umm, if I could go in like right now. I'm not feeling well and I can't wait here too umm, too long." Every word came from my mouth breathy, because I was two seconds from crying.

"Oh okay, honey. Let me see what the doctor is doing." She turned around and picked up the little phone. "She was eating her lunch, but she said to come on back," the nurse receptionist said once she got off the phone.

"Thanks so much." I tried to smile.

I rushed to the back and then got ready for my appointment. As my doctor showed me my baby on the monitor, a few tears were able to escape. Kantwan was supposed to only become better, yet somehow he made a change for the worst. He treated me better when he was just a fuck buddy of mine, but now that he and I were everything but married, he didn't give a fuck. I took the picture that said I would be having my baby in just five months, and then left to go home. I was driving like a bat out of hell, all the way until I got home. As soon as I got into the door, I broke down and cried, sliding down the wall.

"Baby, what the fuck is wrong with you?" Kantwan walked in from the garage, and placed his keys into his pocket. He made his way over to me, and attempted to help me up from the floor.

"Get the fuck away from me!" I barked and he furrowed his brows.

"Why? Is something wrong with the baby? Please tell me nothing—"

"The baby is fine! It's you! You fucked that bitch that I told you I fought? You fucked her and your co-worker?" His mouth opened, but then it closed right back, because he had nothing to say. "I am done with you, Kantwan, it's over." I sobbed. My face was drenched.

"Cheyla, I'm sorry, baby, come on. I don't know what the fuck was going on with me. I just man, I don't fucking know. I was bugging about some shit I did, and I just did some shit I shouldn't have. Baby, I love you. Fuck!" He sounded so damn dumb.

I just chuckled angrily and then went upstairs. I sat down on the bed, wondering where I could sleep, because being here with this nigga wasn't an option. Kantwan walked his pitiful ass into the bedroom, and sat down next to me as I pondered over my options of where I could go until I got on my feet.

I glanced over at him and then looked away as more tears rushed down my cheeks. I knew this would happen. This is why I didn't want to fall in love. All you did was get attached to people just for them to hurt you. I was stupid enough to not only give in to

Kantwan, but I allowed him to get me pregnant. Now here I was with no money, because I wasn't using the shit he'd put into my account, and a baby who would be here in less than six months.

"Cheyla, I don't know what to say, but please don't leave shorty. I promise you this will never happen again. I was tripping, but now I'm good; I'm good and nothing will make me go back to how I was." I ignored him and then stood up to get my suitcase. I began putting clothes into it, along with some underwear, bras, and baby books I'd bought. "Whoa, wait, where the fuck are you going?"

"I'm leaving you. I told you it's over. There is nothing you can say or do to make me be with you, so please just get the fuck out of my face before you end up like Jersey's father."

"You ain't going no fucking where." He stood up and locked the bedroom door, before leaning up against it. "I'd like to see you get past me."

I admired his handsome face, and then went back to packing. Once I finished, I stood up and walked towards the door. He gave me a look saying to try him, so I looked around the room trying to remember if that was the only door, which I knew it was.

"Kantwan, please let me go," I sniffled. "Why do you want to keep me here when I don't want to be with you?"

"You didn't wanna be with me when I first met you, but I changed your mind," he grinned and licked his lips as if that were supposed to make me smile.

"But the difference is that then, I secretly did want to be with you."

"And you wanna be with me now too, you're just angry and hurt, and I get that. I promised you I would never hurt you and I did. But you have my baby growing inside of you and I know you ain't just over me that quickly. You love me as much as I love you. I haven't shown it in the past couple of months, but like I said, I'm over that. I don't wanna be with anyone else but you, shorty, I swear. I promise if you forgive me it will never happen again."

He moved closer to me and gripped my face to kiss me. I was crying and trying to move my face, but he was too strong. He kissed my wet lips, and I kicked towards his groin. He caught my leg, and then made me lie down on the bed.

"I wanna leave!" I screamed.

"And I told yo' ass no! You ain't going no muthafuckin' where! From now on I'm gonna drop your ass off at school *and* pick you up. And don't think of trying to run either, Cheyla. It'll take me two minutes to find you, and when I do, it'll be hell to pay."

He sat down on the bed next to me, and I just laid there crying like my life was over. I wanted to leave so badly, but tonight I couldn't. As soon as I got away from him though, I was gone.

I pulled my phone out when he wasn't looking and text Sonny.

***Me:*** *Kantwan is keeping me hostage, and his brothers plan to kill you. Run, please. But let me know where you go, I may need a place to live.*

***Sonny:*** *I got you, baby girl, and thanks for the heads up.*

THIRTY-FIVE

# Raleigh

_______________

"Mmm, shit," I whimpered as Ka'Shea pounded into me under the shower water. His shower contained three showerheads, one up above and two on the sides. The water felt so good against my body as Ka'Shea invaded it with his long, thick dick. "Fuck I love you!" I cried out as I spilled my juices onto him.

"You love me?" he quizzed as he adjusted his strong grip and drilled me like a maniac.

"Yes! Ahh uhhh!"

"Fucckkk shorty," he groaned right before we came together.

Once he'd caught his breath, he planted kisses all over my neck and collarbone. I was still a bit out of it, and my body felt so damn weak from that orgasm. It took everything out of me it seemed. He finally let me down, and we actually washed off before getting out.

"You don't have anything to say?" I asked as I wiped my face down with some toner.

"About?"

"What I said."

There was silence, and I immediately began kicking myself. I should've never said what I said, but I couldn't help the way I was feeling at the moment. I couldn't help the way I'd been feeling for a while now. Although I dated Sonny longer, I felt stronger for Ka'Shea. He was the man I'd been yearning for, and something I wasn't getting while with Sonny.

He still hadn't said anything as he continued to dry himself off, and then spray Axe all over his body. I loved the scent of Axe that he chose. I finished my face routine, and then walked out of the bathroom to find him sitting on the bed using some off brand lotion. I laughed because I remembered him saying he just needed lotion with absolutely no scent, he didn't give a fuck who made it.

I wanted to talk to him, but I was too embarrassed about admitting my feelings and getting no response. I slipped into my panties and bra, then went to look into my side of the closet that I kept here. It was only a few things since I wasn't officially moved in; I was just here a lot. After picking out some jean shorts and a simple white t-shirt, I spread lotion all over my body and then put the clothes on. By the time I turned around, Ka'Shea had his gray joggers on, with the band of his boxers showing. He was shirtless and taking down his two French braids, which I knew he would be asking me to fix.

"Would you like some breakfast, Shea? I was gonna make pancakes and an omelet," I offered after spritzing my body with a few bits of perfume.

My hair was pressed, so I just removed my shower cap and wrap scarf, before brushing it into a long low ponytail. Make up wasn't my thing really, and on top of that I wasn't doing anything today but chilling. Because I despised my call center job so, I cherished the days off that I got. Yeah, I had my inheritance that was more than enough for me to live off of, but living off of it made me feel some type of way. I felt as if I was walking the same pathway my mother took if I chose to solely live on my father's money. In addition to that, having to get up and work for something made me feel good… sometimes.

"Yeah, that's cool." He scrolled on his phone. "I will eat when I get back, I have to make a run."

"Sure, okay."

I left out, and as I was cracking the eggs for the omelet, I heard the alarm ding letting me know he'd left out. For some reason I wanted to cry, because I felt like I pushed him away by admitting my love for him. Yeah, I know we'd only been together for some months, but those months were bliss and we spent every damn day together. There wasn't a day that I didn't see him, have breakfast, lunch, or dinner with him, and sleep next to him. He was a busy guy, but we never went a full day without seeing or speaking. He stayed face timing me and texting me, and vice versa. What did he expect? He dicked me down phenomenally, showed me attention, was sexy as fuck, and possessed everything else you could want from a man, and yet he expected me not to fall in love? Niggas.

I continued going back and forth in my mind as I cooked. I was cursing him out one minute, and not giving a fuck if the relationship was over. Then the next minute I was sad and hoping whatever I had done wasn't too detrimental to our paradise. I finally finished the breakfast, and annoyed myself as a smile spread across my face from hearing the alarm ding; he was back and just in time.

"Just in time," I said once he entered the kitchen looking sexy as fuck. His long, curly hair was all over his head, and it made me moist between the legs.

"I know, it smells good in here."

"Thank you, sit down."

He did as I asked and then continued checking his phone while I made his plate. I set his plate down, along with some juice, and then got myself situated as well. We began eating in silence, and every so often I caught him looking at me.

"Shea, what the fuck—"

"You wanna get married?" he cut me off, and spoke calmly as if getting married was something as simple as buying a liter of soda.

"Married?" I paused, fork in hand. He stared into my eyes, waiting for my answer. "This isn't the proposal I had in mind, Shea, but are you sure?"

"I am. I'm in love with you and you're in love with me, right?" He slid a ring across the table. His thug ass had no proper etiquette sometimes.

I chuckled and said, "Shea, you're supposed to get on one knee and stuff."

"Why?" he frowned. "Would it make a difference? And I'm trying to get married today."

"Today? Why the sudden rush?"

"Why wait? I'm about to be twenty-six years old. Plus you've been eating a lot lately." He sipped his juice and nodded his head towards my body.

"I always ate a lot."

"You did, but not three times a day. So, since we're in love and you're having my baby, we should get married don't you think? Unless you don't want to."

"No! I do! But where can we get it done today?"

"It's only 9 AM, we can head down to New Castle and get everything done. I just came from seeing my P.O. so I could get authorization for it. A nigga needs permission for everything to do anything when he's on parole." He shoved some food into his mouth.

A huge grin suddenly spread across my face, and it was so wide I placed my hands over my face to contain it. Ka'Shea laughed at me, because I'm sure I looked so stupid.

"Should I change before we go?"

"Yeah I guess, but hurry yo' ass up."

I ate my food quickly, and as I did I thought about how much I'd been eating and on a consistent basis lately. I doubted I was pregnant, but we would see. I finished my food and then rushed off to re-brush my teeth and get dressed. I chose a simple white dress that stopped mid thigh, and had very thin straps. It was sexy, but still classy. I then slipped on some white, stiletto heels, and released my hair from its ponytail. Combing my hair down, I put a few loose curls in it, and then spread some colored gloss across my lips.

"Ready!" I called out as I walked into the kitchen. "That's what you're wearing, Shea?" He hadn't changed.

"Yep." He grabbed my hand and we left out.

A little over five hours later, we were married. To my surprise, Ka'Shea had a wedding band for me already. We did have to stop at a jewelry store so I could get his, and he didn't even care what it looked like, so I just picked something I approved of.

"I can't believe I'm married," I chuckled and looked down at my sparkly diamond. I had never seen so many diamonds on a ring since Jersey's. It was a square diamond, with little ones all around it and down the sides of the band a little. The actual wedding band was more simple, but still full of diamonds. "You did so good with these rings, baby. You picked them out by yourself?"

"Kind of."

"What do you mean?"

"Remember when I bought you a necklace from that jewelry store and you said if you were to pick your own ring, you would pick that one?" he glanced over at me then back to the road. We were headed to the hotel suite we'd booked. We could easily go home, but a hotel made it feel more official.

I looked down at my engagement ring, and a smile tugged at the corner of my mouth as I recalled eyeing the beautiful ring that day. It made me feel all warm inside knowing he paid attention to me like that.

"I remember," I finally whispered as I slipped my hand closest to him into his.

"We need to get your last name and shit changed on your license, make sure you tell your job on Monday." It was Friday, but I couldn't wait to go to work to tell them my name was now Raleigh Amia Camren.

"I will."

Speaking of my job, I felt like I needed to bring a gift to my co worker that convinced to me to sign up for that pen pal shit a while back. If it weren't for her, I would've never dropped Sonny's trash ass, and found the loved of my life, Ka'Shea Calix Camren.

# THIRTY-SIX

# Elijah

The homie Blow kept an eye out for us over on the Eastside, and we were able to find out when and what times Portland came through there. He said he never spotted Sonny, and we found out that was because he'd been busy setting up shop over in our area; Hilltop. We had shit over in Eastside too, but Hilltop and Browntown were our main moneymakers. Unlike Axel, we planned to take over some cities outside of Wilmington too, but that's a story for another day.

We tried to catch Sonny first since he was over here the most, but that nigga had vanished. It was almost like he knew we were coming for him, and he got away. I knew that wasn't the case though, because the only people that knew we wanted him were Blow, Ka'Shea, Kantwan, and of course Kill. None of them would dare spare him, so I knew it was just a coincidence. Since Sonny wasn't available at the moment, we set our eyes on Portland. They both had to go at some point anyway.

It was around nine at night, and Blow let us know that Portland usually visited this trap a little past 9th Street on Kirkwood around 9:45 PM. Kill and I planned to go inside the trap, and wait for that nigga to come in so we could blow his fucking brains out.

"Does Jersey know what you're about to do tonight?" I inquired.

"Nah, she doesn't. We don't talk much these days because her ass been acting weird and shit."

"What you mean?" I twisted the silencer onto my gun, making sure it was on correctly.

"She's been asking me questions and shit like she's suspicious of me, and I don't like that. I don't need that from her. When I come home I wanna talk about regular shit, not business."

"Damn, so she's suspicious of you business wise? I thought you were about to say with females."

"Nah, with my work and I don't like it. I'm hoping the shit will pass, but I'm feeling like after we get this nigga it may worsen."

"Maybe you should've warned her."

"Did you warn Ivy about tonight? You know this is her child's father, and as much as she hates him, I'm sure she will be upset about the fact that he's gone."

"I didn't tell her. I'm thinking we should have though, because now it's gonna look like we killed this nigga just because."

"We should've followed Kantwan's lead, he at least warned Cheyla that it may come down to us versus them. Fuck, it's too late now, this nigga has to die. He had us shot at, well you, so he has to go. I really tried to brush him off as nothing major, but clearly he is."

"Just tell Jersey he hired someone to shoot me and got you, she should understand."

"Here's hoping," he chuckled lightly and then pulled on the lever to exit the car.

I did the same, and then we made it across the street to the trap. Knocking on the door, the both of us slid on our gloves quietly as we waited for someone to answer. No one did, so I decided to try my luck and twist the knob. The shit was open, so Kill and I entered slowly to see two niggas sleep on the couch. We both put one in the back of their heads, before heading to the back of the trap to wait for Portland to show up. Around 9:43 PM, we heard keys jingling in the door, and two people talking; male and female.

"Fuck, y'all in here sleep?" Portland hollered, unaware that his two workers were dead, just like we wanted. "Aye!" he yelled again before yelping along with the female. It was obvious they both realized the two boys were dead.

"Hurry up, bitch," Kill whispered as he adjusted the grip on his gun.

He and I were in the back bedroom, waiting for Portland to enter and collect the money. I knew it was in here, because the wall he kept it in was obviously a hiding space. He needed to do better. Too bad he wouldn't live to progress in the drug game. I was beyond ready to dead his ass; it had been a long time coming.

"Who did this?" The woman yelled as footsteps neared the bedroom.

*BOOF!*

*POP! POP! POP!*

I left off three shots as soon as Portland walked into the room; two in the chest and one in the forehead. He slumped to the ground, as some pregnant bitch screamed and tried to run. Before I could react, Kill hopped up, caught her, and slit her throat from behind. This nigga was merciless. She dropped to the ground, bleeding out on the floor.

"Damn, nigga, she was pregnant," I said.

"Ain't my fucking baby." He stepped over her and called Rogue to bring the clean up.

We let Rogue in through the back, and once he and his people were done fixing shit up, we all departed. On the ride home, I just laughed and shook my head at Kill's psycho ass. He let the windows down, and sparked a blunt as we raced through the streets, headed to the warehouse so we could get our cars. The closer we got to the warehouse, I knew we would be closer to me getting home and facing Ivy. I wasn't sure if I was going to say anything tonight though.

"Good work." I dapped Kill up before we got into our cars and went our separate ways.

Like always, when I got home, I went to take a shower, and then slipped into some boxer like pajama pants. I then went to kiss Donovan, and apologized to him in a whisper. I wondered if he would hate me when he grew up, I hoped not. I then went to the bedroom I shared with Ivy, and was surprised to find her up, reading one of her self-help books in bed. The room was dark, but she had a book light clipped to one of the pages.

"I thought you were sleep, ma."

"Almost, I kind of wanted to wait for you." She cut the book light off and set the book on the nightstand next to her.

"Thank you for that." I climbed in the bed, and we both laid down to face one another.

"I love you, Elijah, do you love me?"

"Of course I do. Why do you ask?"

"Because I want to ask you something, and I want you to be honest."

"Ask."

"Are you feuding with Portland? Or threatening him?"

I swallowed hard. I thought she was about to ask me some shit regarding fidelity, which is why I was so confident to answer any question she had. What are the odds that she would ask me this the night I popped the nigga?

"Uh, nah, why?"

"His paranoid ass tried to tell me you were coming for him, and to convince you to back off, but I told him you weren't worried about his low budget ass. I'm glad I was right. You know, even though I don't like Portland, Donovan needs his daddy. I want him to decide on his own that he doesn't want him in his life."

"Makes a lot of sense. I'm tired as hell, baby, so I'm gonna go to sleep. We can eat lunch tomorrow after your classes if that's cool?"

"I'm actually studying with a classmate, we can go to dinner though, with Donovan."

"That's fine, can Shamece come?" I joked and she punched my chest. "I'm kidding shorty, damn," I laughed.

"You like her now? I know she was your favorite when you came to Starzz."

"Where did you get that impression?"

"Because the night I met you I saw you throw her a lot of money and shit."

"Because she had a fat ass, but I was more interested in your weird ass. Hopping up out of my lap after I gave you my name and shit," I replied, making her giggle. "Nah, but you're my favorite."

"I am?" she half smiled as I brought her body closer to mine.

"Of course." I dipped my tongue into her mouth, and then proceeded to fuck her nice and hard as celebration. Damn, I killed the nigga then went home to fuck his baby mama. Life.

## THIRTY-SEVEN

## Jersey

---

*I* was in the den typing an assignment, when my phone buzzed letting me know I had an Instagram DM. I rarely got them, but sometimes the thirsty niggas ignored the posts about my man and still slid up in them to try and get at me. I tickled Alexsia's little belly, making her giggle, and then picked my phone up to check it. I saw it was from this girl that I went to high school with, but we hadn't talked since we graduated.

*Avila: Hey, I heard someone killed your brother. Is it true?*

*Me: What? What the fuck are you talking about? Where did you hear that?*

*Avila: My brother's homeboy works for your bro, and he said Portland went to check on one of his traps and never came back. Before he left he was saying that he needed to get away for a while because someone vicious was coming after him.*

My mind immediately went to Kill, and how Portland warned me to help save him. I didn't want to believe that he had killed my brother, but I knew deep down that he had. I really hoped he could prove to me that he hadn't somehow, because I loved him and I wanted to be with him. But how could I if he would do something like that? And if Kill did do it that meant I had the opportunity to save my brother and I didn't.

I grabbed my baby, and then went upstairs where I knew he was. He'd gotten into the shower about forty-five minutes ago, and should've been out by now. We hadn't been on the best of terms lately, but I was hoping that he would still think of me and my feelings before committing such a heinous, callous crime.

"Hey, daddy's baby!" he grinned, showing his perfect smile when I walked into the bedroom with Alexsia. "Come here!" He waved her over and she began moving wildly like always when he did that. I hated that shit because she would be fucking me up, thinking I was trying to keep her from him.

"I told you to stop doing that," I frowned and handed her over. He ignored me and rubbed his nose against her little one, making her scream and laugh loudly. "Kill, can I ask you something?"

He sighed and his expression showed that he was irritated as he adjusted Alexsia in his lap.

"Why are you always asking me shit now? And why is it always about my fucking business? You shouldn't even be worried about that shit, Jersey! Fuck!"

"Fuck!" Alexsia repeated, and he and I both stared at her shocked. "Fuck! Fuck! Fuck!"

"No! No, baby girl don't say that." Kill lifted her up and kissed her round cheeks repeatedly.

"Kill, did you murder my brother?"

"Where is this coming from?"

"A friend informed me that my brother has disappeared, and he had mentioned being scared. He said someone was coming after him, and now no one knows where he is."

"What does that have to do with me?"

I paused and said, "He told me he was scared that you were going to kill him. I didn't believe him when he said it, but now I'm not so sure since he's all of a sudden missing or dead."

"Portland had a lot of people that didn't like him, Jersey."

"Answer me," I gritted as tears began to stream my face. He got up to put Alexsia in her playpen, and then made it back over to me after removing his towel and putting some boxers on.

"He hired someone to kill Elijah, but the person ended up shooting me. He wanted us dead, Jersey, and so Eli and I did what we had to do." As the words came from his mouth, my heart rate sped up. "Jersey, baby I swear I tried to prolong it. Usually I would've killed someone like him a while ago. I don't let anyone who I know has beef with me breathe, but I did because of you. I wanted to give your brother the benefit of the doubt, even though I knew I should've deaded his ass an eternity ago," he explained as I sobbed and sobbed.

"Why Kill? That's my fucking brother! Now all I have is Raleigh!" I screamed and Alexsia began to cry. She always cried when someone else did, even when we watched movies together. If an actor cried so did she. She was hilarious with her little fake ass.

"Baby I'm—" he tried to hug me.

"Get off me, you fucking monster!" I shoved him back and then began taking off on him.

He grabbed my wrists and then pinned them to the bed. He climbed in between my legs, as I just laid there crying hard as hell. My brother wasn't shit most of the time, but I loved him. He was my family. It seemed these days that I was losing every got damn body, including the man I'd fallen in love with.

"So, you don't give a fuck that this nigga almost killed me? That don't fucking matter, huh?" he asked, still pinning my wrists to the bed. His beautiful chocolate face was twisted up, but still sexy. I shut my eyes, not wanting to admire him while hating him.

"Why did you have to kill him?" My eyes were closed as my body jerked from weeping.

Finally, he let go of my wrists, and wrapped his strong chocolate arms around my torso to hug me. He nestled his face into my neck, and I tried to hit his back but I didn't have the strength. I just let him hug me as I cried and cried for my brother. He'd had a hard life, just for him to die the way everyone knew he would. Alexsia's little fake ass had fallen asleep in her playpen, since fake crying had tired her out.

"I'm sorry, baby, I know this shit hurts. I'm sorry." Kill kissed my neck and cheeks as I sniffled. He then gripped my face lightly and pecked my lips. I didn't dare reciprocate. I loved him and despised him at the same time. Lying next to him would make me feel like a trader. I felt disgusted even now as he hugged me in his arms and kissed all over me.

I sat there paralyzed as he pulled my shirt over my head to reveal my B cups. I stared at the ceiling, as his lips collapsed around my nipples, and once he'd gotten enough, he made his way down my torso. His hands tugged on the waistband of my sweat shorts, as he brought them down my legs, along with my panties. I was still, not moving, not even in this moment. My mind was somewhere else.

All this time I ignored my brother and refused to talk to him. I wished I had known his time here would be cut short, because I wouldn't have made him suffer so long. My thoughts caused tears to drip from my eyes again, as Kill sucked and licked between my legs. It felt good, but I was in no mood. I laid there silent, lost in my thoughts as he made love to my box with his mouth. Holding my legs apart, he really got in there, making me arch my back slightly.

"Mmm," I moaned subtly, almost inaudible as I came.

"I haven't tasted you in a while, I miss you," he whispered before diving back in.

I wasn't sure I could continue to be with a man who would betray me in such a way.

## THIRTY-EIGHT

## Kantwan

______________

A Couple Days Later...

*J* pulled up to the house that bitch Miami lived in, ready to take care of her. She was dumb enough to invite Rachel and I over to fuck, but then ran her mouth to my girl like it was cool. I admit I'd been on some other shit lately, but I was done with that. I loved Cheyla, and for a minute I got caught up in my status, and the new high caliber of bitches in my pathway. The old me wouldn't have touched Miami with a ten foot pole, but I was twisted, horny, feeling neglected, and in the mood to do some freaky shit. I would pay whatever to be able to go back in time and right my wrongs, but that wasn't how life worked. I could only pray that my baby forgave me, because I couldn't lose her. I loved her more than anything, but I knew she didn't believe any of it.

"Can you just take me to Jersey's?" she requested as we sat outside in the car.

I told Cheyla she couldn't go anywhere, but her ass didn't listen. I dropped her off at school one morning, and she tried to catch the bus to Linwood, a city in Pennsylvania. As soon as her ass hopped off that fucking bus, guess who was waiting on that ass. She almost jumped out of her skin when she walked her pregnant ass off that bus and saw me. She wasn't going nowhere and I meant that shit. So, since she didn't listen, I made her go everywhere with me. If I had a meeting, she came too, and just sat in the other room with Rogue's twin brother and partner, Race. When she went to class, I sat outside of every got damn one until she was finished, and if I couldn't, Race did.

"Why would you even ask that when you know the answer, shorty?" I frowned, irritated by her.

"I hate you, Kantwan, I just wanna be alone for a bit. I can't think being around you all the time. Doing this is not gonna make me want to be with you!" she shouted.

"What will make you forgive me, Cheyla? Huh? Tell me? I will do anything, but let you leave. Just tell me what the fuck I have to do to make sure that we don't break up? I miss being cool with you. I miss loving on you and shit, and I especially miss being inside you." I kissed her cheek and neck. I felt her tears hit my cheek, as she silently cried. Rubbing her belly, I continued to ask her what I needed to do.

"You need to give me some time and space, Kantwan. You cheated on me, and I'm sure more than once, while I'm pregnant with your baby. You left me home alone so you could go out and live freely. That's obviously what you'd rather be doing, so I'm giving you a chance to do that," she sniffled and nudged me.

"But I'm telling you I don't want that, Cheyla! I thought I did, but I don't! I was tripping, I admit that, but I'm good! I did some shit that had me on one, on top of other things that were fucking with me! Then I couldn't even come home and talk to you about it, because you were too busy being Kilexis' number one fucking cheer-leader! The fact that I was dealing with some shit is no excuse for my actions I know, but I'm trying to make you understand why I did what the fuck I did!"

"Don't blame me." She shook her head.

"I'm not blaming you. I'm just letting you know, baby, that I love you, but I need you to have my back. I need you to care a little bit more than you do. I don't feel like you really are for me sometimes. I feel like you're only about me when it's convenient for you. I have sacrificed and even put my life on the line for you, and sometimes I just need to know that if it came down to us being against the world, you would be with me. I know you say it, but I don't see it in your actions,, shorty, and I'm just being honest. I love you more than anything in this world, and I would die, kill, and do a bid for you, but I need to see that it's worth it."

"I tried, Kantwan!" She broke down and dropped her head into her hands.

"I know, baby, I know you were trying and that's why I'm still trying to do this with you." I leaned over to hug her. "Maybe we need to get away together or something." I kissed her forehead.

"I just need some time, Kantwan," she sobbed into my chest. "You broke my heart and I can't even look at you right now. I need to be alone!"

As much as I didn't want to let her little ass go, I knew if I wanted the slightest chance of getting her back, I would have to. I was afraid that she would flee, and if she did a nigga would go crazy. It'd be easy for me to find her, but I didn't want to spend my years keeping her in a relationship she didn't want to be in. I knew we were meant to be, and once she cleared her head, she would return. But I can't hold her hostage anymore, because I ain't even getting the outcome that I'd hoped for by doing so.

"Okay, baby, you wanna go to a hotel? Or you wanna stay in my old parent's home for free?"

"I like free," she responded and I chuckled.

"I was gonna go in there and kill Miami tonight, but I guess I shouldn't. It's my fault I was doing dirt and got caught," I sighed.

"We're at Miami's?" She looked out of the window, and then back at me. I just nodded in response. "You were gonna kill her for me?"

"Yeah, shorty, but I'm not gonna do that. She doesn't deserve to die because she's a hoe and a snitch. But look, I already told Kill to put Rachel in another position or to fire her. I know you don't want me working with her anymore."

"Nope."

"I love you."

"Take me home to get some clothes please."

I kissed her cheek and then cranked the car. I took her to the house where she packed a bag and then I drove her to my parent's home. I had cameras and security systems installed since I was rarely there, but I was now gonna use it to make sure Cheyla wasn't entertaining. I let her in the house and then she went into the bedroom, which I followed.

"This is where we made love the first time," I chuckled. She said nothing as she began removing her toiletries from her bag. I came and hugged her from behind, inhaling the passion fruit scent she always smelled like. "I love you, baby, I promise I will never do anything to hurt you again," I whispered. I could feel her body jerking very subtly, so I knew she was crying.

"Please, Kantwan," she cried.

"Aight," I sighed and let her go, before walking out of the house.

I peeled down my street, and then decided to stop at the store since I was craving some Sweet Chili Doritos. Getting out of the car, I closed the door behind me and hit the alarm.

*POP! POP! POP!*

Three bullets flew into me, one to the shoulder blade, one hitting my arm, and the other in my rib cage. I fell back onto my car, and then climbed back in before anymore bullets could hit me. I heard a few people screaming as I fumbled with my iPhone. I dialed 911, and before the operator could even finish her greeting I was talking.

"Aye, I've been shot. I'm on umm fuck." My mind was fucking up as I bled all over my seats. I couldn't remember where I was for shit.

"Sir! What is your name?"

"Kantwan, aaahh, Kantwan Camren!"

"Okay, where are you, sir? Hello! Hello! Mr. Camren! Mr...."

THIRTY-NINE

## Ivy

______

The Next Day...

Elijah and I were just getting home from seeing Kantwan in
the hospital. Cheyla was crying her eyes out, and I felt so
bad for her. He was doing okay, and we were just happy he was
strong enough to be able to call 911. I don't even know why the fuck
he was over in Hilltop to begin with. Niggas moved out of the hood
to prevent shit like this from happening, yet stayed visiting.

"I'm happy he's okay, but I'm just upset because we've been slipping." Elijah plopped down on the couch in the den, and then put
my feet into his lap.

I'd just come from lying down a knocked out Donovan upstairs
in his bed. My baby was getting bigger now, and could talk well
enough to beg Elijah for a bed. I didn't want him to grow up, but of
course I had no control over that.

"Slipping on what?" I frowned.

"Finding Sonny," he replied, catching me off guard.

"Why would you need to catch Sonny? What does he have to do
with this?"

"He is the one who had Kantwan shot, Ivy. Someone from his crew got snatched up by Kill and he admitted it. He'd been staying in Linwood, but when we got there his place was cleaned out. We don't know where the fuck he is."

"Linwood? As in Pennsylvania's Linwood?"

"Yes."

"Maybe Portland knows where Sonny is. He and I haven't talked in a bit, but I'm sure if he sees me calling he will answer. I don't wanna give Sonny up, but if he's setting people up, he needs to be handled."

Cheyla would try to whoop my ass if she were hearing me say this shit. But then again, her brother had her baby daddy shot, so she would have to feel some type of way about Sonny once she finds out.

"That's the thing, ma, we can't exactly use Portland for any information."

"Please tell me he hasn't fled with Sonny's dumb ass."

"Well, not exactly. Baby remember when Kilexis got shot? Well that was actually a person paid by Portland to kill me. He wasn't too good obviously, because all he did was injure Kill."

"How do you know this? Portland doesn't do shit like that! He's a jack boy and nothing else, Elijah."

"Dante, Axel's son told us. And we had to take care of him and his baby mama, Ivy."

I gasped as I searched Elijah's eyes, waiting for him to say Portland survived. He lied to my fucking face. I asked his stupid ass if he was coming for Portland and he told me no. He lied to me and then proceeded to tell me he loved me. I just kept shaking my head 'no' as he stared into my eyes with a worried expression. Snatching my feet from his hands, I stood up to stare down at him.

"I asked you—"

"I know, Ivy, and coincidentally I had just done it that night." He got up and tried to touch me, but I moved back.

"You killed him and then got in the bed with me like it was nothing? And then Breesha? She was pregnant, you callous fuck!" I hollered and chucked the remote at his head. He ducked and then walked towards me like it was nothing.

"I know, and that wasn't a part of the plan. Niggas don't usually bring their women to the traps, but he did. She saw me kill Portland, so Kilexis had to get her. Ivy, it was either me or him, ma, and that's on everything. We all tried to spare that nigga because of you, Raleigh, and Jersey, but he just wouldn't quit while he was ahead. He would've killed me that day in the restaurant had he hired someone who knew what the fuck they were doing, Ivy."

"What am I supposed to tell Donovan when he gets older huh? That the man I'm with murdered his father behind my back? Huh! Let me know!" I screamed.

"No! You tell him that his father is right here!" He pointed into his chest. "You tell him that I killed that fucking sperm donor, because that is all that he was! And that I tried! I tried Ivy, I really did! There were so many times where I wanted to end his fucking life, but I didn't because of you, Jersey, Raleigh, and little man. Not to mention the fact that he hadn't quite done anything to me. But having me shot at, during a time he knew I would be relaxed and caught off guard? Come on now?"

There was silence in the room as we started at one another with intense glares. I was angry at him for killing Portland behind my back, and he was angry with me for not caring that Portland could've killed him. We were both right, which made everything so fiery.

"I'm sorry, Eli, I know it must've been hard for you to keep him alive, and I thank you for trying. And I also thank you for taking me from him, and being a father to my son. I'm sorry about my reaction, I was just surprised. But if he had have gotten you that day, I would've wanted him to be dead anyway."

"You mean that?" He looked to me, but was still scowling a bit.

"Yes, I mean that. I told you I love you, not him. I wanna be with you and not him. If it comes down to choosing, you will always win over him. I love you, Eli, and whatever you choose to do I will be behind you."

He pulled me closer, and I draped my arms over his shoulders.

We darted our tongues into one another's mouths, and let them dance with one another. I hated that Portland had to die, but to be honest I would rather him go than the man I loved. Elijah was a better father to Donovan anyway, and if he had to choose, I'm sure his choice would be the same as mine.

As Elijah led me upstairs, my mind drifted to Jersey. No wonder her ass had been M.I.A and not talking to anyone. I couldn't blame her for not telling me about her brother, because I'm sure she was grieving. As for Raleigh, I'm not too sure why she said nothing, but I feel it was Elijah's job to tell me since he's the one who put a bullet in him.

As for that hoe, Breesha, I feel bad for the innocent unborn, but that bitch got exactly what any bitch deserved when they decided to ride for a nigga like Portland. He was nothing but trouble, and that's the only thing he could bring the woman in his life. Letting her have Portland was the greatest revenge on her that I could've gotten. Bitch.

FORTY


# Ka'Shea

---

"How are you feeling?" I said to Raleigh.

We were sleeping at her home as of late, because she was a bit depressed over Portland. I hated to see her so down, especially when we were supposed to be enjoying the married life. I guess my vows were being tested already.

"I'm doing okay I guess. I just miss him and all his trifling ways," she smiled and then sniffled. She was sitting inside her walk in closet, doing something with her shoes.

"I can't even imagine how you feel shorty, especially since it was your brother in law who did it." I got down on the floor and began massaging her pretty feet.

"I thought you said it was Elijah who shot him?"

"It was Eli, but that's more of a little brother than my cousin. You know that."

"Yeah," she whispered. "Did they have to kill him? Be honest with me, if he was your brother and you knew what you knew, would you have let him live?"

"No, I wouldn't have and I'm being honest with you, shorty. Portland was lucky because he was surrounded by people who cared for him and loved him, even though he didn't deserve it.

You, Jersey, Ivy, and her baby loved him, when he didn't love you."

"He loved us."

"He did, but he didn't love you as much as he should have. If I were him, the last thing I would have been doing was trying to start a war with my sisters' boyfriends. All he cared about was making big money, even when he didn't even have to."

"True. I guess I was just used to him being that way. For as long as I've known him, he has always been pretty selfish you know? That was Portland, his feelings and needs came before anyone."

"And as a man you can't be like that, especially when you're out here making babies," I half smiled and touched her stomach. "Did you tell anyone yet?"

"No, I haven't mentioned the marriage or the baby. I will though, once things calm down a little bit."

"You talked to Jersey?"

"Just a little. We got into an argument, because I was trying to explain to her that you guys did what you had to do."

"She ain't going for that shit I know. Kilexis already told me she's pretty much off him."

"Yeah, my sister is very loyal, almost to a fault. If you can count on anyone being loyal despite it being an unpopular thing, you can count on Jersey. My sister won't turn against you, even if the world has."

"That's dope. I think you're the same way. That's why I wanted to marry you, I know you will always be there for me, like I will be for you."

"I will. You just better stay your ass out of jail."

"I am, baby. This time around shit is being handled much more properly, and I'm not as close knit with the streets like I was before. Plus, you know that hoe set me up."

"Mercedes, yuck. She hasn't popped up since that last time I saw her. She stopped making little videos about me on Instagram, too," she chuckled, flashing her pretty smile. She had her real hair pressed, and I liked the length, which was a little bit past her shoulders.

"I handled it. Didn't I tell you that? I told you if anybody got in the way I would get rid of their asses. I wasn't playing, shorty."

"I know," she giggled. "I can't believe you slept with her, she's so ghetto and disgusting. She's pretty though, until she opens her mouth."

"Not to talk though, to suck on this dick," I half joked and she pinched me. "I like it better when you do it though." I pulled her down into my lap, so that she was straddling me.

"What about Sonny?" she questioned as she caressed my face. I pecked her a couple times before thinking of what to say.

"Gotta take care of him, too, he had someone shoot, Kantwan."

She just nodded, so I dipped my tongue into her mouth. Moving her panties to the side, I released my dick and slid into her. Watching her face twist as she whimpered had me ready to bust. Raleigh's pussy was always on some other shit. She got wet as hell every time and I loved it. I don't know if it's just me she got that wet for, or if that's just how she worked, but I was happy to being the only one to experience it from now on.

"Slow, baby," she whispered as I gripped her waist to move her up and down my shaft. Her pussy had a strong grip on my dick like it had been lifting weights and shit. "Mmm, oh, oh shit."

Moving the straps of her shirt down, I released her breasts and took her nipple into my mouth. I sucked like my life depended on it, switching back and forth between each one as she continued to glide up and down my rod.

Life as a married man had been pretty good to me so far, and once we got rid of Sonny, a vacation was definitely in order.

# FORTY-ONE

## Kilexis

—————

onight Jersey and I were out to dinner because I was still trying to make up what I had done to her. She didn't really say much to me, and we didn't sleep in the same bed. I hated being like two ships passing in the night, but that's definitely what we were. We were basically co-parenting, but in the same household. I felt like I was in some stale ass marriage, and we weren't even married yet. My love for her was keeping me around though.

I didn't sit across from her at the table, I sat next to her, and since the booth was long enough, Alexsia's carrier fit on the other side of her. I kissed her cheek lightly, and she tilted her head to the side a little to get my lips off of her. I didn't know what the fuck to do, and I was constantly wondering if there was another way I could've went about killing Portland. I couldn't even fathom the thought of her hating me forever.

"Jersey."

"Yes." She raised her brow as she looked over the menu.

"How long are you gonna ignore me, shorty?"

"Kill, just stop." She turned her lip up in disgust as she continued to look over the menu. I just sighed and focused my attention back on the menu as well.

"Wow, what a coincidence that I'd see you two here." Sophie appeared wearing a big smile.

She was wearing some tight number, and her hair was messily hanging down her back, but not in a bad way, a very sexy way. Her body looked even better than it did before, which I attributed to the fact that she'd had a baby. Damn, and a nigga hadn't had any pussy since I fucked Jersey a week ago. And it wasn't all that great since she just laid there like she was dead or some shit. I had to just put her ass on all fours and fuck her from behind until I busted. Looking at her with that glum expression was making my dick soft, so I had no other choice but to put her face in the pillow. Shit at least she was moaning very lightly that way.

"Hey, Sophie, how are you?" I asked.

"I'm doing okay. I was having a hard time dealing with Carter being killed, but me and my daughter's father are gonna try to work things out and see if we can be a family," she chuckled lightly and glanced at Jersey, who was ignoring her and looking at the menu. I mean, did Sophie really expect Jersey to be elated to see her?

"That's good, how is Kilenna?"

"She's great, but we changed her name to Serenity. I didn't think it was appropriate to keep that name because of the reason I named her that." I just nodded approvingly. I really didn't like the little girl being named after me, and I was happy she'd decided to change it. "But, Kilexis, Jersey, I wanted to apologize to you both for anything I may have caused. I honestly thought Kilexis was the father, because the times just matched up in my head. But again, I'm sorry about everything." She pushed her hair behind her ears.

"You're good, Sophie, and thank you for the apology."

"No problem. Have a good night, guys."

"You too."

She turned on her heels to walk away, and damn did I like what I saw. I knew it was just because I was horny as fuck, but still was it a sight to see. I just had to remember how weak the pussy was, and I'd be able to contain myself.

"Could you watch her walk away any harder?"

"Jersey—"

"Can you sit across from me? I really don't want to be next to you. If you'd like, you can also go sit over there with her and her man, since you were looking so hard at the bitch's ass," she snapped.

"Aight." I slid out of the booth and then sat across from her.

Literally, the whole dinner we said nothing to each other. This shit was fucking with me because Jersey and I were like best friends, and now it was obvious that she hated me. I missed being close with her, and I wasn't sure if we would ever go back to that. I would hate to have to parent from separate households with Alexsia, but that was clearly where we were headed.

I paid the bill for the food, and then we left the restaurant. After buckling Alexsia's car seat in, I got into the driver side and cranked up. As I sped down the street, all kinds of thoughts ran through my damn mind. Was it really over? How could I make her understand that Portland had to go? Did she really not care that the nigga could've killed me the day he had someone attempt to shoot Elijah?

"You know, I was getting blown up on Instagram, and I looked to see what it was. Some girl named Yameeka says she's having your baby too. You remember her, Kilexis?" Jersey quizzed, and when I glanced at her she was looking out the window of my car.

"I've never met anyone with that name, Jersey."

"Tell the bitch to stop tagging me in her little Instagram videos and shit."

"How? How the fuck am I gonna tell her when I have no idea who she is? I have never had sex with some chick named Yameeka. I haven't been with anybody since I've been with you, so there is no way someone could be pregnant by me," I scoffed and shook my head as I made a left turn.

"So, you remember every single bitch you had sex with, ever?"

"I may not remember every damn one, but I would remember someone with the name Yameeka. Come on now, we're not talking about some Ashleys or Britneys, Jersey. You know what, why the fuck am I even responding to this shit? This is dumb, Jersey. You know bitches are gonna act dumb because of who I am. Why the fuck are you with me if you think I cheated, huh? You have plenty of money, and even a house to go to, so it can't be that you need money or a place to stay, so why are we together? And if you say because of Alexsia, we can end this right now."

She was silent, and when I looked over she had tears falling down her face. I pulled into the driveway, and then hit the button to enter into the garage. I shut the engine off, and then looked over at her. I had no idea what the fuck to do, but if this was how she was gonna be now, we could just kill this shit.

"Did you kill Sophie's boyfriend?" she whispered as she stared straight ahead.

"I'm not doing this." I was about to get out the car until I heard light sniffles coming from her.

"Why did you have to kill him, Kilexis?" She began sobbing.

I felt so damn bad, not for Portland though, because he deserved that shit. Any nigga that tries to kill me gives me the right to do the same, and unfortunately for him, he lost. I felt bad for my girl because she loved her brother, even though he didn't give a fuck about her. She was simply a chess piece in his little game, and he only pretended to care for her to get on her good side. I wished I could make her see that.

"Baby, I told you I tried to keep him alive, but what did you want me to do? What would you have suggested I do to a nigga who had me shot?"

"He didn't mean to shoot you! The bullet was for Eli!"

"Eli is my fucking cousin, Jersey! Even if the bullet hit him like it was supposed to, I would've still went after Portland. Elijah is my family, my fucking blood, and I'm not gonna allow anybody to try and harm him, and vice versa."

"He's more important than me?" She looked to me with her pretty wet face.

"No, baby, he's not. You, Ivy, Raleigh, and Donovan are the reasons Portland even got the chance to do what he did to me. Elijah and I were thinking about y'all. We put y'all first before ourselves, even though we knew Portland and Sonny would pull some shit. We knew it was risky to let Portland live, yet we did it, because of the love we have for you four."

"I'm a horrible person for being with you," she said in a low tone as she stared out the front windshield.

"I totally understand why you feel that way, I do. Jersey, I love you, shorty, and I want you more than anything, but not if you're gonna be unhappy or feeling guilty about it. I wanna be with you, and make you feel good. I want you to feel a certain way when we're together, and guilt or shame isn't one of them. So if you feel like you can't be with me without being ashamed, then I have to let you go. Just know, I love you and I really really really don't want to be without you. If I thought getting on my knees and begging like a bitch would make things better, I would do it."

She wiped her face with the back of her hand, and then got out of the car. I let out an exasperated sigh, before exiting and getting Alexsia out of the backseat. Jersey took her when I got inside, and then changed her and put her to bed. I went into the bedroom to shower, and when I got out, Jersey wasn't in the bed like usual. I checked all of the five extra bedrooms, and found her in the one downstairs. I just shook my head, and went up to bed. I couldn't do this anymore.

FORTY-TWO

# Cheyla

———————

I sat there next to the hospital bed where Kantwan was lying. He was still sleeping, and I was waiting for him to wake up. A part of me felt like I shouldn't have even been here after the way he'd betrayed me, but unfortunately, I still loved him. Unfortunately when I looked at him I still got butterflies and felt warm all over. I wanted to be with him, but then I didn't. I wanted him because I loved him, but I didn't because I wasn't sure if he deserved me. Yes, he cheated, which in my book was unforgivable, but was I really doing what I should've been doing as a girlfriend? During one of the rare times that my mother was lucid, she used to always say that a man cheating is bad, but when he cheats for absolutely no reason at all, it's the worst. By saying that, I can't one hundred percent say that Kantwan cheated because he was just horny and out and about. He cheated because he was a horny idiot, *and* because I wasn't giving him what he needed from me emotionally. He felt disconnected from me, and I totally get that. However, I feel he should've made more of an effort to talk to me about it, or just break up with me instead of sticking his dick in *two* different bitches.

He moved a little bit, and then finally opened his eyes slowly. He looked to his left and smiled when he saw me. He was so gorgeous, and just as fine he was the day that I met him.

"Baby, you should go home and rest," he yawned.

"No, I'm fine. I took a nap already."

"You don't want to sleep in a nice warm bed? You can even go to our home in Alapocas if you want."

"I'm okay. I'm sorry, Kantwan."

"For what, shorty?" he furrowed his brows.

"That my brother had someone do this to you."

"It's not your fault, baby, that nigga hasn't liked me for a while. I knew something was gonna come from him sooner or later."

"I know, but I think I added fuel to an already burning fire when I told him you were keeping me hostage and stuff. He was very angry about it, and I also told him you guys were looking for him, which is why he went to Pennsylvania in the first place."

"That's fucked up, ma, but I can't even get mad at you. I guess we both betrayed one another. I deserved mine though, you didn't." He stared up at the TV.

"You didn't deserve to be shot, even if you did do me wrong." I fidgeted.

"Yeah, I did. I broke my promise to you, and then had the nerve to hold you against your will as if you were obligated to give me another chance. I do wanna let you know though, we're gonna catch your brother and it won't be pretty."

"I know. Ugh, I just wish Sonny came out of jail with a new mentality. I wish he wasn't such a fuck up, and I wish you guys could have gotten along. That would've made me so happy."

"I know. I wish we could've too, honestly. It's a small world though, and unfortunately Sonny, Portland, Shea, and Elijah all have the same taste in women," he chuckled and then grabbed his water to down it.

"Yeah." After a couple moments of silence I said, "I found out we're having a boy."

He snapped his neck to look at me, and he was wearing the biggest smile I'd ever seen on his sexy face. It caused me to smile as well, even though I really didn't want to.

"A boy, shorty? I wish I could hold you and kiss you, but one I'm not strong enough, and two, you wouldn't let me touch you."

"True," I replied and giggled.

"I miss you though, do you miss me?"

"I miss the old you, the one who only had eyes for me."

"I still only have eyes for you. I got a little cross-eyed for a bit, but I've always only had eyes for you, Cheyla. Despite my actions and what your pretty ass thinks, I love you."

"Good to know. I have to go, I will come back later tonight." I suddenly felt the need to take him up on his offer to rest at our home in Alapocas.

"Kilexis is having me moved to another location because of it being too dangerous right now. You can come there though, if you want. You don't have to, I know you wanna be away from me."

"I will think about it."

I turned to leave out, and once I got to the doorway he said, "I love you so so much, shorty, and I need you in my life. I hope you believe in second chances, I promise it will be the last one I'll ever need."

After standing with my back to him for a few seconds, I just walked out. When I got out to my car, I closed my eyes to rub my belly and think. I didn't know what I wanted to do about us, but for right now I had to take care of something else. I placed a phone call, and when they answered I asked to come by. Once I hung up, I sped out and headed to my destination.

I entered the home and then followed him to the den so we could talk. What I was about to do was against everything I stood for, but I knew it had to be done. I was warned that it would come to this, but I still wasn't as prepared as I thought I would be. Tears began to run down my cheeks as he waited for me to speak.

"Did you want some water or anything?"

"No, I just wanna get this over with."

"I appreciate this, Cheyla, I really do. And I promise you this is the right choice."

"I know. Sonny is in Concordville at the moment. He just let me know his new location and said I could come see him. I wrote the address down on paper, because I didn't want to have this in my phone." I handed the paper to Elijah.

"Thanks, baby girl, and if Kantwan ever thought you weren't for him, he knows now."

"I didn't tell him."

"He'll find out though." I just nodded and then he pulled me into a tight hug before rubbing my back. "Did you wanna chill here for a bit?"

"No, I better go before Ivy gets home." I stood up to leave the den. "Oh and Eli, can you do me a favor?"

"Anything, shorty."

"Don't make him suffer, he's suffered enough."

FORTY-THREE

# Elijah

_______________

*I* appreciated Cheyla for giving me the location on her brother. I knew that shit was hard for her, but like I explained, she was doing the right thing. Sonny was a destructive ass nigga, and he was bound to take down anybody that fucked with him heavy. I mean look, his whole damn crew was dead and he was the only one standing. He didn't even have enough loyalty to let Portland come with him when he escaped the first time. Instead, he dipped and let a nigga that he was supposedly cool with, walk right into the fire. At least he had enough decency to shoot Kantwan for his sister, but even then, someone else did it, not him.

Speaking of Kantwan's assailant, we caught up with his ass, but he refused to give his boy's location up before we killed him. He told us Sonny sent him though, and that was better than nothing. Cheyla was a Godsend right now, and had proved her loyalty to us and to Kantwan like a muthafucka.

I sat in the all black Ford Explorer, waiting for Kilexis to come get in. He'd just pulled up to the warehouse, and was getting something out of his car while I waited. Once I saw him walking over, I cranked the truck up and then hit the unlock button.

"You good?" I asked once he got in.

"Yeah, man, I'm straight. You know Sophie showed up while Jersey and I were out to dinner together," he sighed as I sped out of the area. He lit a blunt and took a pull as he waited for me to respond.

"Wait, what did her ass say? I hope she wasn't trying to start no shit, because we can get her ass, too."

"Nah, she was actually apologizing for pinning her baby on me. She apologized to Jersey, too, but her ass ignored the fuck out of her. It was awkward as hell."

"What did she expect? She's lucky Jersey didn't knock the shit out of her," I said and we both laughed.

"That's the same thing I said. But umm, she was looking good as hell. I had to remind myself that I wasn't no cheater, and that her pussy wasn't even good."

"She was looking that good to where you contemplated cheating?"

"Nah, I mean, nah no I didn't contemplate cheating and I just got some visions of doing a couple things. But like I said, her shit is weak and if I'm gonna jeopardize what Jersey and I have, it's at least gonna be for some good good."

"I feel. So Jersey is still angry?"

"Yeah, she's mad as fuck. I don't think we're gonna last, and that shit pisses me off. I was for real about her, and I still am but I can tell she's over it and ain't shit I can do about it. Is Ivy mad?"

"She was for like ten minutes," I chuckled as I switched lanes on the freeway. "But after I explained to her that it was either him or me, and that he'd already tried to murk me, she understood and she was cool. I know a part of her wishes I didn't have to, but she gets why it had to happen."

"See, man, and Shea said Raleigh was the same. I thought it was because Shea didn't pull the trigger nor was he there, but I'm seeing now that Jersey just can't be convinced. I still wonder if I hadn't have gone, and let Kantwan go instead, would she still hate me."

"Fuck yeah she would, because she would know you sent us, and that you were aware that the shit was happening."

"True." He took another pull, and blew the smoke out into the night air as we went flying down the freeway. "This truck ain't got no bricks in it, right?" He looked over his shoulder.

"Nah, we pushed everything. I've been meaning to tell you to talk to Darrow about upping our shipment. Now that we got some more areas locked down, we're pushing product fast and niggas are restocking way more than before."

"Fasho, I'll get at him."

He leaned his seat back, passed me the blunt, and then I turned up the music in the car. We both needed to think to ourselves before we put this bullet in Sonny. I planned to grant Cheyla's wishes by not making him suffer. Lord knows I wanted to, but that was the least I could do for the girl since she did give up her own brother. I couldn't imagine having to make that kind of choice.

We finally made it to this home in Concordville, Pennsylvania, and I parked so I could double check the address. The last thing I wanted to do was run off up in here and it be a single mom just chilling with her kids. I wanted this shit to be smooth and quick. Run up in there, and kill this nigga so I could get back home to my shorty quick.

"This it?" Kill asked as he looked around through the window.

"Yep, this the one."

I stuffed the paper into my pocket as Kill grabbed the duffle bag from the backseat. He handed me a gun, and then grabbed his multifaceted pocket knife, and gun as well. Once we had our silencers on, we pulled our clear masks down, then exited the car. Running up the driveway, we made our way down the side of the house. On the gate it said *Beware of Dog,* so I looked back at Kill.

"That muthafucka would be making some noise, ain't no damn dog," he spat, but in a whisper.

I nodded and then proceeded. We both hopped the gate, and just like he said, there was no dog in the backyard. There was loud music playing in the house, and I could tell it was coming from whatever room was closest to the backyard we were in. Under the loud Boosie music blasting from his room, you could hear a woman moaning faintly. Kill twisted the back door knob, and it fell right out, meaning the damn shit was broken. Tip toeing inside, we realized there was a bedroom right next to the backdoor.

"Aaah uuuh fuck! Sonny!" some bitch yelled out, making me smile. It was like fate, she basically confirmed that we had the right home, even though I knew we did already.

*BOOF!*

We burst into the room, and the girl jumped off Sonny hollering. I shot her in the head in one try, and blood splattered all over the window she was sitting in front of. Sonny hopped out the bed, and tried to reach for his gun, but Kilexis shot him in the hand, and then the shoulder.

"Ahhh! Fuck!" Sonny grabbed his shoulder, and then screamed while looking at his hand. He was panicking like a muthafucka, and when I looked at Kill, I could tell he was ready to kidnap and torture this nigga.

"Kill, man she asked us to spare her brother," I said to him, as Sonny cried like a bitch.

*PHEW! PHEW!*

Kill shot Sonny in the throat, and then the side of his forehead after sighing. I was happy he complied, because we needed to get the fuck out of here without arguing or debating. We crept back out into the backyard, and I peered through the gate to see if anyone was outside of their houses. It was quiet and empty still, which wasn't too surprising, because I'm sure no one heard our silenced gun, or their screams because of the loud music.

We made our way out to the truck, and then got inside. I drove off at a regular speed, because I knew peeling out of there would cause a scene. Once we got back on the freeway, Kill lit another blunt for us to smoke on the way home. This shit was pretty much over, but I knew there was one more person that we might have to get rid of.

# FORTY-FOUR

# Jersey

Two Weeks Later...

*I* was going to workout today at my trainer's home. He said he had a new machine, and he wanted to work me out on it since it was supposed to be really good. Like I said, I enjoyed the fact that he tried to keep our sessions new and different. In addition to that, my body was looking better than it did before I even got pregnant. I had a little more meat, but I was still slim, and everything on my body was tight. Too bad Kill wasn't able to enjoy it, but I know I was.

I pulled up to Harold's house, and then grabbed my two water bottles and Gatorade so that I could get my workout on. He said he had some energy bars for me, so I decided to save the ones I had at home. Those muthafuckas were expensive, so anytime I could make a box last longer, I took advantage of that.

I made my way up his driveway, and nodded my head approvingly at his home. It was a nice size home on Market Street, located in Brandywine Village. It wasn't as upscale as where I lived, but it was definitely better than where I used to live before I moved in with Kill.

"Hey, just in time," Harold answered the door and then hugged me lightly.

"Nice place, I'm surprised you have this much taste in interior design," I joked.

"Thanks, and I can see you're already in the insulting mood. Just for that, I'm gonna work you out real hard today," he bit his lip and let his eyes wander down my body. If I didn't know him, I would think he wanted to fuck.

"I ain't scared, I'm prepared." I flexed my small biceps.

"You smell good, what are you wearing?"

"Umm, nothing. Maybe it's my fresh cream body wash, the scent lingers awhile. And my deodorant is unscented, so it can't be that. But where is this killer machine you have?"

"It's in the garage, but first you need to have an energy bar." He started towards his kitchen. Once we got in there, he reached into his cabinet and pulled out an unopened box of the same energy bars I had at home. "There you go." He slid the box onto the counter.

"Thanks."

I cracked open the package, and then took one out before scarfing it down. He ate one as well, and then after a few sips of my water, we headed towards his garage area.

"You're gonna love this shit, yet hate it. It hurts after a while, but once you start seeing the results from it, you're gonna wanna buy one for your house," he chuckled as he stuck his key into the knob. When he did, the knob was loosened, and kind of limped down out of the hole it was supposed to be screwed into. "The fuck," he said before pushing the door open slowly.

We both hesitantly stepped down into the dark garage, and then Harold flipped the light switch up.

"Ah!" He and I both jumped when we saw Kill sitting on the weight lifting bench, holding a gun and a bottle of Jack Daniels. This nigga was crazier than a dog in a hubcap factory.

"Yo, what the fuck! Who are you?" Harold yelled with his hands up.

"This is why you've been acting the way you have been, Jersey?" Kill barked as he pointed the gun at Harold.

"You know this nigga, Jersey?" Harold looked to me with a frightened expression.

"Kill—"

"Kill! Yo, you're Kill? Man look, I'm just her trainer—" Harold tried to explain.

"Shut the fuck up! I'm about two seconds away from shooting yo' ass, you bitch ass nigga! You've been sticking your dick in my bitch?" Kill stood up, and because he was so tall he looked scary as hell. "Hello, nigga!" he hollered and cleared one of the shelves of everything on it.

"You told me to shut… Nah man, I'm just working her out! Please, Kill, man it ain't nothing like what you're thinking!" Harold began to sob like a bitch.

"Kilexis, baby, put the gun down. I am just here to workout. I love you, baby, I would never sleep with someone else and you know that," I said to calm him down. Everything I said was true and factual, but I was still angry with him and only saying it to keep him from murdering, Harold.

"Then umm, get your stuff and let's go," Kill slurred, letting me know he was a bit tipsy.

I took Kill's hand in mine, and then we walked back through the house and outside. As soon as we got out, Harold slammed and locked his door behind us. I knew he wouldn't tell on Kill, because he'd already told me prior how niggas were scared to snitch. We both got into our cars and headed home. I had to pick Alexsia up from Raleigh first, so when I arrived, Kill's car was already there.

When I entered, I went straight to the kitchen and put her in her high chair, so that I could feed her. While I was doing that, Kill walked in looking sexy and psycho.

"I'm sorry, shorty, I just, I didn't know what to think."

"Whatever, Kill. I knew you were unhinged."

He was about to speak, but instead he just left the kitchen. Like always, we went the rest of the day without speaking.

## A Couple Days Later...

I'd had some time to think, and I realized I was on some bullshit. If I were in Kill's shoes, I would've done the same damn thing. Regardless of who the bullet was for, Portland obviously wanted one of them dead. I know deep down in my heart that if that bullet that hit Kill had killed him, I would've been trying to murder Portland myself. So honestly what's the difference? I know if Kill chose to keep Portland alive, he would've eventually killed someone, and whether it was Elijah or Kill, I would've been angry with him. So by saying that, I was choosing to forgive Kill.

Not only was I going to forgive him, but I was gonna make it up to him for being such a damn bitch. We hadn't touched, talked, or done anything in a while besides that awkward ass dinner where we ate in silence. We were pretty much broken up in a sense, because fiancée and fiancé had only been simply a title as of late.

I opened my robe to look over my body, and smiled at my cute lingerie set. I hoped Kill was even interested in sleeping with me, because with the way I'd been treating him, he was probably turned off. I knew he was the type to wash his hands of people and never look back, and I just prayed that wasn't the case here.

Alexsia was in bed already, so I had the rest of the night to make up all my wrongs to Kill. I had the rest of the night to convince him that I was sorry and would never question his motives again. As I lit the candles on the small round table I'd bought to put into our room for the night, I chuckled thinking about Harold. That nigga blocked me on his phone, and when I went to the gym he acted as if he didn't even know me. No other trainer there would work with me either. I didn't care though, my body was in great shape, and there was no need for a trainer anymore. I was just gonna go back to running in the morning to maintain.

"What's all this?" Kill walked into the bedroom, surprising me.

"Sit," I grinned and pulled a chair out. He sighed and then walked over to sit down. I inhaled his cologne like it was Grade A oxygen, and then started massaging his shoulders.

He sat there as I massaged him without saying a word. I was trying to think of how to start, but before I could say a word, he yanked me over to him, and began tearing my clothes off and kissing my neck.

"Kill!" I chuckled as he ripped my panties like he was the Hulk. He did the same to my bra, and then pushed me onto the bed once I was butt naked. I stared up at him as he undressed, and then walked over to the bed with his sexy, naked, chocolate self.

"Show me you're sorry," he demanded and pointed to his dick. I just nodded and crawled to the edge of the bed to take him into my mouth like an obedient servant.

I began bobbing up and down on his rod as he moaned loudly. I was putting my all into it, and sucking his dick like I never had before. I loved hearing him groan, and feeling him massage my curly hair. Once he gripped it, I knew I had him ready to nut. He pulled me off his dick, and spun me around, before pressing my face into the bed. He gripped my ass, and then bent down to French kiss my pussy from the back for a bit. I came so hard at the feeling of his soft lips sensually kissing my lower ones. How was I able to go without this for so long?

I gripped the sheets as I felt his thick head pressing into me. I hadn't had him in a bit, so it was a slight painful struggle, but once he got his rhythm, it was all good. His big hands gripped my small waist as he wound his hips into me from behind. He then grabbed a handful of my curly hair, and began slamming into me, but not too hard.

"Uuuh uuh mmm," I tucked my lips in to muffle the cries I wanted to let out. This felt so good, and it made so much sense why Margo was still craving it even after three years.

"Tell me you're sorry." He pounded into me.

"I'm sorry, baby, I'm so sorry!"

"Tell me you love me," he grunted, making me release.

"I love you! I love you so much!"

He kept beating it up until I exploded yet again. He then slipped out of me slowly, causing me to fall on my stomach out of breath. He flipped me onto my back, and climbed in between my legs. Wrapping his big hand around my neck, he began sucking my lips while pulverizing my center. I rubbed my hand up and down his biceps, but he stopped that when he roughly pinned my wrists to the bed without slowing up his powerful, wonderful thrusts.

"Don't you ever act that way towards me again."

"I won't!" I was saying whatever the fuck this nigga wanted me to say,

"You forgive me?" He slowed down, giving me long deep strokes while sucking my nipples hungrily.

"I forgive you, baby, I forgive you."

"Good."

He got up off me to get in a push up position, and then fucked the shit out of me, making me cum three times before he filled me up. As soon as he got close to me, I hugged him tightly and rubbed the back of his head as he kissed and sucked on my neck. His big hands groped my whole body as I lied under him panting like I'd just run twenty miles. If there were ever some kind of Olympic competition for fucking, Kill would come in first damn place. Like I said before, better than anything else, he could fuck.

"Kilexis, baby I love you."

"I love you, too. Now we can eat."

We chuckled in unison, before kissing nastily just how I liked.

## FORTY-FIVE

## Kantwan

———————

*I* was out of the hospital now, and feeling a lot better. I still had random sharp pains in my shoulder and rib cage every now and then, but all it took was an ice pack and for me to sit down for a little bit, and it would subside. When I got out I was hoping that I came home to my shorty, but that wasn't the case at all. She did pick me up from the location Kill had moved me to out in Hockessin, Delaware, but when we got to my home, she just made me some food, made sure I was good, and then left. I wanted to beg her to stay over, but I knew she wouldn't.

Elijah told me how she gave Sonny up because of what he'd done to me, and I was beyond grateful. I felt even worse now about how I cheated on her. I loved Cheyla and I missed her more than anything. I have never regretted something so much in my life. If I had one wish, it would be to go back to the nights I slept around and make a different choice. I was excited to have a little family of my own with Cheyla, but she'd made it clear that it wasn't gonna happen. She was done with me, and it almost made a thug cry.

I sipped my water, and then got up once I heard the sound of the delivery trucks bringing the product to the warehouse. I walked slowly to the door so I could let them in, and then gripped my rib cage because I had a little soreness. Letting them in, I explained that I couldn't help unload, but they weren't tripping. As the last guy walked in with the barrel, I saw Rachel coming in behind him. She was no longer needed on this side of things, because Kill moved her like I'd asked, so I was wondering why she was here.

"What you doing over here?" I questioned.

"Why did you have Kill move me?" She stepped into the warehouse, and I closed the small door behind her. Limping back deeper into the warehouse to supervise, I let out a sigh as I listened to her follow me. "Answer me, Kantwan, you know how I feel about you!"

"Rae, I'm not feeling well. I just want to work and go home, shorty, aight?"

"I'm sorry, I wished I could've come seen you while you were down, but Kill wouldn't allow me to."

"I know."

"Was it because Cheyla was there with you the whole time?" She twisted her face up.

"She was there, yes, but we're not even together anymore, so stop with the theatrics."

"You're not?" Her face lit up.

"Nah, we're not, but that doesn't mean I want to be with you, Rae. I love her and I'm trying to get her back, aight? You knew how I felt about her and yet you still let me fuck, that's not my problem."

"So we're done? I told you I wasn't that type!"

I looked behind me at the workers, because she'd yelled loudly as hell. I really needed to be watching them and making sure shit was going right, not arguing with her ass.

"Look, get the fuck up outta here with this shit, Rachel. I told yo' little ass I had a bitch and a baby on the way, yet you stayed in my messages begging for me to break yo' ass off. I was drunk and horny a couple of nights so I did, but that means nothing. I couldn't care less about what type you are, shorty, you wanted this dick when you knew it belonged to someone else, so deal with consequences and get yo' ass up outta here," I gritted.

"I ain't going nowhere! And since I can't have you, neither will that bitch. You just wait until I show the police what the fuck goes on up in here!" she cried and pushed me.

*POP!*

I sent one right through her dome, and she slumped to the ground.

"Call Rogue to have her ass cleaned up out of here," I instructed one of the workers and he nodded while wearing a frightened expression.

▭

The driver that Kill hired pulled into my driveway, and when he did, I saw Cheyla was there pulling two plastic bags from the backseat of her car. Once the driver let me out, I gave him a tip and walked towards Cheyla as he drove off. She hadn't noticed me yet, but when I got closer to her she looked up and closed her car door.

"I just thought you may want some dinner, so I came to cook if that's okay." She lifted the bags in the air.

"Yeah, that's cool. Can I have a hug?"

"Kantwan, I'm just here to help you okay?"

"Damn, you got my baby inside you and I can't get a hug?" She sighed and placed her hand on her back. Her stomach was out there, and I knew in just a few short weeks, my little man would be here. I saw she was tired and not in the mood to bicker, so I gave up. "It's cool, come on."

She followed me to the door, and then I let her in before locking it behind us. We went straight to the kitchen, and I just sat at the bar so that I could watch her cook my food. She made spaghetti, fried chicken, string beans, and peach cobbler. Everything smelled delicious as fuck, and my mouth watered as I watched her fix my plate. She couldn't even set it down good before I went digging in. I missed little shit like this, my baby could cook.

"Thank you, baby."

"You're welcome." She sat next to me and began eating.

"So, when the baby comes, can you come here? Or I can come

sleep over at my parent's house with you. I just wanna experience the first few weeks together."

"You can come to your parent's house, because I already have a room there."

"I have a room here, too," I chuckled.

"You do?" She looked surprised, and it kind of hurt because I could tell she thought I didn't really give a fuck about the baby like that.

"Yeah, shorty, I got it professionally painted and furnished. Jersey and Ivy told me everything I would need for the baby, so I bought it. I can show it to you when we're done."

"Okay," she grinned and it made me feel all warm and shit seeing her smile for once. I hadn't seen that smile in forever, and I hadn't realized how much I missed it as well. It was my job to make her smile like that, and the fact that I hadn't seen it meant I was failing.

We ate our food, making small talk in the process, and then she cleaned our plates. I then helped her up the stairs, and took her into the room I'd created for our son. Her eyes lit up like sparkling night stars as she took in the decor of the room that I'd spent many a nights planning to be perfect.

"You have everything here, Kant," she whispered as she ran her fingertips across the edge of the crib.

I came behind her and hugged her while caressing her belly. I couldn't help myself. I kissed her soft shoulder, and then inhaled the scent of her hair while my eyes were closed. I missed her; I needed her here and near me.

"I love you, Cheyla."

"Kantwan, please." She nudged me off of her. I felt so defeated. I contemplated telling her I killed Rachel for her, hoping that would do the trick, but I didn't want to implicate in her something, for safety reasons.

"So you like it? Is it good enough for you to stay here when we first bring him home?"

"Yes, it is."

We left out of the baby's room, and when she tried to go downstairs, I grabbed her small hand in mine. She paused, and then I pulled her into the bedroom we used to share.

"Kantwan, I'm gonna go home," she said once I closed the door.

"Baby, just sleep here with me. I don't want you to have the baby and have to call someone. I wanna be right there, so I can take you." I was clicking my fucking heels at the fact that I'd found a reason to convince her to stay over. And even better was the fact that it wasn't totally a lie.

She looked around the room for a bit and then said, "Okay."

We changed into our nightclothes, and then climbed into the bed. She had her back to me, so I took the opportunity to cuddle up behind her. She tensed up a bit, and then tried to peel my hands from her belly.

"This is all I want, I promise I'm not being fresh."

She sighed and then placed her hand on top of mine. We both drifted off only minutes later. I slept way better holding her like this.

# FORTY-SIX

# Ivy

---

*I* had two more classes to attend, but since I was feeling light headed as fuck, I emailed my professors from my iPhone and let them know I wasn't feeling well. I didn't have to do that, but since I wasn't the type to miss work or school, I decided to let them know. They were both cool about it, and agreed to send me the lecture through email.

"Hey, beautiful," Kevin approached me and grabbed my arm lightly.

"Hey, Kev, how are you?"

"I'm good. I tried talking to you after class, but you rushed off to the bathroom," he chuckled and adjusted his baseball cap.

"Yeah, I thought I was gonna barf, but I didn't thank God."

"Cool, so you're headed to your last two classes?"

"No, I'm feeling a little light headed so I'm gonna start my weekend early."

"Oh okay, did you wanna maybe go get some ice cream or something?"

I smiled, because he was so sweet and so was his offer. I hated to turn him down, but I wasn't feeling too hot. I just wanted to get my baby from Raleigh, get some food, and go home to wait for Elijah, who would then fuck me to sleep. I had the perfect night all planned out, even better was the fact that today was my Friday, so I would be free all weekend.

"Kevin, no I'm not feeling good at all." I shook my head and gave him a sympathetic smile.

"I get it. Well, I guess I will just walk you to your car then."

We went out to the school parking lot, and I saw that my tire was flat. When I looked closer, I saw someone had slashed it, so I checked my other three, which were in tact.

"What the fuck!" I shouted.

"Damn, jealous ex of your man possibly?"

"No, I highly doubt that shit," I scoffed. There was no way an ex of Elijah's would choose to pop up now, especially when he assured me that he didn't play them crazy ex games.

"I can give you a lift."

"No, I'm gonna call AAA and then have my man come and get me."

"But why when I can take you?" He furrowed his brows and threw his arms out. He seemed to be a little bit more annoyed than he should've been.

"Kevin, it's fine. My boyfriend can just come up here and we can go home together. I don't want you to go out of your way for nothing," I responded and shook my head. It made no sense for him to give me a lift when Elijah could. Plus, the sun had already set, and me being alone with another man at night would have Elijah ready to cock his glock.

"Aight."

I dialed AAA and then once I finished with them, I dialed Elijah. He told me he'd be to me in about fifteen minutes once he got Donovan from Raleigh, so I hung up and leaned against my car, preparing to wait.

"Kevin, you don't have to stay here with me, I will be alright," I chuckled. "I know it's getting darker, but my man will be here soon."

"Why the fuck you couldn't just come with me, huh?" he barked, catching me off guard.

"What? I told you why I couldn't go with you—"

I was cut off when he yanked my arm and tried pulling me through the parking lot. No one was out there, and there were only a few cars, since it was the evening time.

"Let me go, Kevin, what the fuck is wrong with you?!"

We began tussling as I tried to get away, and I saw two girls walk by. They looked but kept going, I guess way too scared to interfere. He finally grabbed me and was booking it to his car, when some bright ass headlights caught our attention. He let me go and shoved me to the floor, before running off and dipping through some buildings. The car drove by us, and I assume Kevin thought it was Elijah. I booked it back to my car and climbed in to wait for AAA. What the hell just happened?

AAA came and placed my car onto the flatbed. It was a luxury car and I didn't want them pulling it all over town. By the time they were done, Elijah was pulling in. I instructed the driver to follow us, and then got into the car with Elijah. I pecked his lips and then looked into the backseat at a sleeping Donovan. I couldn't wait to get my hands on him and kiss him before putting him to bed.

We made it home about twenty minutes later, and once the tow truck unhooked my car we went into the house. I started dinner, and then made some quick chicken nuggets for Donovan before bathing him and putting him to bed. I then finished preparing dinner, before sitting at the table with Elijah so we could eat together.

"How was your day?" I asked.

"It was okay. We're still looking for this one guy, and once we find him, we'll be able to go back to living that calm life." He stuffed some of the macaroni and cheese into his mouth.

"Really? Who is it?" Elijah didn't like telling me too much, but he told me enough so that I wouldn't be completely in the dark. I liked knowing some damn things about my man's life, so I appreciated that he trusted me with a few details here and there.

"He's just a harmless nigga right now, but we don't want anything getting out of hand. He's on some revenge shit, nigga named Kevin Smith. We've been looking for him, but the nigga never stays put. When we get one location, he's gone by the time we get there— Ivy, you good?" He began patting my back. I almost choked when he said Kevin Smith, and was perplexed by how I had forgotten about the Kevin Smith I knew, who basically just tried to kidnap me tonight.

"Yeah, yeah I'm fine. Baby, I have a Kevin Smith in my biology class, and he tried to kidnap me tonight. He's been really nice all semester, but now that I think about it, he may have been just trying to get close to me. He got really angry when I refused to let him give me a ride. I don't know, that's a pretty common name, so maybe I'm just tripping."

"Nah, that makes sense. I think he's the one who cut your tire, too. Regardless if he's the same Kevin or not, the fact that he tried to kidnap you is enough reason for me to get his ass. But if he is the same guy that means he's still gonna be hard to catch."

"I could help."

"Ivy, ma I really don't want you helping me like that. If something happened to you because you got caught up in my shit, I wouldn't know what to do with myself."

"Nothing will happen to me, Eli, just let me help you. I love you and I wanna help."

"You're trying to be my little rider?"

"Maybe," I giggled. He leaned over to peck me softly, while groping my thighs. "I want to tell you something, but if I do, you have to promise to still let me help you."

"I can't promise that." He bit his cornbread.

"Well, then I can't tell you."

"Aight, I promise, shorty," he flashed his beautiful smile, while pushing his dreads out of his face.

"Let me see your hands, liar." I knew he was crossing his fucking fingers. "Show them to me and they better not be crossed!"

"Fine, here are my fingers uncrossed. Don't look under the table, you know better than anybody that this dick is too big for me to cross my legs," he said and I gasped making him laugh.

"You are nasty!"

"So are you, all the shit you be saying when I'm in them walls, man—"

"Whoa! Okay! Reel it back in, Eli, I have something to tell you."

"Oh yeah," he chuckled lightly and stabbed some of his food with the fork. Nasty ass nigga.

"Donovan is gonna be a big brother, and you are gonna be a daddy." I waited with bated breath for him to speak.

He dropped his fork and said, "For real, ma? You're having my baby?" I simply nodded with a smile. "Oh shit, I can't let you help me, shorty. Not while my kid is in there."

"Your kid is the size of a pea, Eli, it will be fine. I can still help you," I said while he shook his head 'no'. "But you promised!" I whined and he sighed.

"Alright, Ivy, I will figure out a way for you to help me catch him and still be safe. Come sit in daddy's lap so he can rub your belly."

"I don't have a belly yet, nigga." I got up and went to sit in his lap. He instantly stuck his hand up my shirt, and began rubbing my flat stomach in a circular motion.

"You think you got pregnant during that threesome?"

"Eli!" I yelped as he guffawed and kissed my jawline.

"I'm kidding, baby, but did you?"

"No fool, I didn't."

"Just checking, that would've been weird as fuck, shorty."

"Hella weird," I chuckled.

"Aye, you know the homie, Blow, is fucking with Shamece now? He's pretty serious about her ass too, shit was kind of weird to hear."

"She told me she met some guy named Bryson, is that his real name?" I quizzed and Elijah nodded. "I'm happy for her. Did you tell him that you fucked her?"

"I told him we had a threesome a long time ago. I had to, he's the homie and I couldn't let him go out like that. He wasn't tripping though, she got that nigga's nose wide open."

"She must."

"All of y'all got nigga's noses wide open. I'm still in disbelief that Ka'Shea married Raleigh's ass and is having a child."

"Me too, when she told us I thought she was kidding. I'm

starting to see that when Raleigh is MIA for a bit, something is usually up with her," I chuckled.

"I can't wait to marry you."

"I can't wait to marry you either, Mr. Camren."

"I love you, Ivy."

"I love you more."

# FORTY-SEVEN

## Kilexis

---

A Couple Days Later...

"Good morning, Mr. Johnson is in the back waiting for you," Axel's housekeeper answered the door. She was smiling but I could tell it was forced. It was as if she wanted to cry, but she had to put up a front for us.

"Thanks," Elijah and I said in unison.

We followed her to the back, but instead of going into the den, we went into a bedroom that was so deep into this large home, that we may need to turn on GPS to get back out. She opened the door, and when we walked in, Axel was lying in the bed looking like you could snap him in two. He was frail as fuck, and he looked like he was on his way out in any minute. Even though the nigga wasn't my father, the shit made me feel some type of way. He was the one who helped me get to where I was, and to see him go from this big time, ruthless kingpin, to a weak old man was sad to say the least. I remembered when seeing Axel pumped fear in nigga's hearts, and now you just felt pity at the sight of him.

"Give us a minute, Catharine," he spoke and his voice was very scratchy. Upon saying his housekeeper's name, I realized I never remembered it once I left his home, despite Axel saying it multiple times.

"Okay, I will be back in a second with the nurses," she responded and left out.

"Sit," Axel attempted to gesture towards the two chairs by his bed. Elijah and I sat down slowly, and I could tell we both felt bad about making sure we packed heat before coming in. Then again, just because Axel looked weak didn't mean he didn't have anybody lurking in the shadows. "I know my boys are gone," he cleared his throat. "I guess even though I tried to protect them from a game they didn't know, they still got lost in it."

"Axel, man we just did what we had to—" Elijah tried to explain, but Axel put his hand up to stop him.

"No need to explain. Only a handful of us hustlers are able to make it out alive every now and then. I was lucky to have such a long-standing career without succumbing to it, and that's only because I was smart. My boys weren't meant for this shit, and no matter how many times I tried to tell them that, they refused to listen. I knew this would happen if they started courting the streets, I just didn't think it would be by you guys."

"It was either us or them," I shrugged.

"Oh, I know. That's how the game goes, shit that's how life goes. It's either kill or be killed, and you've always been the one who was too clever to be caught slipping, that's where your nickname came from. The fact that it was the beginning of your name just made it seem like fate," he chuckled lightly, and so did Elijah and I.

"How long you got, man?" Elijah quizzed, wearing an uncomfortable expression.

"A few weeks they say, but that's only if I continue to eat right. I ain't fucking with that shit though. I told Catharine to make me a nice big pork chop with some mashed potatoes," he replied as we laughed.

"Come on, man, nah, you need to be here as long as possible," I said.

"I've been here long enough. Life hasn't been the same since my wife died anyway, and now that my kids are gone too, it's time for us to be together again. Plus, I wouldn't mind going out while eating a good ass pork chop."

"Me either," Elijah smiled.

"My will, that's why I called you guys here today. I had it changed, and I plan to leave everything to you guys except the house. I'm leaving the house to Catharine. Johnson's Cleaners is in the will as well, so once it's rebuilt, it's yours." He winced in pain and then coughed a little bit.

"Axel, nah man, you've done enough for me," I frowned.

"All I did was give you a platform, Kill, you did the rest. And shit, the money I gave you, you paid me back like an asshole, so just take what I'm giving you. I've done a lot of bad shit in my life, and it's time I do something good. I'm trying to make sure I go to heaven where my beautiful wife is."

"Thanks," I replied. I didn't really know what else to say.

I was just gonna take that money and do something positive with it, but I wasn't sure how yet. Alexsia already had a hefty college fund, and I'd started her a savings account. I really had no idea what to do with the money, because I'd made plenty of my own and didn't need it. Is there such a thing as too much damn money? I think so.

We chilled with Axel for a few more hours until it was time to put down one more cat. We needed to get this dude named Kevin Smith before he started to cause trouble. He was nothing in my book, but I knew he would soon try to pull something because he hated Kantwan for killing his brother, and me for killing his other one. I thought he was behind getting Kantwan shot, but we caught that nigga and he said it was Sonny.

Ivy got Kevin to agree to meet at this pool hall that was pretty much abandoned. Nobody really went there and when people did, it would only be like two white dudes. The owner was barely there because he was looking to sell the place now that it made no money. I don't really know what happened, because when I was younger my father and his friends would go there a lot. And when I got to be about ten, my dad would take me and Elijah along with him, and the place would be packed like crazy. Time really changes things. What goes up, must always at some point, come down.

"Aight, let's make this shit quick," I said to Elijah and he nodded.

We were locked and loaded, ready to put this nigga down. We initially only wanted him because of who he was related to and the fact that he was a threat, but now that he'd made that sad attempt at kidnapping Ivy, we had a legit reason to make him take a dirt nap. The sun had set and it was around 8:30pm at night. Ivy confirmed the year, make, and model of his car, so we knew he'd arrived. Rushing inside, we saw him sitting down, scrolling on his phone. Elijah closed the front door of the hole in the wall pool hall, which made him hop up out of his seat.

"Kevin, nice to meet you, man, I'm Kill," I smiled as I neared him.

"Where the fuck is Ivy? That bitch set me up!" he hollered.

*POP!*

"Watch who the fuck you call a bitch, homie!" Elijah shot his ass in the leg.

"Fuck! Shit!" He dropped and gripped his leg. He was breathing like a woman in labor as he rocked back and forth.

"Monty is your brother?" I questioned just to be extra sure, even though it was a bit too late for that.

"Yes, and Kantwan is your bitch ass bro—"

*POP!*

I sent one right through his head. Elijah checked outside of the pool hall to make sure it was still a ghost town, while I called the clean up crew to come clean the scene. Once Rogue and his people were gone, we headed back to the warehouse to get our cars and go home. I planned to eat, play with my shorty a little, and then get my dick rode.

## FORTY-EIGHT

# Cheyla

---

A Little Over a Month Later...

'd had my son, Kantwan Jr., about five weeks ago. I was finally getting used to having to be at his beck and call. He seemed to choose the worst times to cry, but because he was so damn cute I didn't mind. He looked like Kantwan, and only had my nose. Everything else about him was his father, which was slightly annoying since I'm the one who dealt with all the damn pain.

I'd finally gotten his little ass to go to sleep, and was ready for a nice hot bath. He'd drooled and spit up on me all damn day, and I felt like I smelled terrible. I walked out of his room, and down the hallway so I could go into the bedroom for a bath. Kantwan was out handling business, and I was happy because I didn't feel like dealing with him. He was still not my man, and he wouldn't be anytime soon. I felt like because of what he did, he needed to really show me something, and he had yet to do that. I think he thought just because I had his baby that it would automatically allow him to be my man again, well no sir. I laughed as I recalled the time last week I heard him jacking off. He had no choice, because he wasn't touching me. And even though I'd requested paperwork to show me he was clean, which he'd provided already, he wasn't hitting anything.

I stripped out of my clothes, and placed them into the dirty clothes hamper. I ran some bath water, and then used some of my Philosophy body wash to make bubbles. It was in the scent Cinnamon Buns, and it smelled just like it. Once the water was finished, I tied my hair up into a high ass ponytail, and then submerged into the water. I turned on the Jacuzzi's bubbles just so that it would be even more of an experience, and then rested my head back. When I felt I'd relaxed enough, I cleaned myself, and then got out of the tub to dry off. I spread lotion all over my body, and when I walked out of the bathroom, Kantwan was sitting on the edge of the bed smirking.

"Oh, hello," I said dryly, and then walked to the drawer to get some panties.

I hated how attractive he was, and the more I tried to despise him, the more beautiful he seemed to become. I also hated that he was back to the old Kantwan, the one who had me dizzy and in love.

"Hey, baby, can you come sit down for a second."

"Kantwan, I'm tired and I don't feel like talking tonight. We can talk in the morning when I haven't been studying and taking care of my baby all day okay?" I low key snapped as I slipped my panties up. His perverted ass watched me the whole time.

"Cheyla, just sit the fuck down," he stated calmly. "And stop with that *my baby* shit, he's my kid too."

Rolling my eyes, I walked over to him and sat down on the bed. He got up, and then got down on the floor to look up at me. His face was so perfect and gorgeous. His features were perfectly placed on his face, and his caramel complexion was impeccable. He stroked his freshly trimmed facial hair, before running that same hand over his fade and sighing.

"Cheyla, I know I've said this almost a thousand times, but I'm sorry for betraying you. I was in a bad place, and like I said, I felt like I really couldn't talk to you and that you didn't have my back.

Instead of coming to you, I chose to act like a bitch and run to another bitch... or two. But I want you to know that I love you, and my son, and I heard you when you said I needed to do more and really prove to you that I wanted you and only you, so..." He pulled a blue box from his pocket, and then took the top off. Inside was a little gray box, which he removed. I didn't know what was happening right now, so I was just gonna stay quiet and try not to faint. Finally, he opened it, and the biggest diamond I'd ever seen in person was gleaming, blinding me. "Baby, I hope I'm not making a fool of myself right now. I hope that you still love me as much as you always have. I hope what's left of our union is enough for you to say yes to what I'm about to ask you. Cheyla Austin, I want nothing more than to be with you and build a family. So I'm wondering, nah umm, fuck it. I want you to be my wife, baby." I opened my mouth to speak but he cut me off. "Please, Cheyla, if you need time I will let you think, just please don't say no."

"Umm, sure." I nodded and he was just staring at me, astonished. "I said yes, Kantwan," I chuckled.

He shoved the ring down my finger, and then got up to kiss me hungrily, while pulling open my towel.

"Fuck, baby, I have missed you so much." He kissed all over my neck, while spreading my legs so that he could get in between them.

"I missed you, too," I whispered.

I know I just talked all that shit and accepted the proposal. It'd been months, and I felt he'd learned his lesson. He was back to being the man that I'd fallen in love with long ago, and I was ready to be with him again, but as his fiancée and soon wife. Putting my foot down got me a nice big diamond ring.

He yanked down my panties, and once we were both naked, he climbed back on top of me and got between my legs. He was struggling to get inside me since not only did I just get sewed up, but he hadn't touched me in months. Finally he made it in, and it was so painful.

"Go slow," I frowned.

"I am, I wanna savor this before you change your mind," he smiled as he worked the rest of himself into me. "Thank you for my baby, Cheyla," he sucked on my lips as he thrust into me slowly. "I love you."

"I love you too, Kantwan."

He cupped one of my breasts, and then dipped his tongue into my mouth. We began to kiss hungrily and passionately as he moved in and out of me. The pain soon turned to pleasure, making my body shiver a bit. I missed this; I missed us.

# FORTY-NINE

# Elijah

---

Four Months Later...

Today Ivy and I would be finding out the sex of our baby. I truly didn't care what it was, I was just excited to be having a child with her. It was funny, because I used to hate when she would ruin the moment by telling me to pull out, and when she finally stopped, so did I. I knew she was just as elated as I was though.

We entered the doctor's office both holding Donovan's small hands as we entered. Once we got in, I scooped him up and sat him in my lap. Ivy went to check in, and then walked back over to me rubbing her small stomach. It was finally rounding out, and you could tell she was pregnant when she wore tight shirts. Just seeing her belly had me on one.

"Can you believe we're having another baby?" I grinned.

"Another? This is your first one," she smiled.

"Nah, this is my kid too, you know that."

"I know, I know. And his name change went through. I almost forgot when I was registering him for the daycare that his last name was Camren now," she chuckled as Donovan hopped out of my lap to play with the toys in the waiting area of the doctor's office.

The mention of Donovan's last name being mine now made a smile creep across my face. I loved this little nigga as if he was my own, and he was. He had my last name, and as soon as Ivy and I got married, I would officially adopt him. I wasn't sure if he would be angry or thankful when he grew up. Would he hate me for basically taking his father's spot? Or would he be grateful that I took him and his mother from a miserable situation? Who knows, but for right now I could tell he was enjoying this.

"Daddy!" Donovan smiled as he held up one of the action figures. It was of Captain Jake, a character from his favorite cartoon *Jake and the Never Land Pirates*. "It's Captain Jake, Mommy." He looked to Ivy to include her as we both giggled.

After about twenty minutes, we were called to the back. Unlike most doctors, this one didn't have us waiting long, she never did. The first time we went to get Ivy a check up, she had a different one who would leave us in the room for almost an hour. I was able to get a doctor under my insurance, and boy was it a big difference. We hadn't even sat down good before she was already coming in.

We made small talk, and then she started the process. Everyone in the room was quiet, even busy body ass Donovan. I'm sure he had no idea what the hell we were here for, but his eyes were glued to the little monitor like everyone else's.

"We have a girl here, Ms. Horne, and she is very healthy. She should definitely get here on time," Dr. Foster smiled.

"Yes! Now I will have one of each, I mean *we* will have one of each.' Ivy smiled at me, and then turned her attention back to the doctor. I agreed. I felt like Donovan was mine, so in a sense I already had a son so a daughter was perfect.

After finishing up at the doctor, we went out to eat to celebrate, and then headed home. The whole way there, Donovan talked, and refused to let Ivy and I talk to each other. His little ass talked so damn much that he ended up tiring himself out about five minutes away from home. It was crazy how when I met him he didn't say much, but now he was a fuckin' baby talk show host.

Ivy changed him out of his clothes, and then laid him in his "big boy bed" as he called it, for a nap. We then went to lay down ourselves, and since both of us made sure to be free for the day, we planned to take a nice nap like Donovan. Getting into the bed, I cut on the TV so we could find a good movie to watch and doze off to.

"This is perfect," she grabbed my hand and kissed the back of it.

"Which part?"

"All of it. The new baby, our relationship, you and Donovan's relationship, just everything is perfect. I've never been this happy in my life, and that says a lot."

"Damn, never?" I looked into her beautiful blue eyes.

"Nope, for as long as I can remember someone has always let me down. I've had days where I felt happy, but it never lasted too long. With you, no matter how my day went, I'm always happy with you. My problems now are so small compared to what they used to be. Now my biggest dilemma is typing a ten page paper, when before it was getting jumped by random side chicks, or not being able to pay my rent."

"I'm happy I could change that for you shorty. And even though I wasn't as miserable as you, you and Donovan have definitely improved the quality of my life."

"We better have!" she said as we laughed together. "And it's crazy that I met you at the last place I would have ever thought I would meet someone."

"Same. I just came to chill, but ended up meeting wifey."

"Yeah," she whispered as she watched me sift through Netflix.

"What do you think about getting married soon, Ivy?"

"Soon, like when?"

"Like maybe a couple months after the baby gets here."

"Really?" She looked up into my face with a surprised expression, causing me to chuckle.

"Yes, really. I love you, and you love me right?" I asked and she nodded. "Aight then, so what's the hold up?"

"Nothing. I would've married you the day I met you," she chortled.

"Damn, I looked that good?"

"Not really, I just knew you had money," she taunted.

"Nah, it was my looks and flawless charm."

"Maybe. I love you." She straddled my lap, and I rubbed my hands up under her gown to rub her small bulge.

"I love you more, shorty."

FIFTY

Jersey

_______________

*And even through the years, even when we're old and gray, I will love you more
each day, 'cause you will always be the lady in my life...*

Michael Jackson's "The Lady in my Life" played over the reception hall as Kill and I shared our first dance. As I pressed my head against his chest, I inhaled his cologne while listening to his calming heartbeat. I loved this man so much, and now he was my husband. Tears streamed from my eyes as I listened to the beautiful lyrics of the Michael Jackson song. Everything he said described exactly how we felt about one another.

The song ended, and everyone in the room clapped for us, including my little baby, Alexsia. Kill and I shared a kiss, and then he helped me to the back so I could change out of this wedding dress.

"Is this gonna fit?" Kill held up my reception dress and frowned.

"Yes," I chuckled. He bent down to kiss my protruding belly, and then helped me get into the dress. I was six months pregnant with our son, who we already planned to name Kilexis Carson Camren II.

"You look so good, baby," he whispered and backed me into the wall to slip his tongue into my mouth.

"Kill, we have to go back with the guests."

"Real quick."

After unbuckling his pants, he yanked down my panties, and then lifted me up to bring me down onto his dick. I whimpered like a little child as he pumped into me. Thank God I carried small, because otherwise I would throw up at the sight of us in the mirror located across the room.

"Shit, this pregnant pussy, man," Kill grunted in my ear which only made me wetter. "You got the best pussy, Jersey, I swear," he panted.

"Uuuuh aahh uuuh!"

Finally we released, and immediately began tonguing it up. Taking himself out of me, I grabbed my bag and cleaned the both of us up. We then shared another passionate kiss, before washing our hands and leaving out to enjoy the party.

"What the hell took you so damn long?" Cheyla frowned as she bounced Kantwan Jr. in her lap.

"I had a hard time getting into my dress," I lied as I sat down. She, Raleigh, and Ivy gave each other looks letting me know they didn't believe my ass.

We had waiters who began passing food out to everyone who was here, starting with the appetizers. There weren't too many people here, just Cheyla, Kantwan, Ivy, Elijah, Raleigh, Ka'Shea, Shamece, Blow, and their kids. Shamece had just started hanging around us, because she was a good friend to Ivy, a *very* good one. I found it funny that Blow didn't mind the fact that Elijah had slept with her. But hey, more power to them.

The four of us began eating, and enjoying conversation. So much had happened in our lives, and it felt good to just enjoy each other's company. But I was looking forward to my weeklong honeymoon.

After eating, dancing, taking countless pictures, and just having a ball, the limo showed up to take Kill and I to the airport. We were flying to Bora Bora for our honeymoon, and taking our baby girl with us. Just the thought of the massages, scenery, sex, and nice dinners that I was about to enjoy had me all giddy. I was so overjoyed I could've screamed.

Once we landed at our destination, a big, black Cadillac Escalade drove us to the resort, before we had to get on a little boat to go the rest of the way. Each room was like a little hut house with beautiful decor. The floors were laminate, and everything else seemed to have this bamboo look.

"This is so nice," I looked all around.

"I know. Is she asleep?" Kill asked, and I looked into my baby's little chunky face to see she was knocked out so I nodded.

He set up the baby cushion guardrails as I changed her, and then I laid her down so she could continue to sleep. We then changed out of our clothes and got into a nice hot bubble bath in the huge tub. Funny enough, I just then realized that was something we did a lot together.

"We both like bubble baths, I guess," I chuckled as I moved my hands around in the water.

"Honestly, I'm not into baths, I just get in here because I know it's a for sure way to get some ass," he stated honestly. I hated how vulgar his mouth was, but I was very much used to it by now.

"Really, Kilexis?"

"Yeah, I'm serious. What kind of nigga takes baths, shorty?"

I just giggled as he pulled me closer. Our lips met, and like always, goose bumps appeared on my arms, a chill went cascading down my spine, and my clit tingled. We kissed one another more passionately, before he slowly pulled me into his lap, and down onto his dick.

***

Kill, Alexsia, and I walked into *La Villa Mahana*. We made reservations six months ago, because we'd heard this place was phenomenal but hard to get into. We were seated right away, and both began looking over the menu to see what we wanted.

"Everything here is so nice," I whispered because I felt like I had to. "I feel like I could move here and be happy."

"Maybe one day we can. Well maybe not here, but somewhere just as relaxing like Hawaii."

"That would be so nice. Wouldn't it, baby?" I smiled at Alexsia, who was drinking her bottle like her life depended on it. Kill and I both chuckled at her. "Can you believe we went from not speaking to one another in a strip club to being married?"

"That shit is crazy, I thought I would never be in a relationship again, let alone be married to someone. But when we got to talking, I knew I wanted to be with you some kind of way. I knew I wanted to be more than friends."

"Me too after the way you put it down," I half joked. "How did you get so good?"

"Good at what? Sex?" he frowned as if it were an odd question. I guess it was a pretty odd question.

"Yes."

"I'm not sure, I just know what women like I guess. I think a little bit of rough sex mixed with some gentle sex is always key."

"That's why Margo's trashy ass couldn't let you go."

"Is that why? Maybe so. What's the excuse for Tommy not letting *you* go? I mean the pussy is A1, but he never had it ,so I don't get it."

"I think he was so hell bent on getting it, and because he wasn't getting it, it drove his ass a little crazy you know?"

"I guess. I don't feel like that could ever happen to me."

"Unless I cut you off."

"You better not. You better not cut me off in any kind of way." He took my hands into his, and brushed his thumb across my wedding ring.

"I won't, not ever again. I love you too much."

"Same, ma."

"Promise we will never be apart." I stared into his brown eyes.

"I promise."

# JERSEY CAMREN

Two Years Later...

"**M**ommy, why can't I come, too?" Alexsia whined as I tucked her into bed.

"Because this place is only for grown ups, baby," I chuckled when she folded her little arms across her chest. She was three and a half, but knew so much.

"We can get you ice cream tomorrow if you behave and be nice to, Saliyah." Kill walked in holding our two-year-old son Kilexis II.

"Saliyah never makes me hot chocolate like I want," Alexsia replied, referring to the nanny we used on occasions.

"I will tell her to do so, okay?" I smiled down at her and she nodded slowly before giggling. I kissed her cheek, and then got up to grab Kilexis Jr. from his father.

After putting him into his bed, I gave Saliyah the instructions and contact, before leaving out with Kilexis. Tonight was the grand opening of Kill's club *Rain*. This was the second Rain that he was opening in Delaware, and seeing him do legit shit always made me happy. Axel died just three days after inviting Kill and Elijah over, and he left all four of the guys ten million dollars each, as well as the newly built Johnson's Cleaners. At Rain, there were several drinks and food items named after Axel, which I thought was dope.

One of his workers named Race drove us in a big, black Escalade to the club located on the corner of Union and Fourth Street. The place was huge and so damn beautiful inside. The walls around the inside of the club looked to be of glass material, and there was fake rain falling down behind the glass that looked so real. The hue of the club was a beautiful blue, just like the color of the couches, ropes, and anything else that had a dash of color. I loved it here, because when on the dance floor, you really felt like you were dancing in the rain, minus the water.

Once inside, we were escorted to the VIP area designated specially for the boss. When we got to our section, a big smile spread across my face when I spotted Raleigh, Ivy, and Cheyla. Kantwan, Ka'Shea, and Elijah were there as well. We hugged and greeted one another as "Off Da Meter" by Kevin Gates played loudly over the venue. Everyone was having a good ass time down on the dance floor, and even the people up in their VIP sections were going wild. It was a Saturday night, and you could just tell everyone was letting loose, enjoying their days off from a hard workweek.

"Gonna make a lot of money tonight, daddy." I nudged Kill and he nodded as he scoped the scene.

"I can't wait to celebrate tonight," he kissed my lips.

I'd just graduated college and now had a career as a professional art buyer, while studying for my Master's. Thanks to Kill, who had me fix his building, anytime he had meetings with legit clients, they inquired on who had picked the phenomenal artwork for his building. I liked not being contracted to one building, especially because I made way more money by being able to have multiple high paying clients who needed art. For the first time in a long time, I actually enjoyed the way I made money.

"I wish I could have one of those," Cheyla whined as the VIP hostess handed me a martini.

Cheyla was pregnant again, but she had a long way to go until she gave birth to her and Kantwan's second son. She wanted a girl this time, but I guess God had other plans for her. She and Kantwan got married about a year and a half ago, and they've been like two little honeymooners ever since. They've always been in love though, and I'd admired their relationship, even from the rocky ass start because of Cheyla.

My girl, Cheyla, was a senior at the University of Delaware, studying Childhood Education. She eventually wanted to teach younger kids at either a small daycare or preschool. Kantwan was willing to help her open a daycare of her own though, so that was probably what she was gonna go with since it would be much better pay.

"You'll be able to have one soon, but for now I will drink one for the both of us," Raleigh chuckled as she swayed in Ka'Shea's lap to the music.

As you already know, Ka'Shea and Raleigh are married. They had twin boys, which caught me off guard because I didn't know where that came from. My nephews Ka'Shea Jr. and Kalix were the cutest little things, and they were so sweet. Twins usually had a stigma attached to them that they were bad, but not my little nephews. I just wished Kilexis Jr. had taken a page out of their book with his little bad ass. I swear I had to spank his hand at least three times a day, just to feel bad when he cried as if his life was over. I chuckled and shook my head at my baby.

Raleigh was no longer working at the call center. She was the manager of the Westin hotel, which is something she always had an interest in, but she didn't know it. After turning my father's home into a full on boarding house, she realized she loved the hospitality field, and was now studying it at Delaware Tech. She planned to move up in the Westin company, and I knew she would. I've never seen her as happy as she was the day she left the call center. Ka'Shea offered to buy it out for her, but we all know she declined that. My parents' relationship really formed our way of thinking.

"Let's dance!" Ivy sprang up, pulling Elijah with her once "All the Way Up" by Fat Joe and Remy Ma came on. She and Cheyla loved to dance, but for me, after swinging on the pole for a while, dancing wasn't too much of my thing anymore, unless the song was just really my jam.

Ivy, too, was a senior at the University of Delaware, getting a degree in psychology. She wanted to be a psychotherapist, specializing in family therapy. She was gonna get her Master's Degree like me once she graduated though, just to make sure she maximized the amount of income she could get.

She and Elijah just got married about eight months ago, after having their *second* child together, and *third* overall, now that Elijah adopted Donovan. After Donovan, they had a little girl, who they named Olivia, and then a boy, who they named Elysha, a play on Elijah's name in a sense. Speaking of Donovan, he was so smart and talkative, and loved to read books to you or tell you things he'd learned in school. He was definitely gonna be a speaker of some kind. It did bother me a bit that he had no knowledge of Portland, but that was no one's fault but Portland's.

As for his father, he will be missed, but he was the cause of his own demise. Everyone tried to help Portland, but he just didn't want to be helped. And hanging out with Sonny didn't make it any better. Sonny left behind a lot of bullshit, such as his underage baby mama, who as of late was claiming some new guy was the father. Well, not as of late I guess, she'd been saying the new guy was the father for years. I found it funny since prior to that she was adamant that Sonny was the dad. I knew Sonny was though, because the little girl looked just like Cheyla and his other daughter, Sonaya. I wonder what made little Alicia wanna lie all of a sudden. Sonaya and her mother Marley moved to Montana with Marley's boyfriend, Wyatt. I guess she never really let him go. He was a stand up dude though, so I guess both she and Raleigh upgraded. Only bad thing about her move was that Cheyla missed her little niece. Marley rarely let her see her when they lived here in Delaware anyway though.

"Got a guest here for you," Kill whispered in my ear.

I frowned at him because I was confused, so he pointed to the entrance of the VIP. I saw someone wearing red approaching, so I pushed my curly hair to the other side nervously. Who the hell was this? The bouncer guarding our VIP stepped to the side, and the beautiful woman entered the VIP wearing the biggest smile I'd ever seen. Her skin was so vibrant, and I could tell she was happy. She was happier than I'd ever seen her, and it in turn made me grin widely as well. She hugged Kill, Kantwan, Ka'Shea, Ivy, and Elijah, before looking to me, Cheyla, and my sister.

"Mama?" I stood up slowly, along with Raleigh and Cheyla.

"Yes, but you didn't say anything about my dress.' She spun around slowly, and her figure was perfect like it had always been.

"Mama, how? You... you were in jail, and they had evidence, how are you out?" I was so confused right now.

"Girl, hell if I know. Your husband got me some good lawyer, a new trial, and next thing I knew, I was being released. You know me, I don't ask any questions." She shook her head and moved to the music. I chuckled because my mother was never a good dancer, but that didn't stop her. Raleigh hugged her tightly, and my mom kissed her cheek before pulling Cheyla in.

"Kill, how did you do this?" I looked down at him relaxing on the plush blue couch in our VIP.

"Hired a good lawyer, who was able to make it appear like a crime of passion versus something planned. That alone shortened the sentence, and then he was able to prove that your mother and father were happy before Trixie, and made it seem like she purposely went after your father, ruining his marriage. Once the lawyer was done with all that shit, the sentence was only five years, and since she'd been good and served most of it, they let her out after six months," he explained, and Kantwan smiled and nodded the whole time. "That lawyer cost me a lot of bread, but it was worth it. I only required one thing of your mother."

"What was that?"

"That she forgive me for getting rid of Portland."

"And I did once he explained everything. I love my son, but I knew this was coming," my mother chimed in and made eye contact with Kill, before pecking his cheek.

"Baby, I love you for this, but why didn't you tell me?" I frowned at Kill.

"I wanted it to be a surprise, and I wanted to make sure I actually got her out," he grinned. I leaned down to kiss him. Like my mother, I truly didn't care too much, but I was happy she was out.

"Jersey, honey let's go dance.' My mother pulled Cheyla, Raleigh, and me. We all began dancing and laughing together along with Ivy, as "Hold Up" by Beyoncé played over the club.

"Don't ever leave us again, Sabrina," I smiled at my mother.

"Never," she half smiled.

I looked over to Kill, who watched me closely with that perfect smile of his. I mouthed, "I love you so, so, so much."

"I love you, too." He lifted his glass and grinned.

Our once forbidden love had become a love story to be admired...

# Become a VIP Reader!

*To join my mailing list text* **SHVONNE** *to* **66866** *and stay up to date! Also, join* **Shvonne Latrice Reading Group** *on Facebook!*